AF438192

Redeeming

USA TODAY BESTSELLING AUTHOR

BELLA MATTHEWS

REDEEMING

A KROYDON HILLS LEGACY NOVEL

RED LIPS & WHITE LIES
BOOK TWO

BELLA MATTHEWS

Editor: Dena Mastrogiovanni, Red Pen Editing

Proofreader: Emma Cook | Booktastic Blonde LLC

Cover Designer: Val, Books and Moods

Interior Formatting: Brianna Cooper

SENSITIVE CONTENT

This book contains sensitive content that could be
triggering.
Please see my website for a full list.

<u>WWW.AUTHORBELLAMATTHEWS.COM</u>

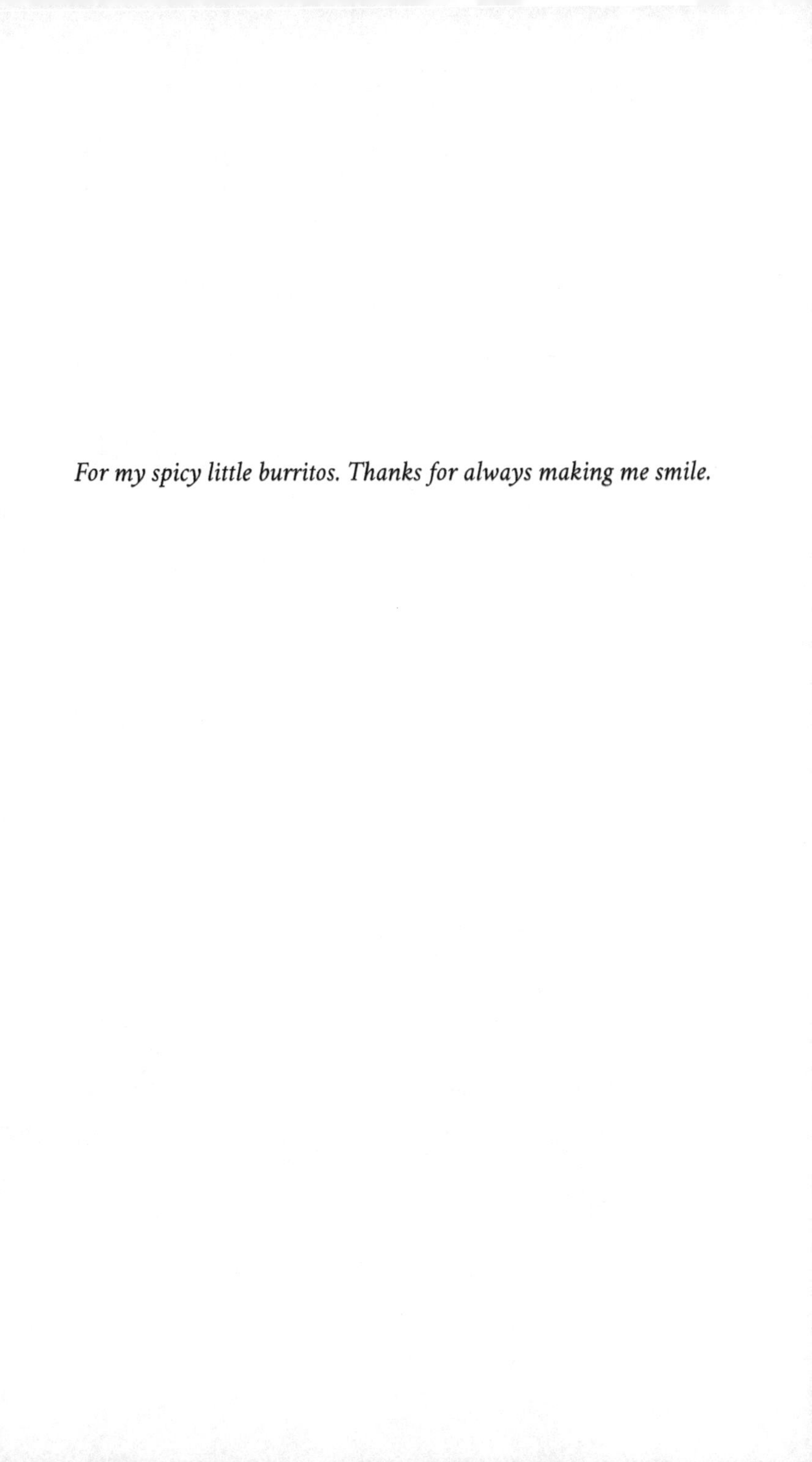

For my spicy little burritos. Thanks for always making me smile.

"Life only demands the strength you possess."

— DAVID HAMMARSKJOLD

CAST OF CHARACTERS

The Kings Of Kroydon Hills Family

- **Declan & Annabelle Sinclair**
  - Everly Sinclair - 28
  - Grace Sinclair - 28
  - Nixon Sinclair - 27
  - Leo Sinclair - 26
  - Hendrix Sinclair - 23

- **Brady & Nattie Ryan**
  - Noah Ryan - 25
  - Lilah Ryan - 25
  - Dillan Ryan - 22
  - Asher Ryan - 16

- **Aiden & Sabrina Murphy**
  - Jameson Murphy -25
  - Finn Murphy - 22

- **Bash & Lenny Beneventi**
  - Maverick Beneventi - 25
  - Ryker Beneventi - 23

- **Cooper & Carys Sinclair**
  - Lincoln Sinclair - 18
  - Lochlan Sinclair - 18
  - Lexie Sinclair - 18

- **Coach Joe & Katherine Sinclair**
  - Callen Sinclair - 28

The Kingston Family

- **Ashlyn & Brandon Dixon**
  - Madeline Kingston - 29
  - Raven Dixon - 13

- **Max & Daphne Kingston**
  - Serena Kingston - 22

- **Scarlet & Cade St. James**
  - Brynlee St. James - 28
  - Killian St. James - 26
  - Olivia St. James - 24

- **Becket & Juliette Kingston**
  - Easton Hayes - 33
  - Kenzie Hayes - 27
  - Blaise Kingston - 17

- **Sawyer & Wren Kingston**
  - Knox Kingston - 21
  - Crew Kingston - 18

- **Hudson & Maddie Kingston**
  - Teagan Kingston - 22
  - Aurora Kingston - 19
  - Brooklyn Kingston - 14

- **Amelia & Sam Beneventi**
  - Maddox Beneventi - 27
  - Caitlin Beneventi - 24
  - Roman Beneventi - 22

    ○ Lucky Beneventi - 20

- **Lenny & Bash Beneventi**
  - ○ Maverick Beneventi - 25
  - ○ Ryker Beneventi - 23

- **Jace & India Kingston**
  - ○ Cohen Kingston - 21
  - ○ Saylor Kingston - 16
  - ○ Atlas Kingston - 13
  - ○ Asher Kingston - 13

For family trees, please visit my website
www.authorbellamatthews.com

SINCLAIR
81

Part I

I don't know if I could ever complete someone. But driving another person batshit crazy seems completely reasonable to me.

—*Caitlin's Secret Thoughts*

"You ready yet, kitten?"

In through the nose.

Out through the mouth.

I will not kill Callen Sinclair on my birthday.

I will not kill Callen Sinclair on my birthday.

I will not kill Callen Sinclair on my birthday.

"What was that?" My older brother's ridiculously hot best friend leans against my door frame and crosses his stupidly big biceps over his chest . . . and dear lord, I think my eye might actually twitch a little as I repeat my mantra for a fourth time like I'm in the middle of my hot yoga class.

You'd think after living with Callen for four years, we'd have gotten past this love-hate relationship we've had since we were kids.

I mean . . . you'd be wrong, but you can think it.

I take another deep breath in and step into my closet.

"Nothing," I snap back at him while I grab my hot-pink Jimmy Choos, then sit down at my vanity to put them on. I lean down, then toss my hair over my shoulder to look up at the big oaf. "Remind me again why you're driving."

Callen's eyes linger a little too long on my legs before he looks away.

Good. I like to remind him that I am, in fact, a woman, and not some little girl to be ignored anymore. Even if I'm pretty sure most days Callen doesn't even realize I have tits and a great ass. One I'm definitely going to be shaking at the bar in a few minutes while he's probably hitting on some skank.

Not that I'm jealous or anything.

Lucky skanks.

To him. I'll always just be *Maddox's little sister.*

"I'm driving because your brother and Killian are going right from West End to the airport. Does Vegas ring any bells?"

I nail him with a glare.

"Yes, dumbass. I know they're flying to Vegas. But half my family lives in this building. How did I get lucky enough to be stuck with your sparkling personality?" I slide on my shoes, buckle both ankle straps, then stand and adjust my dress before grabbing my clutch.

His eyes stay hard as they follow me across the room until I'm in front of him, and the sexy jerk finally smiles. It's a *really* good smile.

Dark jeans and an even darker green t-shirt shouldn't look that good on any man, but then Callen's never been just *any man.* He stands more than a foot taller than my own five feet, four inches, with thick brown hair and eyes the color of the most vibrant football field he's probably ever played on . . . *Not that I've studied his eyes or anything.*

If that wasn't enough to have half the women in Kroydon

Hills panting after him, his body is a work of art. And I'm not just talking about the intricate tattoos inked on his golden skin. No . . . that would be too easy. It's the whole perfectly chiseled, endlessly tanned and beautifully muscled package under his artwork that could make a woman stupid. And I'm not a stupid woman.

It's not fair.

But then again, nothing about Callen has ever been fair.

"After you, Cait."

"Whatever." I close my eyes and shake my head, clearing my thoughts. I might not kill Callen Sinclair today, but no one said I couldn't objectify him . . . just a teeny, tiny bit. "Let's just go."

I reach around his big head to hit the light switch, and he catches my wrist in his deliciously calloused hand before his lips tip up further on one side.

Like I said . . . not fair.

Callen turns off the light, then drops my hand and presses his to the small of my back, ushering me out. At the first touch of skin on skin, I command my body not to shiver. Maybe a backless dress wasn't the best design to go with, but when I designed *this* dress, I did it with tonight in mind, and I'm not changing now.

His warm breath skirts over my ear, and his hand slides down just a touch further onto pink silk as he rests it on the swell of my ass, and I officially lose the fight.

"No cat ears tonight, kitten?" he asks with a gravelly, sexy voice, and I yank my hand away.

"Fuck you, Callen."

The ass laughs, low and long. "Come on, Cait. It's a joke."

"One year. *One birthday.* And you're still calling me kitten." I smack him in the gut with my purse and leave him behind as he bends at the waist, laughing.

Callen Sinclair has been the bane of my existence since I

was six years old and he saved my damn cat from a tree before turning to my brother and making fun of me for crying.

I didn't know what a crush was back then. I was just a little girl who thought he hung the damn moon. I no longer have that crush. I wouldn't say no to an orgasm from Kroydon Hills' biggest manwhore . . . but I'm one of hundreds of women who probably feel the same way.

The difference is they're not his roommate.

Callen

"*I* swear to God, it's like she *wants* to get in trouble," Maddox groans as he hands me a beer and looks out at the dance floor where Caitlin and Bellamy are laughing and dancing without somehow sloshing their pink martinis all over the floor.

I look at them again and ignore the fact that I know exactly what she's doing and how good she looks doing it—because it's burned into my fucking retinas like a once-in-a-lifetime solar eclipse—and shrug instead. "They're fine. You're here. I'm here. *Fuck,* even Jude's here . . . somewhere."

Caitlin hates having her bodyguard anywhere near her, cousin or not. But her parents have never let up on that one. Probably the only time the princess has ever been told no.

Just then, Killian shimmies his way between the girls, making himself the meat in a sandwich consisting solely of our roommates.

If someone would have told me years ago that I'd end up sharing a penthouse with Maddox, his sister, her best friend, and their cousin Killian, I'd have said *the fuck I will.* But here I am, four years after Maddox and I swapped our two-bedroom condo for the five-bedroom penthouse with four fucking roommates and two goddamned dogs. For someone like me, who was basically raised as an only child because all five of my siblings are about twenty years older than me, I'd have sworn on everything that's holy there'd be no fucking way. No fucking chance. Not happening. But when that girl out there, in that tiny little pink thing she's calling a dress, marched into the penthouse with her own roommate, two brand-new puppies, and her brother glaring behind her, what the hell was I going to say?

Okay, yeah . . . I probably could have said no.

But it wouldn't have just been telling Caitlin no.

Something I've never been good at. None of us have.

It would have been telling her mom no because she was who struck some kind of deal with Madman that ended with Cait and Bellamy taking our extra bedrooms. And I gotta say, no one tells Amelia Beneventi no.

Fuck me . . .

I sip my beer, knowing it's one and done tonight. Football is already in full swing. Our first preseason game was yesterday, and after a bitch of a season strife with injuries and late-season losses last year, the eyes of fans everywhere are on the Philly Kings.

We won yesterday, but that doesn't mean a goddamn thing.

Not yet. Not when everything can change with one single play.

Some dude I don't know makes his way over to the girls and Killian. "Who's the douche?"

Maddox drops his bottle to the bar and shakes his head. "Guess that's Bellamy's new guy. I think he's a physical therapist at the hospital."

He looks like a strong wind could knock him over.

"When did Bellamy get a new guy?" I ask as I watch them closely.

The girls might be pains in the ass, but they're *our* pains in the ass.

Maddox shakes his head as the song changes, and Killian joins us. "She went on a date with him last week," Maddox tells me.

"Ross?" Killian asks as he looks back at the girls. "She's bored. He'll be gone by the third date like all the rest of them."

West End's newest bartender puts three more beers on the gleaming mahogany bar and smiles at Maddox, like she's hoping he'll tip her by bending her over that bar later. *He won't.* He never fucks around at work. *Smart man.*

"Hey, are Kenzie and the girls coming tonight?" Killian asks us he looks around.

"Nah, man," I tell him. "I helped her hook up her TV in the condo earlier. She's moved in and set up and she starts her new job at the hospital with Wren tomorrow. But it will be nice to have her back from DC."

Maddox looks up and grins. "Pretty sure we're all getting together to celebrate her being home after we're back from Vegas."

My phone vibrates in my pocket as Maddox and Killian discuss getting out of here to head to the private airstrip nearby. I pull it out, wondering who the hell is texting this late on a Saturday. Pretty much everyone I talk to is somewhere inside this bar for Cait's birthday.

DAD

Can you all come over tomorrow?

DECLAN

What time?

Of course, my oldest brother is the first to answer. Par for the course. Dec's always been the overachiever brother. He's the oldest of my three brothers and two sisters. He followed in Dad's footsteps on the field and eventually *off* the field. Now he coaches the Kings too. Rumors have been swirling he's going to be Dad's replacement for head coach when the old man finally retires. Not that *that's* happening any time soon.

MURPHY

We won't be back from Alabama until early afternoon. It has to be later in the day.

Guess Murphy went to see his son Finn play football this weekend. Murph is the same age as my sister Nattie and Brady. They all went to school together, and that's how our parents met. That's also why my siblings are all twenty years older than me. I was a surprise.

NATTIE

Like a family dinner?

COOPER

We bringing the kids?

CARYS

I can bring dessert.

Did I mention my brother Cooper married my sister Carys?

Because that's not awkward as fuck to try and explain to people.

Coop was already out of the house when Mom and Carys moved in with Dad. So technically, they were stepsiblings, but it's not as gross as it sounds. Not that it's easy to wrap your head around when you're a kid. Luckily, I've had twenty years to get used to it.

CALLEN

Just tell me when and where.

There. Answered. I just wait for them to tell me what to do.

It's always how we work.

DECLAN

Aren't you out with the kids? Better not overindulge, Callen. The season's started.

Lucky me. I basically have five siblings who all think they're my parents because I'm closer to their kids' ages.

COOPER

You know your kids are all grown ass adults?

NATTIE

Just you wait, Cooper. Giving your babies freedom sucks.

MURPHY

Dude, Declan. Your babies are grown with babies of their own.

DECLAN

Nat's kid is a rockstar, and she still has her on Life360. Don't give me shit.

CARYS

How about Callen's almost thirty? Are you seriously asking him what he's doing out this late during football season?

I fucking love my sister.

DAD

Some things never change. Just stop by when you can tomorrow. Just you kids. Text or call before you come. I'm going to bed.

And Callen . . . don't drink too much. You were slow yesterday.

I shove my phone back in my pocket and grind my teeth as Killian claps my shoulder. "We're getting out of here, man. See ya in a few days."

I nod and look from him to Maddox. "Don't worry. I've got Meatball," I joke, because when Caitlin moved in with Cupcake, she also came with Meatball. Her mom tried to say Meatball was for Cait, but really that damn dog is Maddox's dog. Fat, lazy little shit with a strange little mean streak when you piss him off.

"Thanks, man." He lifts his chin, then looks out at Caitlin one more time. "Keep an eye on her for me?"

"Pretty sure that's what Jude's for." I let my eyes trail back over the fucking wicked little goddess on the dance floor. The way her hips sway. The curve of her breast, along with the fantastic glimpse of side boob she's giving me, as well as every other red-blooded man and probably most of the women in the room.

Fuck me.

It's been too goddamn long since I've gotten laid.

"Jude's gonna keep her from getting shot or kidnapped. Not from going home with a piece of shit."

I silently groan.

The thoughts I've been having more and more recently are enough to get me killed.

By Maddox.

And let's not forget his dad . . . Sam Beneventi is feared by the whole goddamned city.

Or worse . . . by his mom, who's killed at least one person I know of since she moved to Kroydon Hills. She did it to save Declan's wife, Annabelle, while she was pregnant with the twins. She didn't hesitate. Killed the crazy bitch with a single bullet. So yeah, I keep my thoughts to myself.

"Thanks, brother," Maddox tells me, like I have a fucking choice in the matter, before he walks away.

He and I have been as close as brothers since we could walk. Our families are tight, and as the two oldest guys of our generation, we were always together.

When Caitlin came along a few years later, we both took on the big brother role. At that age, of course we would because seriously, we were four fucking years old. We thought she was cool as shit. By the time we were eight, we'd sliced our palms open with Madman's first pocketknife and called ourselves blood brothers. That made Caitlin as much my sister as his in both our eyes. So when Maddox declared Caitlin was the worst a few years later, I hopped right on board that train.

Even if she never really annoyed me. Not then. That shit didn't start until college, and it was for way worse reasons.

Ones I've been trying to forget ever since.

It was easier before.

Before she grew up.

Before she lived with us.

Before I let myself watch her when no one else was looking.

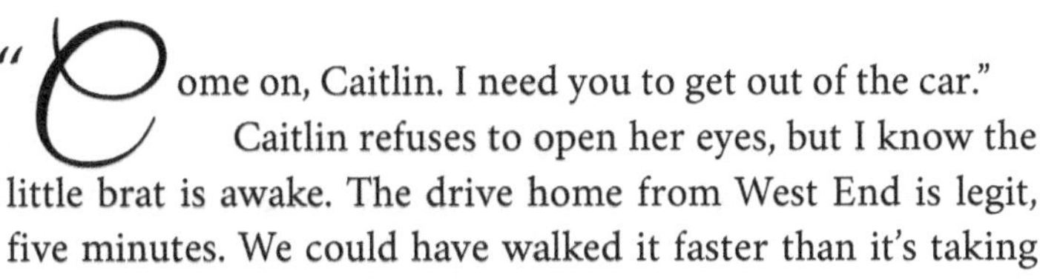

"Come on, Caitlin. I need you to get out of the car."

Caitlin refuses to open her eyes, but I know the little brat is awake. The drive home from West End is legit, five minutes. We could have walked it faster than it's taking to get the drunk birthday girl home.

"Cait . . . Come on," I groan through clenched teeth.

"I'm fine," she mumbles. "Just leave me. I don't wanna walk."

"Maybe if you didn't wear six-inch heels, you'd want to walk." I get out and slam my door before rounding the truck to her side. Her pale skin is practically glowing under the fluorescent garage lights when I open her damn door. "Kitten . . ."

She doesn't even bat an icy-blue eye at the nickname she despises.

"All right, up you go." I scoop her up, and her eyes stay closed, but the troublemaker smiles and wraps her arms around my neck as I hip-check the door closed. "Hang on."

"Hmmm . . ." she hums deep in her throat, content with having gotten her way, and I ignore the way my dick jumps in my jeans. Her soft hair tickles my face and envelopes me in her sexy scent. Vanilla, honey, and spice. I always thought it reminded me of bourbon. But it's pure Caitlin as it wraps around me.

I ignore our ancient doorman as I walk through the lobby to the elevator.

"You really not gonna walk, kitten?" I press as I move us into the elevator, and her smile grows just enough for something deep inside me to fracture. She used to smile at me like that all the damn time.

"Am I too heavy, Callen? Not strong enough to carry me to our condo?" One eye cracks open as she giggles. "And stop calling me *kitten*."

She scrunches her eye closed, and I lose the fight entirely.

My head thunks back against the elevator wall as I pray for patience until the doors open again on our floor. I adjust my hold on her and type in our key code, then walk into the kitchen.

"Here you go." I sit her down on the counter. "Don't move."

Caitlin reaches out for me until I stop and hold her in place. "What are you doing?"

My normally prickly black cat looks soft and pliable and so damn good in front of me. "Taking care of you. Now lean back. Don't move. And let me."

I wait until she does as she's told. "Good girl. Stay."

"Make up your mind, Sinclair. Am I a dog or a cat?"

I look at her from the fridge and grab a water bottle.

Fucking gorgeous.

That's what she is.

Fucking gorgeous trouble.

"Here. Take these." I open a bottle of ibuprofen and pop two pills into her hand, then crack the water bottle. "Now swallow."

Her eyes pop wide open. "Oh, I could swallow."

"Jesus Christ, Caitlin. The damn pills. Swallow the damn pills."

In slow-motion, she follows her orders, her drunk eyes focused on me the entire time, and her pink-stilettoed feet swinging back and forth against the lower cabinets. "Stop doing that," she tells me softly.

I scrub my hand down my face, absolutely fucking exhausted as I stand in front of her. "Doing what, Cait?"

"Looking at me the way you are." Her voice softens. "The way you used to."

Shit.

"Caitlin . . ."

She reaches her hand out and rests it against my chest. "You gonna ask me what I wished for, Callen?"

I don't answer. I can't.

But as if tethered to her, I feel myself being reeled in and move closer.

"I wished—"

"Don't." I press my thumb over her lips, silencing her.

Big fucking mistake.

She presses her lips against the pad of my thumb before her tongue darts out.

"You're drunk, Caitlin."

I'm a goddamned beast, I'm so strong, but turning this woman down takes more strength than I ever could have hoped to have. And I'm pretty sure she can see it on my face.

"I miss you, Callen."

Like a dagger to the heart, she strikes hard and fast, knowing exactly what she's doing.

"I'm right here," I say the words, even as I take a step back.

"Not the way you used to be," she pouts, even if she's right. "Not since—"

I pick her up and set her on her feet. "Time for bed."

Caitlin's eyes flash with hurt, but it's better this way.

"Come on, kitten." I guide her to her room in silence.

Neither one of us ready to admit defeat.

And make no mistake. We both just lost this little battle.

Ten minutes later, she's changed—*not that she cooperated*—and tucked into her bed with her water bottle next to her on the nightstand, a trashcan by the bed, and Cupcake and Meatball both snoring at the foot of her bed.

Her heavy eyes close again. "One day, you'll tell me why, Callen."

I shake my head, knowing she's wrong, and wait until she falls asleep before moving across the hall to my own room and into a cold shower, where I jerk off to thoughts of her lips wrapped around my dick instead of my thumb.

There's not a doubt in my mind Caitlin Beneventi is going to be the death of me.

I'm not built for someone soft. I'm loud and opinionated. I talk back, refuse to listen, and sarcasm is my love language. Don't waste my time if you can't handle that. I won't be changing for you.

—Caitlin's Secret Thoughts

Oh . . . My . . . God . . .

I roll away from the sunlight shining so obnoxiously bright through my windows, it's stabbing my eyes with a million tiny pinpricks. So much for not overdoing it last night. *Oh, who am I kidding?* I knew exactly what I was doing . . . At least I did until—*wait . . . did I?*

I look under the sheet, and *sweet baby Jesus.*

No.

No. No. *No.*

Noooooo.

Tell me I didn't.

I throw the blankets off, and it's still there.

Callen's shirt.

Shit.

Stars light up my now completely non-existent vision as the room spins, and I press the heels of my palms against my eyes, begging the universe to show me I didn't really untie my dress and let it fall in a puddle of Italian silk on the floor in front of Callen *fucking* Sinclair. But I already know the answer. I can smell it all over my body. Because me naked wasn't enough to get Callen's attention. No . . . Instead, he was horrified enough to rip his own clothes off to cover me up.

You'd think I'd have learned this lesson his senior year in college.

Guess Mom was right. I always do have to learn things the hard way.

Oh. My. God.

I bury my red-hot face under my pillow and pray for a do-over.

I don't get it because karma is an asshole. A big, fat, hairy asshole.

Seriously . . . no woman would let me make this big of a fool out of myself.

Twice.

Nope. Karma is obviously a douchey dude.

After quite possibly the longest, scalding-hot shower of my life . . . one I spend the majority of sitting on the tile floor —which *hey*, at least I wasn't in a full-on fetal position—I slide on a pair of soft sleep shorts and an oversized tee. Then I stare at my door for a full five minutes, working up the courage to face the consequences of my less than stellar decision-making skills.

It takes longer than that for me to make my way down to our kitchen, where my walking, talking nightmare is standing in drool-worthy gray sweatpants, shirtless, and looking like a daydream. He's flipping chocolate chip pancakes on a skillet, while a piping-hot coffee pot sits freshly brewed next to him. Two mugs are steaming on the kitchen table with a glass of orange juice sitting next to a bottle of ibuprofen, and I offer up a silent prayer of thanks as I pop two pills and wash them down with the cool OJ, then slide quietly into one of the chairs.

Neither of us says anything until he walks my way and slides a plate of pancakes and bacon in front of me. "Eat, Cait. The carbs and grease will help with the hangover."

I lift my chin in an attempt at defiance that might help save my dignity, if I had any left, but actually just hurts my throbbing head instead. "Who says I have a hangover?"

Callen's smile is cocky and gorgeous.

The ass.

He reaches out and runs a hand gently over my head and down my hair. *Damn.* Even that hurts. Not that I can focus on the pain. I can't. Not when I'm too shocked he's touching me. Something he used to do freely before I threw myself at him when I was eighteen. *"Eat, Cait."*

Like I didn't hear him the first time.

So bossy.

I bring my knees up to my chest and pick up a piece of bacon while I watch the muscles on his back move gracefully as he fills another plate and sits across from me. Callen raises his brow and waits until I actually eat mine before picking up his own fork. "Good girl."

Damn him and his stupid sexy voice.

Time to be a big girl and face the music.

"Can we just forget about last night?"

Okay . . . maybe not my most *adultish* reasoning.

Whatever. Adulting is bullshit.

Callen's eyes sparkle. "Not a chance, kitten. It's not every day your best friend's little sister strips naked in front of you." He stabs half a damn pancake and shoves it into his mouth.

"Callen . . ." And, *yes*, I do hear how pouty I sound, but I can't stop myself.

He washes the pancake down with coffee, watching me over the massive mug. "We don't ever have to talk about it again. But you're gonna need to keep your clothes on from now on."

I roll my eyes, and he groans. "Best friend's sister or not, Cait, you're a beautiful woman, and you can't go pulling that shit in front of me and expect me not to react."

His hoarse voice holds me captive as my brain struggles to process his words, but I seem to be stuck on only one . . . *beautiful.*

I drop my feet to the floor and push my plate away, whispering, "You think I'm beautiful?"

Callen raises his eyes to the ceiling, and his chest expands with his deep breath.

"You know you're beautiful, Caitlin."

He says it so nonchalantly . . . like it's the easiest thing he's ever said but also somehow pains him to say. Meanwhile, his words just rocked me to my core. This man. The one I've wanted to look at me as *more* since I was old enough to know what a crush was. The boy who used to slay my dragons and may have managed to save me a time or ten before he turned into Kroydon Hills' biggest manwhore just told me I'm beautiful. And now I'm just as pissed off as I am shocked and confused.

"If I'm so beautiful, why the hell did you put clothes back on me last night, Callen? I'm guessing that was a first for you. You don't exactly go around town turning anyone else down."

I regret the words the minute they leave my mouth, but it's too late to take them back.

Callen's jaw clenches as he stabs another stupid pancake.

"Nice to know exactly what you think of me, Cait." He

pushes back from the table, furious. *Shit.* "I've never taken advantage of any woman—drunk or otherwise impaired. I don't need to, but thanks for that."

"Callen. I'm sorry. I shouldn't have said that."

He shakes his head. "Happy birthday, Caitlin."

My stomach churns as I watch him walk away.

Damn it.

There's a soft knock on my door hours later before Bellamy opens it, takes one look at me sobbing on my bed, kicks off her ugly orthopedic sneakers, and curls up next to me. She looks at my TV for a moment, then fluffs the pillow behind her back. "Has he taken her out of the boat yet?"

I shake my head no. "She just saw the picture of the house in the paper."

She slips her legs under the comforter because I like to keep the condo cold, but she hates being cold and snuggles up next to me. "Good. The boat and the swans are my favorite part."

I turn to face my best friend. The only one I've ever had, and I didn't even find her until my freshman year of college. She was new to the school and to the town so she wasn't scared of my family the way everyone else around here is. By the time she found out who my dad is, we'd already cemented our friendship, and she's been stuck with me since. "Did you finally bang Ross last night?"

Her half-assed shrug tells me all I need to know.

"That good, huh?"

Bellamy tucks her hands under her head. "Good is in the eye of the beholder."

"Sorry," I whisper and look back at the TV.

"Yeah. Me too. How was your night?" When I don't answer, she reaches over me to grab the remote and pauses *The Notebook*. "Caitlin . . . what did you do?"

"You can't tell anyone, Bellamy. No one. You understand? Not one of your brothers. Not one of the girls. No one . . ." I trail off, too exhausted to bother coming up with a forced threat I'd have no need to follow through on because my bestie would never tell a soul anything I wanted kept between us. Bellamy Wilder is awesome. Everyone should have a friend like her in their life.

"Well, don't leave me hanging. Oh. My. God. Caitlin Beneventi—did you and Callen *finally* give in?"

I drag my white comforter up over my head, only for her to pull it down. "You didn't," she gasps, shocked.

"No," I squeak. "We didn't."

"Then what aren't you telling me?" she demands, and my stomach takes a nose dive.

"Cone of silence, Bellamy. Swear it."

She glares back before slowly flicking me. "Really?"

"Fine." I'd roll my eyes if I weren't worried the motion would make me throw up. I hate hangovers. "I was really drunk and might have made Callen carry me upstairs."

"Caitlin." She smacks me as her shoulders shake with quiet laughter.

"Hey," I flick her back. "Stop hitting me."

"You made him carry you?" Her giggles grow, and now my hangover isn't the only thing making me want to die . . . Okay—maybe just a teeny bit. I bite down on my lip and don't answer. "Caitlin . . . what else happened?"

I contemplate not telling her for a hot second, but I need to tell someone. I'm good at a lot of things. Dealing with men isn't exactly one of them. They tend to get scared away by my bodyguard or my father. "I kinda stripped in front of him."

She tries to smack me again, but I catch her wrist this time.

Guess my reflexes aren't totally shot.

"Either you stripped or you didn't, Cait."

"Fine. *Yes*. I untied my dress and stood there as it fell to the floor in my pink, lace thong and nothing else," I admit while secondhand embarrassment washes over me *again*.

Wait . . . is it secondhand if it happened to me the first time?

Shit.

Maybe I'm not hungover. Maybe I'm still drunk.

"Good lord, woman. Are you going to make me work for every damn detail? What the hell happened next?"

"He stripped out of his shirt, basically forced it over my body, then shoved me into the bathroom before he put me to bed." A niggling of something scratches at my brain just beyond my memory, but I can't put my finger on it.

Bellamy's eyes are alight with frustration. "Alone?"

I nod.

"Then this morning, I managed to call him a manwhore instead of thanking him for his help."

"Oh shit," she whispers, and I echo the sentiment. "What are you going to do?"

I blink. "I've got nothing . . ." I rest my head on the pillow next to hers and lie on my back. "You want to tell me what to do?"

She leans her head against mine, and I groan.

Yup. Hair still hurts.

"I'd start with an apology and go from there. It'll just be the two of you tonight. I'm going in at six and working a double."

"Oh come on. Seriously? You've got to work?"

"I already told you I'm working a double today and

tomorrow, then leaving to spend a week in Maine with my mom," she scolds me.

"Listen . . . My head is loud enough to be the drummer during a Lilah Ryan concert right now. Cut me a break if I'm processing a little slow," I sulk.

"You'd be a sexy-as-fuck drummer," she smiles.

Always my ride or die.

"I would, wouldn't I?" I agree.

She laughs at me. "Uh-huh. And I'm thinking Callen's out right now. The dogs were both snoring on the couches, but there was no sign of him. So you've got some time to figure out your move."

"You mean my apology."

Bellamy rolls away and does something on her phone. Probably setting an alarm so she can take a nap before going to the hospital. I wish I could fall asleep as easily as she does.

"I mean your next move. You've had a thing for Callen Sinclair for as long as I've known you, Cait. You'll have the house to yourself and a big fat apology to make. See where it goes." She pulls the blanket up under her chin and closes her eyes. "Now, watch the movie so I can catch a few hours of sleep before work."

How come when she says it, it sounds easy, but when I try to do it, I mess it all up?

COOPER

What time are you heading over to Dad's today? I'll meet you there.

—Text from Cooper to Callen.

Cooper stands, leaning against his big ass SUV—his thick arms shoved into the pockets of a pair of cargo shorts, and aviators pulled low, hiding his eyes—when I pull into Dad's driveway a few hours later. He looks fucking exhausted. I guess that's what happens when you have three eighteen-year-olds at home. You probably never stop worrying long enough to sleep.

"What the hell, man?" I ask as I walk up to him. "Worried I was gonna ignore Dad's summons?" Coop smiles and pulls his glasses down to wink at me. Fucker. "Dude, I don't need another Declan, okay?"

Cooper and I have always had an easier relationship than what I have with Murphy, Declan, or Brady. I think it's because football isn't the god Coop bows down to the same way my other brothers and brother-in-law do. He probably could have gone pro if he wanted to, but he only ever wanted to be a Navy SEAL. Well, that and to marry Carys. *Yeah.* Family is so fucked up.

Being good at football and football being your life are two completely different things.

Some guys live to play. Some play to live. I play to play.

"Nah, kid." He throws an arm around my shoulder and rubs his knuckles over my head until I shove him off me. "Not my style. Just wanted to spend time with my baby brother."

I eye him warily. "I just spent a week with all of you at the beach last month."

We knock three times and call out as we walk in, just to be safe. It's an unwritten rule you never walk into Mom and Dad's house unannounced. Not since Murphy walked in on Mom and Dad half-naked on the kitchen table. The one they've refused to replace. My asshole siblings like to say that's where I was conceived. Isn't family fun?

"Hi, boys," Mom calls out from the kitchen. She moves around the island in the center of the room and cups my cheeks in her hand. "You look thin, Callen. Are you hungry?"

I'm six foot six and two hundred and fifty pounds.

No one has *ever* told me I look thin.

"I'm good." I drop a kiss on her cheek, and my stomach growls from the delicious scent of rosemary sourdough bread sitting on cooling racks stacked on the counter. Mom took up bread baking during the pandemic and is very proud of her sourdough starter.

This room has always been the heart of the entire house, but today, it's quiet. "Where's everyone else?"

"I think Dad's in his office. Declan and Murphy are coming over later tonight. Nattie and Brady were already here," she tells us with a sad smile.

"Come on, kid brother." Coop slaps my back.

Everything about this feels off. *Stilted.* Like someone's trying to force a round peg in a square hole. Like I'm the only one not in on a secret. "You guys want to fill me in on what the hell is going on?"

Like is Dad finally ready to retire?

I keep my thoughts to myself because I've got mixed emotions about the whole thing, even if I've been expecting it for a while. There's something about playing for your father. A different level of pressure put on you by everyone. But none of that has ever bothered me the way playing for Dad bothered Declan. Maybe because I grew up wanting to be Dec and knowing in my bones one day, I'd play for my father.

The press had a field day with it when I was drafted, but I ignored them.

It's easy to do when you've been trained to deal with them your entire life.

Coop knocks on Dad's office door before he pushes through.

Dad sits behind his desk with game tape playing on the TV hanging on the other side of the room. He seems as tired as Coop as he takes his glasses off and rubs his eyes. "Hey, guys." He looks between Cooper and me and nods as if agreeing to something. Or maybe bracing for impact. "Are you hungry? I think your mother is making lunch."

"Not really . . ." I trail off, my stomach no longer interested in food.

Nothing about this feels right.

"How about you have a seat, son." Dad motions to the couches in the corner of the room.

"Could someone please tell me what the hell is going on? Are you retiring, Dad?" I ask, refusing to move. The energy around us is wrong. It's heavy . . . *broken.* Every instinct in me is suddenly braced for a fight.

Dad stands across from me, not answering.

Cooper grips my shoulder, and my world falls out from under me.

"You're not retiring, are you?"

A small sniffle slips past Mom's lips as she moves into the room, next to Dad. A united front, as always.

I hadn't even realized she'd followed us in.

"Callen—" Dad stops abruptly. "I *am* retiring. I'll be around to help Declan with the transition this season, but the team is his. It's already been decided with the Kingstons."

I grip the chair for balance, not a fucking doubt in my mind *that* isn't the bomb he's dropping. That was just the warning shot.

"*Why* are you retiring, Dad?" Unwelcome anger courses through my veins like it always does when I'm preparing for a fight on the field. A fight for the ball. For the play. For the win. If you're not fighting for it, you don't want it bad enough. And this . . . this right here feels like the worst kind of fight. The kind you don't ever recover from. "What aren't you telling me?"

Dad's eyes close as he presses his lips to Mom's forehead before he looks at me and Cooper. "I've got cancer, son."

Caitlin

Some people stress clean.

Others stress eat.

I stress bake.

That's what happens when you grow up with a baker as a mother. I rarely crave sweets. Coffee—yes. Sweets . . . not so much. But something about the act of baking. The formulas in the recipes that need to be followed precisely . . . Most I know by heart. The familiar movements I could go through with my eyes closed. The memories of sitting on Mom's counter with my hands in cookie dough while she iced cupcakes. The whole thing calms my mind when nothing else will.

I guess that's why my kitchen looks like something out of the *Great British Bakeoff* when my phone vibrates. Where is it? It's not hard to find when I see the trail of flour moving next to my glass canister.

BELLAMY

Are you up and showered?

CAITLIN

Are you my mother?

BELLAMY

I mean . . . your dad is a total DILF, so there are worse women to be.

CAITLIN

I hate you.

BELLAMY

You love me. Now get showered, get dressed, and get your shit together. I'm about to go into surgery and just wanted to check on you. You gonna be okay?

CAITLIN

When am I ever NOT okay?

BELLAMY

Last night?

CAITLIN

Twat waffle.

BELLAMY

> I prefer French toast.

I look around at my mess and decide maybe I should have made French toast instead of chocolate chip cookies. Hmm . . . there's still time.

CAITLIN

> I'm okay. I've already taken the dogs for a run and showered, and now I'm eating a perfectly healthy dinner.

BELLAMY

> The dogs don't run, and neither do you. And you wouldn't know a perfectly healthy dinner if it smacked you in your face. You're baking, aren't you?

CAITLIN

> Whatever. I've showered and gotten dressed. That's as good as it's getting today.

BELLAMY

> Triple chocolate fudge cake?

CAITLIN

> Ha! No. Chocolate chip cookies.

BELLAMY

> Now who's the twat? You should have made them yesterday so I could have one.

CAITLIN

> You shouldn't have left me.

BELLAMY

> Tits up, you spicy little burrito. You've got this. Take the problem by the balls and yank.

CAITLIN

You've got to stop with the Instagram reels. They're warping your brain.

BELLAMY

Whatever. You like them too. They're funny.

Apologize to him, Cait. Let me know how it goes.

CAITLIN

Tell Momma Wilder I said hi when you get to Maine tomorrow.

I shove my phone into my shorts pocket and look around at my mess.

Maybe rage cleaning would have been more effective.

*M*eatball pops his head up from where he's been sleeping next to me for the past hour and stares at the door before I hear someone fumbling with the key, followed by a distinctly Callen curse. I guess it's time to face the music.

I wait another minute, but unease washes over me when there's still no Callen.

"Come on, Meatball." I shove his chubby body off me and watch as he stretches into downward dog and slides off the couch in slow-motion, then trots over to the door where Cupcake is two steps ahead of him, already whimpering.

What the hell?

With my hand on the doorknob, I check the peephole, but there's no one there.

Huh . . . Maybe he changed his mind and decided not to come home.

Great. I guess I screwed up so bad he doesn't want to be alone with me.

Cupcake scratches at the door and whines, and Meatball sits his fat ass on my feet.

The needy little fucker is always like this whenever Maddox is gone.

"He's not here," I tell the dogs and try to kick Meatball off, but he's a legit sixty-pound lump, and if he doesn't want to move, he's not moving. "Okay. Fine. I'll check," I growl, then roll my damn eyes because I am, in fact, arguing with a dog.

I crack the door, and it pushes all the way open as Callen's big body falls backward into the foyer. "What the hell?"

Callen opens his glassy green eyes as he lies flat on the floor, confusion dancing in his dazed eyes. "Hey, kitten. What are you doing up there?"

"What the hell, Callen? Are you drunk?"

Meatball licks his face, and Callen licks him back.

Oh. My. God.

He lifts his hand and pinches his fingers together like he's trying to show me an inch, but in reality his thumb and pointer are smooshed together. "Just a little bit. Wanna help me up?"

I look him over, trying to figure out how the hell I'm supposed to get him up before I grab his hand. This is never gonna work. "Come on, you big oaf. Let's get you up."

I tug, but he doesn't budge. Instead, he smiles a sloppy smile. "You know it would only take one pull, right?"

I kick his butt. Not hard. Even I'm not that mean, *but seriously* . . . what the hell?

"I just tried to pull, Sinclair. Your fat ass didn't budge." I yank my hand away, but he doesn't let go.

"One pull and you'd be down here with me, kitten. One time. Just once."

Holy shit.

Callen's grip on me tightens. "It would be so easy to give in."

Ummm . . . what?

This time when I kick him, it's hard.

"Oww." He wraps a hand around my ankle, and a shiver runs up my spine. "Kitten has claws. That wasn't very nice, Caitie."

"Jesus Christ, Callen." I pull my leg away from him and yank my hand free. "Get up, and I'll make you a cup of coffee."

In a move that shouldn't be sexy but really . . . really is, Callen stands and somehow picks me up with him, then leans me against the wall. My breath catches in my throat as he strokes a hand over my hair. "That's an urban legend."

"What?" I ask, completely confused. What the hell is happening right now?

Callen drops my feet to the floor, then wobbles a little, and I grab the front of his shirt to steady him. "Coffee doesn't sober up a drunk. It just gives you a wide-awake drunk."

"I don't think that's what urban legend means, Sinclair." That sloppy grin from moments ago turns wicked, and I can't stop my body from taking notice. And based on the way Callen is looking at me, my reaction isn't lost on him. "What's going on, Callen? This isn't like you."

His smile vanishes, and he takes a step back out of reach, then turns away from me and walks away.

What the actual hell?

"Callen," I call out and follow him down the hall and into his room, like one of the dogs. "What are you doing?"

He strips out of his shirt and tosses it on the bed. "I'm taking a shower. Wanna join me?"

I mean . . . the logical answer is yes. But *yes* isn't an option. Not now.

What did he say this morning about taking advantage?

Concern creeps it's way in . . . I've watched this man for years, and this isn't like him.

"You gonna stand there gawking, kitten? Or are you gonna join me?"

He shoves his shorts down his legs, thankfully leaving his boxers on. But oh my, I now know why every woman in a fifty-mile radius wants to fuck Callen Sinclair. And his tight black boxers do very little to hide the very big reason. His shorts get tangled around his ankles, and I see it all happening in slow-motion before either of us hits the bed.

Callen stumbles, trying to step out of his shorts, and I reach for him, trying to steady him again. But this time, instead of staying put on his feet, he tumbles backward onto his bed, taking me with him, and I land with an *oomph* on his chest. And instead of either of us moving, we both lie frozen in place, holding our breath.

"You're so damn beautiful, Caitlin," he whispers as his fingers play with the long strands of my hair hitting his face, and I could cry. I've spent so many years wanting to hear those words from this man. But not like this. Not after last night and this morning.

Is this because of that?

Did I do this?

Without giving myself time to overthink it, I push up out of his arms. "All right, Romeo. No shower for you. I think it's bedtime."

I pull his shorts off his ankles, yank his comforter down, and move his legs under it. But it's like trying to move dead weight. "Help me here, Sinclair."

Callen blinks, and his eyes clear. "Stay with me, Cait."

"What? You can't be serious." My heart cracks, and I want to scream.

Where has this Callen been for years, and why the hell does it only come out when one of us is drunk?

"It's been a shit day." He swallows, and his green eyes plead. "I don't want to be alone."

My hand shakes as I gently brush his hair away from his face.

Is it possible to love and hate someone equally?

Because this man is all I've ever wanted . . . but not like this.

Not when he doesn't know what he's doing or saying.

Not when he has no clue he's breaking my heart.

"Just let me lock the condo up, okay?" I run my thumb along his brow, and he closes his eyes and relaxes. "I'll come back after."

"Promise?"

"I promise," I whisper back and know there's no way I'm making him sleep alone tonight. I might not get a minute's sleep, but I'll be doing it right here.

She remembered who she was, and the game didn't change. It ended.

—Caitlin's Secret Thoughts

Okay . . . So maybe following through on my promise and actually getting back in bed with Callen wasn't my smartest move, but hey, at least I grabbed my Kindle before I came to bed.

Who the fuck am I kidding?

That was mistake number one hundred and fifty-two where this man is concerned.

Because lying in his bed—with his face buried against my stomach, and his arms wrapped around my waist like I'm a lifeline as he sleeps off whatever this drunken bender of his is—is only one piece of this absolute mind-fuck of a night.

When he wrapped himself around me hours ago, I didn't move. Didn't breathe. *Honestly,* couldn't figure out what the hell was happening and figured he'd shift away eventually.

He didn't.

Being surrounded by his scent, his blanket, his body, in

his space. The one I've never seen him bring a woman into in all the years I've lived here . . . yeah. That's all fucking with me enough that five hours and three-quarters of the way through the new A.J. James romance my friend sent me earlier tonight, and I'm a hot mess.

I didn't think it was possible, but this book is even spicier than her last one, which means basically, I'm in hell. I'm turned-on, and pissed off—because *really*? What was Callen thinking? Preseason started a few weeks ago, so getting drunk like this isn't like him. And getting drunk and saying what he said—well, that was just mean. And confusing. So damn confusing.

Callen pulls me closer as his hands slip under my tank top just above the waistband of my shorts, and I inch backward.

Uh-uh. No way this is happening, not like this.

But apparently, he has other plans.

His hands sear my skin as they smooth up my back, and I close my Kindle and smack him on the head with it. "Down, boy."

"Ow, Cait. What the fuck?" he groans, and I'm kinda impressed he knows where he is and who he's with. I guess thank goodness for small miracles and fast metabolisms.

"Sorry, Sinclair. I'm not about to let your drunk ass molest me in your sleep," I snap, impressed with myself because I really, *really* want his hands on me anyway I can have him. But this is Callen . . . and he'd never forgive himself, and I'm a better friend than that.

Stupid morals.

There's pain in his green eyes when he pulls back. A pain I didn't cause him. "What happened, Callen?" I ask softly. Completely unlike me because again . . . this is Callen.

People might like to tease that I'm all hard edges and smart answers, but no one is like that all the time. Not even me. And if there's ever been someone I wanted to be soft for . . . To let my guard down with, it's him. "This isn't you. You don't drink until you pass out. And you sure as hell don't ask me to stay with you. You usually don't want to have anything to do with me."

He drags his hand down his face and pushes up next to me so we're sitting side by side, with our backs against his tufted brown-leather headboard and our legs lined up next to each other. Not saying anything. No smart-ass comeback or quick-witted argument. He doesn't look at me, just stares down at his hands for a long time while I wait in silence—something I've never been good at.

"Callen . . ." I wrap my hand around his, unsure what I want to say, so I do what I do best and wing it. "Do you remember when I was little, and my mom told me I wasn't allowed in the tree house?"

A crooked smile tugs at the corner of his lips.

One I could draw with my eyes closed, I've seen it so many times.

"Which time?" he asks with a hint of quiet sarcasm that eases my mind just a little.

"The first time when I followed you guys up there anyway and asked you and Maddox to let me play with you." I picture it so clearly in my mind. Six-year-old me, already in love with ten-year-old Callen, who cared about exactly two things. Football and his friendship with my brother. He barely knew I existed back then . . . at least most of the time.

Guess some things never change.

Callen flips his hand over, and strong, calloused fingers lace with mine and squeeze, making my heart squeeze right along with them. "You mean the time you followed us up there, even though you weren't supposed to and demanded you be allowed to play too, then stomped your foot when Maddox told you no?"

I take a measured chance and rest my head against his

shoulder, needing to give him whatever kind of comfort I can right now. "I mean the time the two of you left me up there after Maddox said he was going to tell Dad."

I close my eyes and fight back a tear when he presses his lips against my forehead.

Callen and I like to tease each other.

We like to bicker and joke and make fun of the other one.

It's what we do.

What we don't typically do is touch. Not like this. *Never* like this, no matter how much I wish we would. No matter how many times I've hoped and wished for it. He touches everyone else so freely. His friends. His family. But never me.

"The time you were too scared to climb back down the ladder and sat at the edge, crying." His voice is hoarse from sleep as I hold my breath, soaking it in.

"Until you came back up and told me to climb on your back and hold on to you so you could climb us both down," I whisper so quietly, it's nearly inaudible, still able to remember exactly what it felt like to have him save me—and exactly how much it hurt when he pulled away after Maddox showed up. "You were so sweet until Maddox came back with Dad. Then you agreed with him that I was just a stupid girl and walked away."

He's so close, if I lift my head just a little, we'd be face to face and lip to lip.

"You like to do that, Callen. You like to say things when no one else is here to hear them and do things when we're alone and there's no one here to witness." I pull away because we wouldn't be Callen and Caitlin if there weren't a push and pull between us, even if no one but us ever knows it's there. "Well, there's no one here now, so how about you tell me what's going on, and we'll act like you never said a word after. I'm worried about you, Sinclair."

Callen

*T*his woman has no fucking clue.

Not about the day I've had, the fucking shit news I got, or the way I feel about her.

How could she? I haven't told her any of it.

I can't.

I shouldn't.

"Cait." Her name is jagged like glass ripped from my throat. "I—"

"You do, Callen. Don't bother saying you don't do it. Look around you. Where am I?" She lifts her head and moves away, facing me instead of beside me. Her arms wrap around her knees, and she lifts her beautiful face and nails me with nearly violet eyes. "I'd never be in here if Maddox was home. Seriously . . . I wouldn't be here if anyone were home, and you know it. You would have never asked."

It's not the honesty in her words that bothers me. How can it when she's right, and I know it? I've always fucking known it. It's the hurt in her voice. In her face. In the way she's holding herself. "I'm sorry . . ."

Cait shakes her head and tucks her hair behind her ears.

"Don't, Sinclair. Don't apologize. That's just a half-assed Band-Aid. Fix it. Tell me what's wrong. What happened today?"

I think back to my conversation with my parents earlier.

To the one I had with Cooper when we went to West End after.

Fuck.

"I can't, Cait. I made a promise," I might as well plead with her not to ask me again. Dad doesn't want word getting out. Not yet. He wants to keep this private for as long as he can while he works out a plan with the owner of the team, Killian's mom, Scarlet Kingston-St. James.

She closes her eyes and drags perfectly white teeth over her pouty pink lip as her hair dances over her shoulders with a shake of her head. When she opens them, there's a fire there that was missing before. It's burning hot and beautifully pissed. Rightfully so. "I'm so fucking sorry, Cait."

"For what, Callen?" she whispers, and somehow that's worse than if she were yelling, because this woman is never quiet. It's not her natural state. Caitlin is loud without ever uttering a word. She's vibrant and demands all the attention in every room she's ever walked in, just by standing silently in the center. It's as natural as breathing for her. The rest of us are just lucky to orbit around her, but I can't get too close. My friendship with her brother would never survive the fire.

"For what I said. I shouldn't have—"

She climbs off the bed and whacks me with a pillow. "Fuck you, Callen. Fuck you for saying I'm beautiful, then acting like you were wrong to say it." The moon glints off her wild eyes as she hits me again. "Fuck you for asking me to stay with you because you didn't want to be alone." Her voice never gets louder. That's Caitlin's style. She doesn't need to yell to get her point across. She smacks me one more time— while I sit here and take it because she's right—before she drops the pillow and steps back. "Fuck you, Callen. You made me feel like shit this morning for what I said, then you turned around and made me feel like every other unimportant woman in your life and in your bed. But you know what? At least they get an orgasm out of it."

She groans and grabs her Kindle.

"Figure your shit out, Callen, because one of these days—" She stops and stares at me with so much disappointment in her eyes that it weighs me down. But not her. No. She stands with her head held high, every inch of her the princess she was raised to be. "Do you feel anything at all for me, Callen? Anything?"

"*Caitlin—*" Fuck. Yes. I feel it all. I always fucking have . . . That's what I want to say. But I don't, feeling like an utter piece of shit who doesn't even deserve her anyway.

"How the hell am I supposed to answer that?" I stand up and take a step toward her, my frustration over this entire fucking day boiling over. "What do you want to hear, Cait?"

We do a dance. For every step I take forward, she takes one back. "You want to hear that I got the worst news of my life today, and I can't even talk to you about it because I made a goddamned promise, and I'm a man of my word?"

Another step forward and another one back.

"You want to know that I promised my best friend years ago that I wouldn't touch his baby sister? Because I did, Cait. I made him a fucking promise. My best friend. Your brother. The one person whose always been there for me. Through all the fucking shit. The Heisman shit in college. The pro shit show after. Christ, Cait. I practically lived at your goddamned house." I can't stop the way my voice booms louder with each new revelation until she's backed up against the wall.

My chest vibrates with anger.

At her.

At Maddox.

At myself.

Fuck—I can't.

"But . . ." Her voice trembles with hesitation.

"No buts, Cait." I cup her face, even though I know I shouldn't. Her soft skin feels fucking perfect in my hands. "Four fucking years, Caitlin. I've lived with you for four fucking years. I've had to act like your presence doesn't affect me. Like you're not the most gorgeous woman in any room.

Like I don't fucking want you when I do. I can't fucking do this anymore."

I lean my forehead against hers.

"Then don't," she whispers back.

If only it were that easy.

"It's not that simple." No matter how much I wish it was, and fuck, I wish it was.

She reaches up with one hand and wraps it around my neck, anchoring herself to me as unshed tears pool in her glittering eyes. "Nothing worth having is ever easy. I've heard you say that a million times, Callen. I'm worth having."

Caitlin presses her lips to mine, and before I can react, she ducks under my arms and opens the door. "Figure it out soon, Callen, because I'm not going to wait around forever."

Orgasms are like baking. I *can* do it myself, but I'd much rather have someone do it for me.

—*Caitlin's Secret Thoughts*

"**K**nock, knock."

Everly looks up from her sketch pad and puts down her colored pencil as I walk into her office, coffee in hand. "Bless you." She smiles and pops her grabby hands into the air and takes the raspberry-mocha-caffeinated goodness from my hands. "I swear your mother is a goddess."

She's not wrong.

Sweet Temptations, the bakery my mother has owned my entire life, is just a few doors down the street from Everly Wilder Designs offices and flagship showroom. Callen's niece is one of the hottest wedding gown designers in the last five years. Needless to say, I jumped when I was offered the chance to work with her after graduation.

She can have the brides. I focus on bridal party couture and formal wear.

I also dabble a little in styling on the side. When you have friends as high-profile as I do, it's fun to dress them for everything from a low-key photo op to the ESPYs. Most of the clueless athletes in my life send me off with their credit cards and let me update their wardrobe whenever I think they need it. Like real life Ken dolls. In some ways, I enjoy styling more than designing.

Clothes can tell you almost everything about a person.

Like today, my clothes are like a shield from a shitty day.

My heels are high. My skirt is short black leather, and my white blouse is perfectly starched. It also makes my boobs look significantly bigger than they are.

Thank God for push-up bras.

I carefully cross my legs as I sit in the icy-blue velvet chair opposite Everly's desk, careful not to spill my black coffee. I like my sweets in the form of food. Not drink.

Caffeine should be strong and dark and freshly ground with a splash of cream.

Not *give you a cavity* like Everly's will.

"You look terrible, Cait. Did you get any sleep?" She leans back in her chair and hums as the caffeine hits her bloodstream. "Ohh . . ." A calculated smile stretches across her face. "Or did you not get any sleep because you were *busy?*"

"Excuse me? Glass house meet stone . . . I do not look terrible. I look tired, thank you very much. I didn't sleep well last night." It's not like I can tell her I didn't exactly sleep alone for the majority of the night. Not with how close she is with Callen and Maddox.

I swear this whole damn town is interconnected.

And gossip spreads like wildfire.

Next thing I know, the *Kroydon Kronicles* will be talking about it.

Whatever *it* is.

I think back to my fight with Callen and the complete

lack of sleep I got after and wonder, *for the millionth time,* what I could have done differently.

The answer is everything.

How the hell did this weekend go so wrong?

"Listen . . . I have three kids keeping me awake at night." She picks up her sketchbook and tosses it my way.

A dark, deep purple ball gown is sketched, but nothing about it looks at all like one of Everly's typical wedding gowns. "What's this?"

She raises a perfectly arched blonde eyebrow.

"I swear to God, Everly. If you say a design, I'll make sure my mother never serves you another cup of coffee again." That's basically the seventh level of hell for my overly caffeinated boss.

The bitch laughs.

"I hate you," I quip back, joking. Well, for the most part. I don't hate her. I grew up in constant awe of her and her twin sister, Grace. They were pretty and popular with a million friends, and Maddox and Callen adored them. The twins were allowed to do everything with the guys, unlike me.

But that's what happens when your moms are best friends.

My mom actually saved her mom's life when she was pregnant with Everly and Grace.

What can I say . . . my mom's a great shot.

I mean, I'm better. But with Amelia Beneventi as a mother, it's expected.

"You make it so easy, sometimes, Caitie." Everly laughs, and I bristle. Not many people can get away with calling me Caitie. Everly is one of the few. "It's an idea. My cousin Lilah called me yesterday. She's agreed to do a short stadium tour. It's going to be her last one for a while. She's getting tired and wants to spend some time home . . . But first, her label wants her to spend the next six months touring the world, and she wants us to design every costume for the show. Every dancer. Every performer. Every costume she wears. And she wants to kick it off in three months."

"Holy shit," I whisper. This is huge. Lilah is basically the biggest pop star in the world. My hands itch for my pencils already. "Where do we start?"

"I was hoping you'd say that. Lilah will be coming in for a meeting at ten this morning. You ready for this?" she challenges, and my skin prickles with excitement.

"Are you?" I counter, and Everly nods as I hand her back her sketchbook, suddenly wide-awake and brimming with excitement. "Am I pulling any fabric samples for the meeting?"

"Purple is the only input she's given me." She hands me one of our swatch sample books. "Go get inspired and bring you're A game. She wants it all. Gowns and dresses. Short. Long. Tight. Flowy. It's to promote her *Sixteen Dresses* album."

"What's the name of the tour?" I ask as I pull out my phone to capture a few notes and ideas I already have.

"The Captivating Tour."

Callen

J've had concussions that didn't mess up my head the way it is today.

Thank fuck we don't have to be at the practice facility for a few hours.

Yeah . . . it's gonna be a shit day.

I throw on shorts, grab my sneakers, and chug a vitamin water, ready to go for a run and sweat the whiskey out of my system, right along with a certain five-foot-four blue-eyed beauty when my phone vibrates in my pocket.

I consider throwing it across the fucking room when I see who it is.

NATTIE

Hey, little brother. Heard you talked to Dad last night. How are you doing?

Leave it to Nattie to mother-hen me when even my mom hasn't done that today.

MURPHY

He's fine, Nat. Don't baby him. Dad is going to be fine. We're all fine.

NATTIE

None of this is fine, Murph.

COOPER

How about you all stop saying fine. It makes you sound psychotic.

DECLAN

Fighting about it isn't going to help, guys. Dad's gonna get through this, and we're all gonna help him do it.

NATTIE

I don't doubt that, Dec. I just wanted to check in on Callen. And maybe to remind him we haven't told the kids yet. So maybe don't mention anything to them. Okay?

CALLEN

Really, Nat? The kids? Most of your kids are in their twenties. And Dad asked us not to say anything. Did you really think I was gonna run my mouth?

Sometimes having such a big age gap with my siblings isn't the worst thing.

This isn't one of those times.

CARYS

Callen . . .

CALLEN

Don't, Carys.

They love to baby me.

Always have. And I get it.

But seriously . . . Now's not the time for that shit.

COOPER

Dad said business as usual until he announces his retirement. We've got our orders.

NATTIE

Some of us aren't former SEALs used to taking orders, Cooper.

MURPHY

Should have played team sports, Nat.

NATTIE

Shut up, Murph.

CARYS

Aiden Murphy! Don't be a bully.

NATTIE

Declan – when is Dad announcing his retirement?

DECLAN

He's not sure yet.

NATTIE

Okay. Well I think we should all take turns checking on him.

MURPHY

Uhhh . . . He'd hate that.

CALLEN

And Mom's there. I don't think he needs us acting like he's sick.

NATTIE

He is sick, guys.

I stare at my sister's words as they eat away at me like acid.

He. *Is.* Sick.

I'm not sure if it's the hangover or the way Cait left me spinning last night, but I can't wrap my head around those three words.

He didn't look sick.

He looked the same.

Strong. Healthy. Immortal.

You meet a shit-ton of guys with daddy issues when you play football. Some guys have dads who tried to relive their glory days through them. Those guys resent the sport.

Some felt like the only way to get their old man's attention and approval was through the game. They're generally douchebags with a chip on their shoulders. They make great defensive line guys. They're angry. Anger works on the field.

I've met a few who've used football as a giant fuck you to their father because they didn't want to be the doctor or lawyer their parents expected them to be, and this was the best way to get away from the expectations.

It was never like that for me.

There were constant expectations, but they were the kind that make you a better athlete and a better man. If you're going to do something, you give it everything you've got. There's no such thing as half-in. If you're in, you're 100 percent in. And I was in from the first time I held a football in my hand.

Late-night practices? Bring it on.

Extra time in the weight room? Works for me. Strength makes everything better.

Study tapes? I'm gonna study those fuckers until I know how many fucking freckles the dude lined up across from me on game day has. I'll know every play. I'll know plays they haven't come up with yet. No one is ever going to accuse me of being unprepared. And they're sure as hell never going to question my right to wear the Kings black and gold. It's the only colors I've ever wanted to wear.

When Declan was drafted to the Kings, he resented the hell out of it. I've heard the stories. The press used to say it was *daddy ball.* Yeah . . . that lasted one season until Dec took that ball and shoved it down all the doubters throats during the Super Bowl.

Dad likes to talk about the legacy you leave.

Our legacy is dominance.

Joe Sinclair took a mediocre team and created a dynasty.

One I'm proud as hell to be a part of.

Football is the greatest sport in the world, and I'm one of the best to ever play it.

I didn't do it for my father or my brothers.

I did it because I fucking love it.

I've played battered, bruised, and injured, and there's never been a single moment in my career where I haven't wanted to be on that field . . .

Until today.

The Philly Press

WHAT'S IN THE WATER?

What happens when you take three hot hockey players and add one bad boy baller?

Well . . . every woman and more than a few men sitting at West End tonight were treated to the sum of that very equation when four incredibly gorgeous Sinclair men had dinner while the rest of us mere mortals sat wiping drool from our chins.

What is in the water in Kroydon Hills, and how do I get some?

#WhatsInTheWater #IdLikeToBeTheSumOfThatEquation #KroydonKronicles

Callen

"Swear to fuck, guys. It's not like this everywhere. You've got to get the hell out of this town. They leave us alone in Chicago. I'm not in a constant fish tank." Hendrix, Declan's youngest son, looks between his older brothers and me, disgusted by the constant attention the *Kroydon Kronicles* shines on the local celebrities. Especially our friends and family.

"Dude, I'd be one of those little sucker sharks in a fish tank. Top of the food chain."

"Leo . . . seriously, man, you know they attach themselves to the glass and eat the algae, right?" I shake my head, then laugh as Nixon shoves Leo.

"What the hell is wrong with you?" Nix asks as we walk back to the condo. "Did Dad drop you on your head as a baby or something?"

"You gotta look past the *Kronicles*. The rest of the town doesn't give a shit who we are or what we're doing." This town protects their own, for the most part, but I wonder how bad the attention is going to get once word gets out about Dad.

Leo claps me on the back. "And that's coming from a frequent *Kronicles* headliner."

"Fuck off," I grumble, unable to talk to these guys about what's going on. Only a year separates Nixon and me, but these guys are part of *the kids* my sister *so eloquently* told me not to tell about Dad's diagnosis.

"What the hell's going on with you tonight, *Uncle*?" Leo pushes.

He always pushes.

Hendrix snickers, and I groan.

"Dude, didn't you two walk in on your mom and dad getting it on during vacation last month?" I push back to get them to shut up.

I want to get the hell home and go to bed. We don't have practices on Tuesdays, and right about now, I'm living for tomorrow.

"Too soon, Callen," Hendrix bitches, and I side-eye him.

Nixon's chest shakes with laughter as we walk into the lobby of our building and wave at the doorman. "We're never letting you live it down either, little brother."

"I'm never gonna look at a washing machine the same way," Hendrix mumbles, and yeah . . . it might make me crack a smile. "Fuck, man. I'm gonna have nightmares again now. You gonna comfort me, Nix?"

Nixon shoves him away as we wait for the elevator. "You're on the couch tonight, shithead."

"Come on. I'm flying back to Chicago tomorrow. You're not really making me crash on a couch, are ya?"

Leo flicks Hendrix's ear. "Could'a slept at Mom and Dad's. I'm sure your noise-canceling headphones would have been fine."

"Dude . . ." Hendrix closes his eyes. "I'll take the couch."

I lean my head back against the wall, tired as shit, and watch the dynamic play out between the brothers before the doors open on Nix and Leo's floor, one below mine. They file out, but I grab Hendrix and drag him in for a hug. "See you soon, man."

"See ya, *Uncle.*"

"Fucker," I mumble and shove him through the door.

Cupcake and Meatball greet me at the door a minute later, shaking their little asses, demanding to be given the attention they want, and refusing to move until I give in. Kinda like someone else I know. I lock up behind myself and chug a bottle of water in the kitchen, hoping no one else is home. But I know *she* is. I can feel it in my bones. That's what it's been like since the day Caitlin moved in.

I move into the dimly lit, quiet family room, where the woman who haunts my fucking dreams as much as my days sits, curled up in the corner of the couch. Her delicate frame is lit by a single lamp as her hand moves furiously over her sketchpad. Cait's dark hair is piled on top of her head with a pencil sticking through the center of it, holding it in place. A single strap of her black tank top has fallen off her shoulder, giving me a glimpse of way too much creamy, perfect skin.

Skin I want to mark.

To claim.

But I can't.

Not with this woman.

Not now.

Not ever.

"Callen . . . Callen—"

Her words are hushed, like she's in a vacuum.

Shit.

"Earth to Callen." She looks up at me, annoyed that I'm standing between her and the lamp. "Are you ignoring me or have you just taken too many tackles to the head?"

Fuck—she's beautiful.

"You don't take tackles to the head, kitten." My feet don't budge as she puts down her sketchbook and purple pencils and stands to face me. Her tits push the boundaries of her soft-looking tank, with her peaked nipples holding my gaze like oncoming headlights I can't look away from. Jesus Christ, I can't do this anymore.

"I know." She smiles as if last night didn't happen and she hadn't walked away, pissed and hurt. And it's the hurt that killed me. Pissed Caitlin I can handle. Hurt is a whole different game, and I swear to fuck, I can't keep up with her. "I was calling your name, and it was like you were lost somewhere else. I knew if I got a football term wrong, you'd correct me."

She reaches out and tugs my hand in hers, and something about her touch breaks me in a way I'm not sure I want to recover from.

Before yesterday, I thought I was un-fucking-breakable.

"Cait—it's been a shit day . . ."

Her fingers brush my temple, and I close my eyes and soak in the touch I know I shouldn't allow.

"Talk to me, Callen." Caitlin's voice is soft and so unlike her. "We used to talk."

I did that to her, and damn, I don't like knowing she's now hesitant with me.

"I gave my word, Cait." I don't know how I'm going to shoulder that weight though. Not when it's already a million-pound anchor drowning me.

Her pale cheeks flush with fiery anger. "My brother—"

"It's not Maddox," I cut her off. I owe her that much. "It's my dad," I utter, so damn frustrated.

"Coach?" She takes a step closer, and all the anger that was there a second ago is washed away like the change of the tide. "Is he okay?"

No one ever gives Caitlin the credit she deserves for being as intuitive as she is. They all see her as a flaky socialite, more interested in designer shoes and clothes than anything that matters. They don't know her. They never took the time to watch her. Their loss.

I grab her nearly naked shoulders, tangling my fingers in her straps, unable to think straight while she's touching me.

"I won't say a word, Callen. Something is eating you alive. It's enough that you stumbled in blackout drunk last night." Sadness laces her tone as her icy-blue eyes shudder at the mention of last night. She's not yelling at me like I expected, and that's somehow worse.

"You're wrong," I tell her, and she laughs a silent laugh.

With a determined tightness settling in, she takes another step toward me until only inches separate us. "I'm not. Whatever *it* is, it's already consuming you. You need to talk to someone, and I'm the only one here, buddy."

"You forgive me for last night then?" I'm not sure why I even ask, but I do it knowing I might not like the answer.

She shakes her head. "I'm choosing to be the bigger person. You're still my friend, and you're hurting."

"You're not wrong about *that*, Cait." I can hear the exhaustion in my own voice, but there's nothing I can do about it. Not now. Not when I'm so fucking tired. Tired of fighting this. Tired of just the idea of fighting everything that's coming. Fucking tired of fighting her.

She cocks her head to the side, working through what I mean.

"I wasn't blackout drunk. I remember all of last night. I knew what I was doing. It's the only part of the whole fucking day I don't want to forget." I slide my hands down to her waist and breathe her in like she's the hit of pure oxygen I need to get through the night. "I knew I shouldn't have done that. And I know I shouldn't be doing *this*, Cait."

Her breath gets caught in her chest as a tremor runs down her beautiful body.

The tips of her fingers skim over my lips, and my control frays at the edges as it pulls tight, trying to hold strong. *But failing.*

"Careful, Callen. You're not getting another chance." She presses up on her toes and wraps her arms around my neck. "Be sure this is what you want."

And it's like I can see each individual strand of the string holding me back snapping one at a time.

I'm not good enough for her—*snap.*

Our families are already too interconnected—*snap.*

She's part of my inner circle—*snap*

Until there's only one string left.

"You can't just use me to forget the rest."

That's when the final string breaks.

Fuck it.

Caitlin

*C*allen's mouth is on mine, intense and unrelenting, like an all-consuming fire, sucking all the oxygen from the room and demanding everything I've desperately wanted him to take for years.

His hands slide down to my ass, and I'm lifted in his arms. "Fuck, Cait . . ."

My name is like a prayer violently ripped from his lips like nothing I've ever heard before. Heaven wars with hell as he takes the stairs two at a time, kissing and licking, teeth grazing and hands squeezing. Part of me knows this—*us*—can't happen.

Shouldn't happen. I'm waiting for him to tell me so. *Dreading it.*

But with each touch . . . each kiss and suck, I push my thoughts away because I've never wanted anyone or anything as much as I want this man in this moment.

In every moment.

Callen kicks open his bedroom door and spins us around, pressing me up against the cool wood door. His muscles shake with restraint as he rips his lips from mine and presses them to my forehead, and I close my eyes, thinking—*now is it.* Now is when he's going to stop.

Because we've been *here* before, and that crashed and burned before it ever started.

Only this time, he doesn't push me away. He pulls me closer. One hand bands around my waist, and the other cups my face as his green eyes darken, and he leans his forehead against mine. Our lips are barely a whisper of a breath a part as he licks his lips. "Four fucking years, kitten. I've kept my distance from you . . ."

His voice is deep and strained, but those aren't the words I crave.

"I don't want your distance, Callen. Please. *Please.* Please. Don't stop." I shove my hands under his shirt and drag my nails down his back, clawing to get closer. "Please . . ."

"I've been the better man for four fucking years," he growls and captures my lips as I sink against him. "I can't do it anymore, Caitlin." His words teeter on the edge of barely disguised anger before he swallows my cry and carries me to the bed.

I'm dropped down with a bounce, and before my next breath, my cami and shorts are in a pile on the floor, and Callen is on his knees with my thighs thrown over his shoulders, shaking with a matching need. "You are so fucking beautiful, kitten."

I lose all sense of self-control as rough, calloused hands skim the inside of my thighs, followed by his lips. His hot breath causes goosebumps to break out over every inch of my cool flesh, while Callen's fingers play with the strings of my thong. Tracing them. Snapping them. Running under them. "I like this, Cait. Black lace suits you. My black cat."

His nose glides up my thigh and over the expensive lingerie before he rips it from my body with his bare hands.

I lean up on my elbows and look down at the sinful sight in front of me. Callen's head should live between my legs.

"That was Italian silk lace," I gasp as his tongue licks up the length of my sex, and I lose any sense of control I may have had left and fall back against the bed.

"I'll buy you more," he growls against my pussy, and the vibrations send me skyrocketing.

A moan slips past my lips as my vision darkens, and I bury my fingers in his thick hair.

Every nerve ending is supercharged with an electric current pulsing through my body.

Already on the verge of falling . . .

Of breaking in a way I never have.

A way I might not recover from.

Callen sucks my clit between his lips, and I hum deep in my throat as he slides one blunt, beautifully calloused finger into me, then another. Stretching me.

"So fucking wet for me, Caitlin."

Oh my God.

I see stars as I close my eyes, the sound of his voice threatening to get me off all by itself.

"Don't stop," I gasp as I grind shamelessly against his face. "Please, Callen. I need . . . *more.*"

"I know what you need, kitten," he teases and bites down on my throbbing, swollen clit, sending a shockwave straight to my core.

"Tell me this is for me, Caitlin" he demands as he adds another finger, curling it inside me, and my orgasm tugs at the edge of my sanity. "Tell me this pussy is wet for me . . . Have you been dreaming about me fucking you?" His teeth graze my clit. "Filling you?"

Callen looks up at me and slaps my pussy, then buries his face against me, and I don't have time to even think as I come blindingly fast and hard, shaking and screaming his name.

"Fucking beautiful, Caitlin," he growls as he kisses the inside of each thigh before he drops them to the bed and stands.

I think I'm going to die as I watch him walk away, dazed and confused and heartbroken, thinking he's *walking away,* until he comes back in from the bathroom, carrying a string of condoms.

Thank God one of us is thinking straight because I'm pretty sure I'm incapable of higher-functioning reasoning right now. This—*whatever this is with Callen*—has fried my brain.

The sexy, cocky smile pulling at his lips has ruined me, and that's before he shoves his jeans and boxer briefs down his legs and rolls the condom over his beautifully thick, long, hard dick. My God, my mouth waters at the sight.

"Kitten . . ." He drops a knee on the bed next to me. Two thick, rough fingers drag through my hypersensitive sex before he paints my lips with my own cum, then presses down. "Open for me and suck."

I do as I'm told and eagerly slip him between my lips. My tongue traces the pads of his fingers before sucking them into my mouth, so completely turned-on, it nearly shocks me.

Callen's lust-fueled deep-green eyes grow wild before he captures my lips with his, sucking my tongue and sharing the taste.

My toes curl as every inch of my body sparks, ready for more.

I reach down and wrap my hand around Callen's cock, unable to fist him completely, and the sexy sound that rumbles through his chest at the sight of it is so fucking hot.

I press him against my entrance, then look up, unexpectedly hesitant.

"It'll fit, kitten." His hand covers mine and drags his cock through my sex, coating himself in my wetness. And there goes that smile again.

"Fuck me, Callen." The words are quiet as I get lost in the moment.

"Never could tell you no, Cait," he whispers against my lips and pushes himself inside me in one long, deep stroke. But it's not enough. I want more.

My body throbs with a need I've never felt before as pleasure threatens to pull me under.

Callen stretches me so completely, my body vibrates around his.

"Gonna need you to breathe, Cait."

I hadn't realized I was holding my breath until his hand cups my face, and he takes my mouth in an earth-shattering kiss.

He slides out slowly before pushing in again, and my knees lock tight against his hips as I lose myself in the kiss.

Every night I've ever longed for this.

Every time I've ever wished it could be us.

"Breathe, baby." He pulls back out before inching back in further until he swallows my moan and my hips raise to meet his. He holds me close as his mouth moves down my body, worshipping me.

My hands skim over the planes of his face like I've longed to for so damn long, and I close my eyes, lost in the feel. Overwhelmed in the moment.

"Eyes on me, Caitlin. I want you to remember who's fucking you."

My eyes fly open, and damn this man for being this beautiful.

His eyes soften, and I absolutely melt as pleasure pounds through me. I press my palms flat against his chest and wrap my legs around his waist, digging my heels into his ass. Clinging to him, not an inch of space left between us.

"Fuck, you take my cock like such a good girl." I preen under his touch and his words. "Your fucking cunt was made for me, Cait."

My clit throbs with each new filthy word, and a delicious flush coats every inch of my heated skin.

"So fucking tight." He snaps his hips against mine, picking up speed, driving deeper and harder as I cling to him, unable to think . . . or speak.

I just feel . . . This. *Us*. Him. Everything.

Sensations overload my body, as it pulses around his.

"You like the way my cock fills you, baby? The way you stretch around me?" His voice is deep and harsh and so fucking sexy.

"God, yes," I moan, clawing at his thick, strong shoulders and loving the way his muscles feel under my hands as he fucks me harder. *Faster*. Sending me higher—until I'm soaring.

My orgasm is right there, just out of reach as I moan and gasp.

Breathless and needy.

So damn needy.

My body strung tight, begging for relief. But I never want to come because I don't want this to end. Not tonight or tomorrow. Just. Not.

Callen slams into me, his fingers biting into my skin as he fucks me.

He looks like a savage god.

My savage god.

"Need you to come now, Cait," he demands and flattens my hips to the bed while he fucks into me over and over. I scream incoherently as my orgasm ignites, and flames burst behind my eyes and lick up my skin, threatening to destroy me in the fiery explosion.

He fucks me through my orgasm before my name falls from his lips and this beautiful man takes what's his.

What's always been his to take.

Even if it leaves me irrevocably broken.

It takes a strong man to handle a strong woman.
I don't have an attitude and unrealistic expectations.
I know my worth and refuse to settle for less.

—Caitlin's Secret Thoughts

allen's lips brush my shoulder blades the next morning as I lie naked, my chest against the bed and my face buried in his pillow, exhausted and deliciously sore in the most decadent way. But that's what happens when you spend the entire night being worshipped. And there is not a single doubt in my mind—I was worshipped last night.

All night.

Six . . . No—seven times.

"Callen," I purr, loving his lips on my skin but unable to move. "I need sleep . . . or maybe coffee."

That's when the scent of freshly brewed Lavazza coffee tickles my nose.

Ohh. He's good.

I turn my face to him, and he runs a finger along my temple and tucks a lock of my hair behind my ear. His lips tip up on one side, as cocky as ever. "Your wish is my command, kitten."

"You're dressed?" I murmur as I roll over. The sheet catches, and Callen's eyes immediately darken as my nipples tighten when they're exposed to the cool air. He licks his lips, and I pull the sheets back up. "Down, boy. I'm not sure I'm going to be able to walk today as it is."

"You weren't complaining last night." He puts the cup of coffee down on his nightstand and sits next to me. "I could kiss it and make it better . . ."

Butterflies take flight in my stomach as I trail my eyes from the beautiful Italian coffee to the beautiful man who made it for me and notice, again, that he's fully dressed. "Why are you dressed, Callen?"

The sexy smile slips from his face, and my heart sinks with it.

"Callen . . . You're only ever quiet when something's wrong." I sit up, and he hands me a shirt. "What's this?"

It smells like him, and I slide it down and stand, amused at the way it hits just above my knees. There's no way he's ever getting this back.

Why are guys clothes always so much softer than women's?

"Okay." I cross my arms protectively over my chest, bracing for whatever's coming. Time to face facts . . . I've got a pretty good idea where it's going. "Let's just start this fight. And pay close attention, buddy. This is going to be a fight. And if you say last night was a mistake, it's going to be a fist fight because I'm not scared to throw hands."

Callen laughs, and I'm not sure whether I should be relieved or angry.

"What are you laughing at?" I demand, pissed off that my happy post-seven-hour orgasmic bliss is over.

"You're cute when you're pissed, Cait." He gathers my face

in his hands and brushes his lips over mine, and all the fight leaves my body. "It wasn't a mistake. But we need to talk."

"If that's supposed to make me relax, it's not working," I warn him as I wrap my arms around his waist. "Can't we just stay in our little bubble, please, Callen? It's not like I don't know what you're going to say."

It's also not like my heart doesn't already hurt just thinking about it.

"It's not that easy, Caitlin. I've tried to fight this thing between us for years, and you see where that got us." He pulls me against him and rests his chin on my head. "But he's my best friend, and I've got to talk to him before you and I can—"

"Can what?" I interrupt as anger and frustration battle with an overwhelming feeling of impending loss. A loss I'm not sure I'll survive. How can it have been one night when it feels like a lifetime. "What, Callen? We haven't had twenty-four hours to figure out what a *we* is and if we even want a *we*. How about you take the time to figure that out with me before you worry about how it's going to affect Maddox."

He runs his hands over my hair, and I fight the chill that skirts down my spine.

"He lives here, Cait. He's going to know right away something's going on. I can't let him walk into that. I've got to talk to him." His voice is firm and steady, and if he thinks he's leaving little room for argument, then maybe he doesn't know me all that well.

I try to push away, but Callen's arms are like a steel vice locked in place.

"If you talk to Maddox right now, I swear, Callen, it will be for nothing because I will never talk to you again."

"Caitlin . . ." he groans and loosens his hold on me.

"I know he's your best friend, and I know you're loyal. I get it, I swear." I take a step back, still in his arms but able to see his face now. Needing him to see how serious I am because I'm not sure I'll ever have enough lady balls to get through this again, and I need to see his face when I do. "This is my life. Your life. Not his. I'm the one standing here, in your room, wearing your clothes, with the taste of your cum still on my lips from last night. My feelings matter more than Maddox's do right now. And if you don't agree with that or can't see that, then you're not the man I thought you were."

"Sounds like an ultimatum, Cait." A muscle twitches as a hard line sets in his sharp jaw.

"It's really not. I know you and Maddox are you and Maddox. But if you want there to be a you and me—which, by the way, we haven't even discussed because you came in here, guns a'blazing . . ." I look over at the untouched coffee sitting on the nightstand and wonder how this morning spiraled so quickly. "Not that I thought we needed to have that conversation this morning, or today . . . or at least before you let me drink my coffee. Whatever. What I'm saying is I'm not backing down to him for once in my life. And I swear to God, if you do, you're wasting your breath because I won't be here when you're done."

The alarm on my phone goes off, and I have to hunt through our piles of clothes to find it.

"Shit. I've got a meeting this morning I can't miss."

I refuse to admit the pain I'm feeling in my chest is my heart cracking in two and look at Callen from across the room. "I've got to get showered and get moving. Ball's in your court, Callen. What are you going to do with it? Run or score?"

"I love when you fuck up football, kitten." He wraps his hands around my head and pulls me to him. "They're back at the end of this week. I've got to talk to him before that."

Tears I refuse to let fall sting the backs of my eyes.

I think he just picked me.

Over my brother . . .

Callen has never done that.

I feel my lip wobble as that simple fact sinks in.

"Need a ride to work?"

I shake my head, unwilling to give up this fleeting connection. "Jude will be waiting for me."

"Tell your bodyguard I'll drop you off. I'm meeting my trainer at Crucible. I'll be right there."

Killian's dad expanded what used to exclusively be an MMA gym but now caters to elite athletes as well. Makes sense since our town is overflowing with them.

"You don't have to . . ."

He presses his lips to my forehead. "You might be able to tell everyone else in your life what to do, but that shit doesn't work on me. Now get showered, get dressed, and get your sweet ass in the truck."

He smacks my ass, and I squeal and take a step forward before changing my mind and grabbing his hand. "Your shower's pretty big, Sinclair."

A devilish smile stretches across his handsome face. One I love seeing. It's the same smile he's always had when he gets a surprise. And today, I think that's me. Not sure how he thought this morning would go, but I doubt it was like this.

"It *is* awfully big, isn't it?" Callen reaches behind his head and pulls his shirt off, then runs his hands up my bare legs and under my shirt. Rough palms skim up my ribs and cup my breasts, and need pools deep in my belly. "How fast do I need to be, kitten?"

I look at the time, wishing I wasn't presenting the sketches I worked on last night to Everly today. "You've got ten minutes. Fifteen if I don't blow dry my hair. Think you can make it quick?"

Callen throws me over his shoulder and smacks my bare ass. "I can make you come at least twice in ten minutes."

I hang upside down, laughing as he carries me into the bathroom, and run my hand under the waistband of his basketball shorts to pinch his ass.

"Promises, promises . . ."

Turns out he can make me come *three* times in ten minutes.

LEO

Hey. I need clothes.

CAITLIN

You need a whole wardrobe makeover.
What's your point?

LEO

You made Nixon look good. Think you can
help me?

CAITLIN

Use your words, Leo. What are you asking?

LEO

I need a stylist. I'm not getting the
endorsement deals I want even though I had
one of the highest scoring averages in the
league last season. My agent says it's
because I don't dress well enough. His exact
words were I don't look put together.

CAITLIN

I mean you look put together if frat boy is the look you're going for. But if you want to look classy and understated—like you're not trying but just are . . . Yeah. I can help you.

LEO

You're a lifesaver, Caitie.

CAITLIN

Call me Caitie again and I'll leak the picture of you making out with that blow-up doll in college to the Kroydon Kronicles.

LEO

Cold as ice, Caitlin.

CAITLIN

And don't you forget it, Leo.

I put my phone down as my mother sits across from me in Sweet Temptations.

"To what do I owe the pleasure, sweetheart?" She pushes one of her famous chocolate chip cookies across the table and slides it next to the espresso pick-me-up I needed by three this afternoon.

I break a piece of cookie off and dip it in my espresso, just to see her grimace like I've just committed a crime against humanity. "I'm working on designs for Lilah's upcoming tour and didn't get much sleep last night."

Not a complete lie.

I was working on the designs . . . well, before Callen came home.

Mom moves the napkin with my cookie away. "Uh-uh. I know my daughter, and that smile was not excitement over designs. That smile was for a man."

She reaches for my espresso, but I lift it out of reach and refuse to answer.

How can I when I don't even know what I'd say.

It's obvious she doesn't believe me as she breaks off a piece of the cookie. "Whatever you say. Did you have a nice birthday weekend?"

"Mom, it's not like I didn't spend Friday night with you and Dad and the boys." I eye the cookie and wonder if I can take her. Ha. Kidding. Sort of. My mom is a badass with a capital B. You'd have to be to be my father's wife.

Speak of the devils, and they shall appear.

Rome and Lucky walk into the shop, so completely involved in whatever bullshit they're spewing, they don't even notice Mom and me sitting in the corner until they walk over to the counter and both start hitting on my friend Quinlan when she gets their coffees, then points toward Mom and me. I watch her eyes roll as my brothers make their way over to us and don't bother hiding my laugh.

"You know she's way out of your league," I tell the two of them as they take turns kissing my mother's cheek so she doesn't lecture them where they stand. The Beneventi boys, Maddox included, can be and are cocky shits most of the time, but they will never disrespect our mom.

"I don't know what you're talking about, kit cat," Rome challenges me because he knows I won't start shit over the stupid nickname in front of Mom. "I promised Nonna I'd pick her up some biscotti today. Her hands are bothering her, and she didn't want to make them herself. You got any, Ma?"

"Stop hitting on my employees, and I'll get you whatever you want," she tells him as she gets up before she stops and looks at me. "We'll pick up this conversation soon, principessa."

Rome follows Mom back to the counter, and Lucky steals

her seat and pops the rest of the half-eaten cookie into his mouth, then looks back at Quinlan. "She wants me."

I laugh. "You think everyone wants you."

He shrugs. "They do. No girl can resist the bad boy."

My dumbass littlest brother smirks, and I think I throw up in my mouth a little. "You're disgusting."

"Also true. You coming to the Kings game this week?"

Our family has two boxes at the stadium. One is the official owners' suite. If you're in there, you better be prepared to be working. You're on the whole time and better behave like it. The other one is the family box. Family and friends only. No cameras allowed. As much as I like to tease Callen about football, I grew up in that suite as much as I did in his family's suite. Our moms were always together. Even at the games. I know football. I don't necessarily love the game, but I do love the team. Then there's Callen . . .

"I'm not sure. It's just a preseason game." I choose my words carefully. My brothers maybe manwhore dipshits, but they're also bloodhounds and Beneventis. They can smell bullshit a mile away, and I'm not ready for them to get a whiff of anything just yet. It's Tuesday, and Maddox and Killian come home Friday night. That only gives me three days and three nights to figure my shit out.

Guess it's going to have to be enough.

CALLEN

I need your advice on something.

COOPER

Pulling out isn't effective.

CALLEN

Dude. You're married to my sister.

COOPER

What's your point . . . ?

—Text from Callen to Cooper

Carys hands me a cup of tea, reminding me so much of Mom that it's a little freaky. "You doing okay, little brother? I know it's been a heavy few days."

"Thanks, Carys." I splash some milk in the mug, even though it's a hundred degrees outside and I'd rather be drinking a beer. My sister stands there, waiting me out like she thinks she's preparing for the fall or something. "I'm fine."

Pretty sure I've never said that as much as I have these past few days.

She nods but doesn't believe me. It's written all over her face.

"If you say so." She leans her elbows on the marble counter and stares me down. "You think you'll get any playing time Thursday night?"

"Maybe one series. They'll tell me whether I'm dressing for the game tomorrow." Most teams won't risk their starters getting injured during preseason. These games aren't for us. They're for the rest of the team to evaluate the players and the plays. But preseason games don't count for anything. Not for standings. Not for playoffs. Not for bonuses. And they won't risk the money makers. Why should they? "Why? You coming?"

She looks away and wipes at her eye. "Yeah. We all are. We want to make sure we're there in case it ends up being Coach's last game."

Yeah. There's the fucking purple spotted elephant in the corner of the goddamn room.

"I think it's gonna be," Cooper adds as he walks into the kitchen, looking at something on his iPad. I was too young to remember Coop as a SEAL. After he retired, he managed money for a while. Pretty sure he never has to work another day in his life if he doesn't want to, but you'd never know it. That's not his way. These days, he's a consultant for a private military group. It gives him plenty of time to be involved with his three kids. Especially since Carys's lingerie brand has skyrocketed over the past ten years.

He looks me over skeptically. "Kinda late in the day for a run . . ."

"Yeah. Just wanted to clear my head and ended up here." Cooper and I meet a few times a week for a run. Sometimes Declan will join us. Every now and then, Brady will too.

Never Murphy. He's not a runner. Most of the time though, it's just Coop and me.

"Come on." He slaps my back and heads to the kitchen door. "Let's grab some rods."

I look from him through the glass door out to the lake at the end of the property. "It's hot as balls outside."

Carys giggles and leaves us to it. "Have fun, boys."

She kisses Coop's cheek, and he smacks her ass as I look away.

My entire family is like this. None of them are afraid of PDA.

None. Of. Them.

Growing up, it was sickening. Family vacations were hazardous to your health. At least as a teenage boy. Nobody wants to see their dad grabbing their mom's ass. Or worse. The outdoor showers at our beach compound have seen a whole lot of action. And most of it wasn't from my generation until recently.

Well . . . at least as far as anyone knows.

Not gonna lie. Now I kind of get it. At least I think I do.

I could easily see myself unable to keep my hands off Caitlin twenty years from now.

If Maddox doesn't fucking kill me first.

"Come on, kid." Cooper pushes through the door and grabs the fishing rods leaning against the back of the house and two beers from the outdoor fridge, and I follow him down to his new dock. He and Carys have always lived on the lake. But it was only about ten years ago that the land across the lake from them went on the market. They bought it, built this house, and have used their original house as a rental property ever since. "Want to tell me what's going on?"

I laugh. "You know you have actual kids. Ones I'm ten years older than, by the way."

He casts his rod and cracks his beer. "Did I ever tell you

when you were little and I lived on the other side of the country, I worried you wouldn't know who the hell I was? You, Everly, and Gracie . . . the three of you barely knew me. And I swore when I came home, I'd fix it. Kid, by the time I was your age, I was married with three kids of my own. But getting to watch you grow up . . . Getting to be here for it. Not everyone gets that chance, and I was grateful. So, yeah. I guess you'll always be a kid to me. I don't mean it as disrespect."

"Yeah . . ." I cast my rod and sit in an Adirondak chair next to him, definitely the one grateful now. Not just for Coop but all my crazy-ass siblings. "I don't take it that way either. It just cracks me up."

We sit in silence as the late afternoon sun dips down behind the falls across Kroydon Lake until Cooper finally pushes me. "You gonna tell me what's bothering you? Is it Dad?"

"I mean . . . The stuff with Dad *is* fucking with me."

It's not a lie.

It's not exactly the whole truth either.

"What else is on your mind, Callen?"

"You ever done something you knew was right but you knew it was fucked up too?" I ask, not ready to give him specifics but needing someone to talk to.

Caitlin wasn't wrong this morning.

We rushed into things last night.

But how the hell can it be rushed when it's been years in the making?

Cooper stares blankly at me before his lips curve. "I married your sister. Pretty sure a whole lot of people in our family thought it was pretty fucked up at first."

"I've heard stories . . ." I nod, knowing there's so much I don't know. Probably don't want to know. "How'd you handle knowing it could fuck up your relationship with Murphy?"

He, Murphy, Brady, and Caitlin's Uncle Bash were all best friends growing up.

That didn't change when Murphy's mom married Cooper's dad.

I'm betting it got complicated.

Almost thirty years later, we're a powerhouse family.

Cooper looks at me. "Tell me you're not in love with Bellamy Wilder."

"What?" I laugh. "No."

Bellamy's brothers both married Sinclair sisters. Pretty sure that's enough.

"Good. No need to keep it that much in the family." He looks at my unopened beer, and his look changes. It hardens. "I'm not going to ask then. I'm just going to tell you to be sure. Before you hurt someone. Anyone . . . be sure whatever *it* is, is worth it."

I stare off in the distance, knowing no matter what I do, I'm fucking over someone I love.

And that's the thing about Caitlin . . . She's Cait. Without ever saying it, I love her. I always have. Not in the same sense. But she's always meant something to me. I don't want to hurt her. I don't want to hurt Maddox. I don't want to fuck it all up.

"Can you imagine your life without her? Can you live without her touch?" Cooper asks, and I consider playing dumb, but I came today because Coop's the brother who'd get it. Who would understand me without me ever having to fill in the blanks.

"It's early . . ."

"That's a boy's answer, Callen."

Fuck.

That hits hard.

"A man knows. Be the man you're supposed to be." He pulls his line out of the water and recasts. "You know . . . our old house is empty. The tenant moved out a few weeks ago, and we haven't put it back on the market yet."

I think about that for a few minutes.

"You think you could hold off on listing it for a few weeks? I think I need to figure a few things out." Maybe a little distance would help. Or maybe I need a plan for when Maddox fucking kills me.

CALLEN

Want to grab dinner with me?

KITTEN

Like a date?

Won't people see?

CALLEN

People will see two friends getting dinner.
They won't see what I'll do to you after.

KITTEN

Does this mean you didn't call Maddox?

CALLEN

It means I want to take you out, Caitlin.

KITTEN

Okay.

Caitlin

*W*hen Callen suggested dinner, I assumed he'd meant West End . . . . I hadn't planned on walking around the cobblestone streets of Chestnut Hill. The tiny town not far from Kroydon Hills has a great vibe. White fairy lights are strung from the trees as live music trails out from the local bars. Callen holds my hand in his as we make our way to a small restaurant right off the main street and asks for a seat in the back.

"You afraid to be seen with me, Sinclair?" I tease him, knowing we don't look anything like friends right now. We look very much like a couple on a date, and I love it. This is what it could be. This is what we could have . . . if he'd let us.

"Not at all, Cait." He thanks the waiter, then pulls out my chair. "I don't feel like having fans come up to us all night to talk about tomorrow's game."

"Good answer." I smile as I drape my napkin over my lap and look at the menu, but Callen just sits and stares at me, making my cheeks flush. This man makes me self-conscious in a way I never am. "What?"

"Have I told you how pretty you look tonight, Caitlin?"

I sit a little straighter, unable to tell him how long I've waited to hear those words from him. "You have now."

His leg brushes mine under the table, sending an electric current coursing over my skin as the silence between us reaches almost deafening levels.

"So . . ." I finally say just as he starts at the same time.

"About last night . . ."

"You first," I tell him, hating this weird awkwardness between us.

We're good at acting like the other doesn't exist.

It's how we've coexisted for so long.

Ignorance is bliss, and all that crap.

But this . . . this is painful.

This feels strangely forced. Not the being with Callen part. The part where we're supposed to act like nothing happened.

"We—"

The waiter interrupts us to read the specials and take our drink orders, but Callen's eyes never leave mine, locked on me with an almost predatory glint.

When it's finally just the two of us again, Callen grabs my hand. "Cait . . . I'm not saying last night shouldn't have happened. But we should have talked. I should have taken you on a date. I should have done a lot of things before last night happened. Things you deserve."

"Things we can do now," I protest, not sure where he's going with this. "There's no right order, Callen. It's whatever's right for us, not for everyone else."

"Is there an us?" He shutters his eyes, and every inch of my body goes on high alert." We didn't exactly take the time to talk about it."

"No, we didn't talk about that last night, but I'm pretty sure I spelled that out for you this morning," I snap a little more harshly than I probably should have. "What do you want, Callen? Is it me?"

He doesn't answer right away, and my defenses soar. "If it's not me, that's okay. We can go back to acting like we don't matter to each other. Like last night never happened. I've watched you with everyone but me for eight years. I can do it again." I pull my hand away from his. "But make no mistake, Sinclair. I won't be here in another year, waiting for you. This is your chance. You don't get a third."

Callen reaches across the table, palm up, waiting.

When I don't place my hand back in his, he reaches under the table and grabs it, holding it in my lap. "Christ, Caitlin. Not all of us answer as fast as you. It takes most of the rest of the world a few minutes to compose a thought. That doesn't mean I don't want you. It doesn't mean I want to act like nothing happened. I'll never be able to act like that again. I've done that once, and that was hard enough."

"Oh . . ." I lick my lips and lean back as the waiter delivers my wine and Callen's soda.

"Are you ready to order?" He looks between Callen and me and waits.

"Could you give us a few minutes?" Callen asks him.

But as the waiter walks away this time, there's no uncomfortable silence. "I wasn't sure—" I start, before he cuts me off.

"And that's my fault, Cait. I know I hurt you before. But I need you to understand something. In college—"

"God, Callen. Can we not?" I ask, still mortified.

"If we're doing this thing, we need to do it right," he tells me with this quiet confidence I find so incredibly sexy. Callen Sinclair is loud most of the time. He jokes and teases. But it's the quiet moments that I've always thought were at the heart of him. "That means clearing a few things up. Like that night."

I close my eyes. "Like that night."

"You were eighteen, Caitlin. Barely eighteen. And I had a girlfriend. One I'd been with for four years."

I cringe at the memory that's burned into my brain.

The way I snuck into his room . . .

The nerves I felt then and the humiliation I felt when he rejected me.

He squeezes my hand, then slides his under my sundress and rests it on my bare thigh. "And I was twenty-two, about to be drafted."

"Callen . . ." I'm not sure what I even want to say.

"It took every ounce of strength I had to turn you down, kitten." His words are jagged and harsh. "I swear on my life, Cait. I've thought about that night a million times since. But I couldn't. I'm a lot of things, but I'm not a cheat. And I'm not a shit friend. Not until last night. But fuck . . . Caitlin. I wasn't the right man for you then. I was barely a fucking man. I was a kid who was about to get the keys to the fucking kingdom."

"And I was just a kid . . ." I whisper, wishing I could take it back.

"A kid with more confidence than most grown men I know."

I swallow my nerves and somehow manage to keep my voice steady. "And now?"

"Now I'm a man who knows what I want, Cait. It's the same thing I've wanted for four fucking years." God, those words . . . I've waited so long to hear those words and had given up hope I ever would.

"What changed, Callen? Why now?" I can't believe I'm even asking. But I need to know. "Because I meant it when I said I can't keep doing this. Not now. Not after last night."

"You changed it. For four years, I've fought this. I guess I don't have the fight left in me to fight it anymore."

"Wow. Is that supposed to make me feel good about myself? I've worn you down? Seriously?" I glare as the waiter brings the rolls and salads, but Callen refuses to let go of my hand.

I'm not sure whether to laugh or cry.

"It's supposed to tell you this isn't something I take lightly. You're important to me. You always have been . . ." He leaves his sentence hanging.

"Let me guess . . . but so is my brother." I feel like this is a self-fulfilling prophecy.

"You know he is, Cait."

"So where does that leave us?" I ask, getting dizzy from this merry-go-round but not willing to get off it. Unsure if I'll ever be ready.

"You tell me."

"I just want a chance to figure out what's going on before we tell the world," I plead. "We shouldn't have to figure it all out tonight."

"I don't think we have to figure it all out. Just what matters to us. And, yeah, Maddox is one of those things. He comes home Friday, Cait, and I'm not willing to lie to him. Not just because it's him, but because I don't want to start this . . . *us* . . . on a lie. We're going to have enough stacked against us. I'm not letting that be one of the things too."

"He's never going to be okay with this." My stomach drops at the thought of what's coming.

"I'd rather have him pissed because of the truth than furious over a lie."

Well hell . . . when he puts it that way . . .

Not everyone is going to think you're beautiful and perfect. They're wrong though. Stupid twats.

—*Caitlin's Secret Thoughts*

In the end, Callen and I compromised. He's going to talk to Maddox when he gets home Friday. That gives me two more days before this whole thing gets a lot more complicated. But when Callen pulls his phone from his pocket as we walk into the condo later that night, it's not relief I see. It's torture.

"What's wrong?"

He looks up from his phone but doesn't make eye contact as he shoves it in his pocket. "Nothing."

"Callen . . ." I run my thumb over his cheekbone and cup his cheek in my hand as a bad feeling washes over me. This isn't about him and me. This isn't Maddox. It's something else. "The truth. Remember?"

He closes his eyes and sinks into my touch.

"Is it your dad?" I push, gently thinking back to what

started everything yesterday. "You can tell me, you know? I won't say a word. I promise."

His eyes open, and this strong man . . . my strong man, seems nearly broken.

"I can't Cait. We told him we wouldn't say anything," he groans painfully.

"We?" I push a little harder.

"My siblings." He wraps his arms around me, dragging me to him.

"They each have a spouse to help them. Let me help you," I sink into his chest as his chin rests on my head. "Is he sick?" I whisper the words, hoping they're wrong.

"Yeah, he's sick. It's cancer. Multiple myeloma." He forces out the words like a physical fist clenches his throat, and I can't even imagine what that feels like. "We're waiting for the test results so they can come up with a treatment plan. That was Mom letting me know he has an appointment tomorrow after practice."

"Callen . . ." I tip my chin up to look at his face, and the pain in those green eyes is crushing as I press my lips to his jaw. "I'm here. I'm not going anywhere, and I can handle anything you throw my way. Promise me you won't forget that."

"I promise," he whispers as his fingers tangle in my hair. "I'm going to take the dogs out. I'll be back in a minute."

"You sure?" I press up on my toes and ghost my mouth over his. "I can take them out."

The look he gives me speaks volumes and yet manages to tell me nothing new.

This man is protective of everyone in his circle.

His family. His friends. *Me . . .*

He kisses my forehead and smiles against my skin. "Go upstairs, kitten. I'll be back in, in a few minutes."

"Yes, sir," I whisper and bite down on my lip to hide the

grin that immediately springs to my face when his eyes flood with desire.

I watch as Cupcake and Meatball trot over to their leashes, knowing what's coming and waiting with their non-existent tails wagging a mile a minute. I'm not sure whether to breathe a sigh of relief or hold my breath waiting for the next big hit.

Callen

"Caitlin . . ." I reach over her the next morning and hit snooze on her cellphone, silencing the alarm that's been going off for the past five minutes. "Kitten . . . it's time to wake up."

"Hmm . . . no," she mumbles, so fucking pretty, it almost hurts to look at her.

I slide her wild hair away from her face and skim my lips over her temple as she lies draped across my chest, her legs tangled with mine. Her body is cold, like a tiny freezer I wish didn't have to wake so soon.

I spent half the night watching her sleep, wondering how the hell we got here. Trying to figure out the best way to get to the next place with the least amount of damage. Because I know at the end of the day, there's going to be damage. And whether she wants to think about it or not, we'll both be the ones dealing with it.

The thing is, Caitlin Beneventi is worth it.

She's worth it all.

The shit show that's coming from Maddox.

Probably from our families.

Maybe from our friends.

She's always been worth it. I was the one who never was.

I wasn't enough. Wasn't ready.

Not for what I knew came with being with her.

She's not the girl you date—she's the one you marry.

I smile, thinking about it because anyone else would say I was nuts even contemplating it.

Caitlin is loud. She's a smart-ass. Her sarcasm knows no bounds, and her words are cutting like the sharpest knife.

You don't look at her and see soft. You don't see the girl next door who needs to be protected. None of the typical things guys see when they say they know their girl is the kind you make your wife. But she's better than that. She's strong and fierce and protective and fucking capable. She's sexy without even trying. And when no one's watching, she's soft and sweet with the biggest damn heart.

I'm screwed because I'm pretty sure I've been in love with her for the better part of four goddamned years.

"Come on, Cait. You've got to get up. You've got to go to work, and I have practice." I flip her over to her back and take the tip of one nipple in my mouth.

Caitlin's hands slide into my hair and tug as she cradles me between her legs. "Gotta wake up, baby."

"This is so much better than the alarm clock though," she murmurs softly as she wraps a leg around my hips and rubs herself along the length of my morning wood. "I think you should fuck me first thing every morning."

"Oh, kitten, I love the way your mind works." I move my mouth down her chest and over her ribs, dragging my tongue around her belly button. "How about I wake you up with my mouth between your legs, feasting on this pretty cunt every day?"

Caitlin drags her nails over my scalp and pushes my head down, eager for me to make good on my offer.

"Fuck, Cait. Why the hell did we wait so damn long?" I

spread her thighs, settling in, and then lick her hot pussy through damp, silk panties.

So fucking pretty.

My kitten purrs beneath me as her tart taste coats my tongue.

"Callen," she moans without a care in the world. "I think we need to make up for lost time."

"Such a greedy girl. I need to get you ready for me, Caitie." I graze my teeth along her sex, and my girl squirms against the bed.

Her breath comes out in sharp pants as she quivers beneath me. "I've been ready for fucking years, Callen. I want it now. I want you."

Pushing aside the soft silk, I drag my finger through her drenched sex, then push inside as she moans.

I suck her swollen clit into my mouth, and growl against her pussy as her juices coat my face.

Caitlin's knees snap up around my shoulders as she rocks her hips up, fucking my face.

Tugging my hair and pulling me closer until she's coming.

I pull back and look up at this beautiful woman in my bed.

Fuck . . . *She's. Mine.* She's *all* fucking mine.

"That's one, kitten. You ready for two?" I ask as I roll a condom down my fisted cock and drop a knee on the bed.

"Fuck, yes, Callen."

I flip her over to her knees and smack her ass, leaving a bright-red handprint on her perfect porcelain skin. My chest rumbles as I drag my tongue along the mark. "Fucking love seeing my hands on your perfect skin."

Caitlin cries out and throws her head back as she leans her ass into me. "Fuck, yes . . . More, Callen. I want more."

"Gonna take this ass one day too, kitten."

I drag a thumb through the cum dripping down the inside of her creamy thighs, then up around the tight ring of her ass, running it around the puckered skin, and she pushes back against me. "Promise?" she moans, and I push in just a tiny bit.

"Has anyone ever had your ass, Caitie?" I growl and pull my thumb out.

She thrashes against the bed, shaking her head. "No."

"Gonna have to fix that, baby."

Caitlin's forehead falls to the bed as a scream rips from her throat, and I plunge my cock into her pretty pussy and my thumb into her tight, perfect little ass.

Fuck me . . . My cock weeps from the hot, wet, tight grip of her pussy as I set a punishing rhythm, fucking desperate to get us there.

Her black hair falls around her face as she lifts her head to watch me fuck her before I wrap it around my fist and pound into her, tugging her up.

Her back arches as her pussy pulses, and my girl meets me thrust for fucking thrust. "Fuck, Caitie. You're taking me so good. Tell me how it feels."

She drops her head to my shoulder and crashes her lips over mine, pushing her tongue into my mouth between pants. "So fucking good."

She bounces on my cock.

"So fucking full," she mewls and drops down again, her breath catching in her throat.

I grab her face and hold her to me as we kiss hard and hungry.

Desperate for each other.

Caitlin's cunt milks my cock as her body vibrates. "So close, Callen."

I snap my hips against hers, over and over, until she's crying out and shaking.

Fucking her hard and fast until my muscles burn and her body screams.

Caitlin's orgasm is explosive when I finally let her come on my cock.

Red-hot heat tugs at the base of my spine as my orgasm barrels through me, so intense, so fucking perfect, I wonder how I ever went without this woman.

I take her mouth one more time before we both fall to the bed, covered in a sheen of sweat and tangled limbs.

"My God, Callen. Maybe you shouldn't wake me up for work like that every day," she whispered with a raw voice.

I drag her mouth back to mine and lick into it over and over, not willing to let go.

"Why the fuck not, kitten?" I ask when we're both out of breath.

"Because I'm totally calling out of work today so we can do that again."

LEO

At what age is someone considered a cougar?

KILLIAN

Like a cat?

LEO

Like a woman, shithead.

HENDRIX

Thirty.

CALLEN

The fuck? I'm twenty-eight.

HENDRIX

Old man.

MADDOX

Have your balls even dropped yet?

NIXON

Think he may have gotten his first pube hair this summer.

CALLEN

Aww. Did it scare you?

HENDRIX

Dude. What the hell? Leo's the one fucking an old chick.

LEO

Thinking about it. And she's not that old.

KILLIAN

Like older than thirty? Cause I banged a forty-year-old last year, and that woman knew exactly what she needed and how to get it. None of that quiet shit either.

It didn't hurt that she had great tits and was all kinds of bendy too.

LEO

What stopped you?

KILLIAN

Her husband.

MADDOX

That'll do it.

I walk Cait out of the building the next morning with my hand on the small of her back and catch the look Jude gives me as I drop it once we're through the doors.

"Ignore him," she whispers, but I'm pretty sure that's a bad move.

Not that there's anything I can do about it but watch her get into the back of his SUV before I head to practice. At least I'll get to hit something . . .

*H*ours later, after practice is over and my body is tired and sore, I make the mistake of forgetting about the morning.

About the peace before we got out of bed.

About the feel of her in my arms.

About the look in Jude's eye before she got into the car.

I forgot about it all as I cleared my mind and focused on prepping for tomorrow.

That is, until I walk out to the parking lot of the practice facility and see the black, tinted-out SUV sitting next to my truck. I know that car. And it's no surprise when the window rolls down and Sam Beneventi stares back at me with cold calculating eyes.

"Get in the car," he bites out, and I realize I'm no longer looking at my best friend's dad.

This isn't the same guy who used to throw us in the pool.

Right now, in this moment, I'm looking at the head of the Philadelphia Mafia.

"I'm supposed to be meeting someone," I answer, knowing my siblings are going to be waiting for me at Dad's house so they can fill us in on what the doctors said this afternoon. But Sam doesn't look like he gives two shits about what I'm supposed to be doing.

"My daughter?" he asks pointedly.

Fucking Jude.

"Get in the car," he says again, and if it's possible, this time he sounds more pissed off. Fucking fantastic.

I toss my bag in the back of my truck and get in his car, knowing this isn't going to be good.

It's just him and me and his driver.

"Where to, boss?" the driver asks.

"Just drive. I'll let you know when we're done," Sam tells him calmly, like he's not about to kill me.

I guess that's a good thing.

He pulls a folder out of his bag and tosses it my way. "Do you love my daughter, Callen?"

"What the fuck, Sam?" I do a shit job of hiding my anger. "How about you let me tell your daughter that before I tell you?"

He nods, silently assessing me, then reaches over and opens the folder, clearly pissed off at my lack of an answer.

A picture of Caitlin and me walking the streets of Chestnut Hill last night sits on top of the pile. I flip through, and the next is one of us at dinner, then us walking back to the car . . . and one of us this morning.

What the actual fuck?

"You're having her followed?" I growl, not caring that this is her father or that he's probably killed men for less. She's going to flip her shit when she finds out.

"I'm not," he answers calmly, and my brain fucking hurts as I try to put two and two together. But right now, it's not equaling four.

I close the folder and toss it back to him. Over this already. "You want to spell it out for me then? Because I'm not going to stop seeing her. Not now. Not unless that's what she wants. And maybe you should talk to her because I'm telling you that's not what she fucking wants."

Maybe I should be scared, but I'm not. I'm pissed.

I was ready to fight with Maddox.

I was ready for him to tell me I'm not good enough for her.

This came out of left field, and none of it's making sense.

"If you were anyone else, I'd deal with this differently, Callen. If you were just some stupid little shit who hadn't looked out for Caitlin her whole life, I'd force your fucking hand before I'd break it for touching what doesn't belong to you. If you were any other dumb fuck, you wouldn't be in this car testing my fucking patience because I wouldn't give a single shit about removing you from her life. But you're not anyone else. I've watched you grow up. I know your parents. I was at your fucking baptism. I watched the way she's looked at you whenever you were in the same room for years. And I've seen the way you looked at her when you thought no one was paying attention."

I open my mouth but shut it when Sam glares.

"I can't believe I'm saying this, especially with your reputation, but I know you. Probably better than you know yourself. Believe it or not, I've been you. And I know you think you're being careful. But those pictures say otherwise. And Caitlin can't afford that. Not right now. She can't afford careless. She can't afford public."

I hold Sam's controlled glare, refusing to back down. "I'm not trying to be a disrespectful asshole, Sam. But honest to God, I've got no idea what you're talking about."

I'm not stupid, but I'm not wrapping my head around whatever he's trying to get at either, and the sinking feeling in my gut says it's worse than I think.

"There are things happening in this city. *My fucking city*, Callen. Things I'm working on. Things you can't know about, and you can't be involved in. Things I'm going to fix."

He runs a hand down his face, I think disgusted with himself . . . *for what*—I have no fucking clue. But frustration and stress hang heavy in the air, hand in hand, clinging to us both.

I have no clue what I'm supposed to say or do, so I listen and try to read the situation.

Try to zero in on whatever he's attempting to say but doing a shit job expressing.

"Are you telling me Cait's in danger?" Sam's face changes, and my whole fucking world stops spinning as my body goes rigid. "What the hell is going on and why doesn't she know about it?"

"Because I have it under control. At least I did before you stepped into the picture," he snaps, unnervingly calm. "I didn't take those pictures. The *Kroydon Kronicles* did. Lucky for me and for you, I've got friends everywhere, and money shuts most people up. But *this* can't happen again."

"What can't?" I ask, not following *again*. Is he talking about us, or the *Kronicles*, or the danger in the damn city? "Swear to God, Sam. It's like you're giving me half a conversation."

He shakes his head and shoves the folder back in his bag. "You are too high-profile, Callen. The local media loves you. The national media loves you. You make head-lines, and Caitlin can't be in the headlines right now. It's not safe."

He waits, probably gauging whether or not I'm following him, but I just sit, taking it in as he tells me this woman I've finally let myself love isn't safe.

"You make Caitlin *not safe* . . . Do you understand?"

I crack my neck, pissed at him for the life he lives and at myself for being any part of the reason she's not safe. "Spell it out for me," I say as calmly as I can with rage coursing unchecked through my veins.

"If you love my daughter the way I think you do. The way I think you always have . . . you need to break it off. *Now*. Completely. No secret touches. Not hiding it from anyone." His eyes darken as he grinds his teeth. "That includes her brother. Break. It. Off. Without any fanfare or drama. Don't give anyone any reason to talk. Don't make her the center of the gossip rags. This matters, Callen."

"You sure this isn't just you trying to control the man she ends up with? Because I'm telling you that's me, Sam. One way or another, it's me." I refuse to accept this is it. I didn't just get her to turn around and give her up. Not now. Not fucking ever.

"The fact you have the balls to say that to my face is incredibly stupid but incredibly impressive. And I hope one day, if that's what she wants, it's what she'll have. But son, I'm telling you you're too high-profile, and the press hasn't even gotten wind of what's happening with your father. Once he announces his retirement, they're going to be swarming. And that's before they find out the rest." He says it so matter-of-factly, with no care to the way his words just sliced or the fact he's not even supposed to know it in the first place.

"How do you even know?" I ask before I think better, and he laughs.

Fucking laughs.

"I know everything, Callen. And if I know, other people are going to know."

"Fuck you, Sam."

He nods slowly as a vein in his temple pulses. "I'm going to give you that one because I would have said the same thing to anyone who tried to keep me away from Amelia. But here's the difference between you and me, Sinclair. I'd have killed the bastard. You're not me. Be fucking grateful. I'm the man who keeps the monsters at bay because I'm the bigger fucking monster. Now shut the fuck up and do as I say so I don't have to get nasty—because Callen, you've never seen that side of me, and I'd like to keep it that way."

I try to absorb everything he's telling me while every inch of me wants to reject every fucking word but knowing I can't.

He's keeping her safe and asking me to do the same thing.

The only thing.

Because Caitlin not being safe isn't an option.

Giving her up is the only way.

Fuck . . .

"Break it off, Callen. Break her heart. Make her hate you, if you have to. And do it because you love her, and you want to keep her safe. I'll do the rest, but I need you to do this."

The car pulls to a stop, and I look out the window at my truck.

"How long?" I ask, holding out hope.

"As long as it takes."

It's the answer I was expecting but not the one I wanted.

"I'll do it," I tell him and open the door. "But so help me fucking God, Sam. If she gets hurt, I'll be the bigger fucking monster."

Don't announce your next moves.
Just make the damn move and smile because you knew
you could.

—*Caitlin's Secret Thoughts*

I sit at the dining room table, opposite Lilah Ryan, pulling together mood boards we started working on yesterday. We're nowhere near done, but for something with this scope, we need so much more prep than anything I've ever done before. Fabric samples are scattered across the table, with different boards sitting on different chairs around the room.

Shades of purples and pinks and silvers and greens.

Satins.

Silks.

Leather.

And crystals. So many crystals.

"What about this?" The beautiful blonde-haired, blue-eyed girl next door who stole the hearts of the world at sixteen when the rest of us were busy crushing on the cute boy . . . My cute boy was her uncle, but anyway, that girl holds up a pretty piece of grape chiffon. "What if we layer this over a lighter color? Would that be pretty?"

She stands and spins. "The skirt would need to be big and flare out around my legs like a ball gown made of butterfly wings."

"Holy shit, if you start talking about unicorns, I'm done," I joke, and she bites her lip.

"Sorry. I just want it to be magical. The whole show." She sits back down and lowers her voice. "It's going to be the last one I do for a while."

"Okay, well magical I can help with. Write down butterfly wings as inspiration. I have an idea." I go searching through some old sketches, looking for something I worked on last spring as I hear her humming a pretty song. Something I don't recognize.

The dogs bark and run for the door seconds before it opens and Callen walks in the condo. I hear him talking to them and smile as I call out, "Hey, Callen. I'm in the dining room with Lilah."

If we don't want this to go public just yet, I need to make sure he doesn't walk in here naked to bend me over the table.

My God, that sounds like fun, and I have the perfect dress.

I wonder how high my heels would have to be for that to work.

"Callen's home?" Lilah asks. "What about Maddox and Killian?"

"Callen had practice earlier, but that should have been him that just came in. Maddox and Killer are in Vegas for some MMA thing. And Bellamy is visiting her mom in Maine." I move around the table to peer into the hall but don't see him.

"Oh." She puts the fabric down and looks around the

room. "I'm so sorry. I didn't mean to take over your dining room. I should probably get going."

"It's not a problem at all. I like working from home, and I'm really excited for this project. It's going to be amazing. I can't wait to see the show." I smile and close my binder. "Are you going to kick it off in Kings stadium?"

"No. I think they've got me scheduled in Europe first. I'll finish it up in the US." She moves around the table and hugs me, and I try not to stand there stiff as a board. I'm not exactly the biggest hugger. Bellamy likes to tease that I'm broken. "Thank you so much, Caitlin. I really appreciate this."

"Lilah, you could have any designer dress you. It makes sense to let your cousin do it, but for me to be a part of it . . ." Emotion wells, and I have to force the words out just to control the quiver threatening. "Thank you for trusting me. I'm honored."

"Listen, I've seen your work. It's beautiful. And the way you've been styling everyone—perfection. Seriously. I'd love to maybe talk about that if you have time. But I don't want to ask too much—"

"I have time. I've got plenty of time. You let me know what you need and when, and I'm there." *Holy shit.* I'm going to style one of the biggest stars in the world. We may have grown up in the same world, but we weren't close, and this is a big damn deal for me.

She grabs her phone from the table and shoots off a text.

"Yes. That's perfect. Let's get something on the schedule. I just sent you my calendar. I've got to go, but we'll talk tomorrow." I follow her into the hall and watch as she squats down to give each dog a little love. I swear you can tell whether a person is worth anything at all by the way they treat animals, and Lilah treats them like they're tiny humans.

"You've got a flaw, right?" I ask before my filter can catch it.

Who am I kidding? I don't have a filter most days.

"What?" She straightens, confused.

I shake my head. "Nothing."

"I'm not perfect, Cait. That's just my brand. Perfect and pure like the driven snow. It's exhausting but worth it."

"Sorry," I mutter, only slightly mortified.

She plays with the braided bracelet on her wrist, like it's a nervous habit. "I like to be a good person, but being a good person is never going to be enough. I'm never going to please everyone. I gave up trying a few years ago."

"I can see how that could take a toll . . ." I know I couldn't do it.

"And if you want a flaw, I hate coffee. But if you ever tell anyone that, I'll deny it. Apparently, hating coffee is un-American."

I stand there, shocked. "Your mom is the biggest coffee freak I've ever met."

"Yup. And one of her favorite brands is one of my biggest sponsors. Talk about a giant flaw." She opens my front door and smiles at me. "See you soon, Cait."

I lock the door behind her and jump at the sound of Callen's voice.

"She curses like a trucker too. Bet her fans would love to know that."

I turn and find him showered and changed into a pair of navy-blue sweats and a gray tee. His eyes are heavy and hollow as he leans his shoulder against the door frame. *Shit.* "How did things go with your dad?"

He doesn't move. Not an inch as I go to him and run my hands over his chest.

"Stage two. Treatable. *Fightable.* Never gonna be something that's curable. But it's something he could live a long life with. Would have been very different if it was stage three." He cups my shoulders and closes his eyes. "He's got a fight ahead of him, but Dad's always been a fighter."

"He's going to be okay, Callen." I echo back, not sure how to make any of this better for him but desperate to try.

"Yeah . . ." He shakes his head, and that's when I see it.

The resignation in his eyes.

And it guts me.

"Caitlin . . ."

"Don't, Callen." I rest two fingers against his lips as my heart breaks. "I've had a really good day, and I'm not ready to think about Maddox or any of the possible issues between us. I just want to be us tonight."

With exhausted eyes half-closed, he kisses the tips of my fingers. "I'm so tired, Caitie."

Caitie . . .

"Then let's go to bed." I take his hand in mine and lead him upstairs, past my room and into his. "Sit down, Callen." I push him back until he sits on the bed and watches me strip out of my clothes.

I can feel his eyes on me like he's touching my skin.

Like this is the last time he's touching my skin.

"You're exhausted." I grab one of his tees and slide it over my body and breathe in the smell of Callen as it surrounds me, then climb onto his lap and cup his face in my hands. "Was practice okay? Are you ready for the game tomorrow?"

"I doubt I'll play tomorrow," he groans and closes his eyes and drops his chin to his chest as I massage his tight muscles. "That feels good."

"Let me take care of you, Callen." I want to cry because it all feels so wrong. And maybe it's me. Maybe it's what's going on with Coach and I'm making it about myself, but there's been a seismic shift between this morning and now.

Something is wrong. I know it, even if I'm too scared to push for answers.

Instead, I kiss the top of his head and lay him down before I climb into his arms and rest my head on his chest.

We don't speak for the longest time.

Just lie there in the silence as I cling to him.

Feeling him slipping away.

Losing my nerve minute by minute.

Second by second.

Breath by jagged breath.

"I love you, Callen . . ."

"Cait—"

"Don't. Not tonight. Don't tell me whatever you're about to say. *Please* . . ." I beg, and I'm not proud, but I'll own it. I don't want to hear whatever he's thinking. "Just sleep tonight. The world might look different in the morning."

Callen never says another word.

He holds me all night like a lifeline.

I'm not sure he ever actually sleeps.

And I'm fairly certain, hours later, once he thinks I'm asleep, he presses his lips to the top of my head. "I love you, Caitlin. Only you. Only ever you. I promise . . . I'm sorry."

I wake up to an empty bed and cold sheets the next morning, and my heart sinks.

I'd hoped last night was a dream. That I'd been wrong. But then I remember his words whispered in the darkness, and I know they were real. They were a goodbye.

I stifle a sob and get out of bed, half expecting to be alone in the condo. For Callen to have snuck out like a thief in the night, but I guess that's hard to do when this is your home.

Instead, I find Callen in the kitchen, dressed and nursing a cup of coffee. He doesn't look up when I walk in.

"Morning . . ." I mumble as I make a cup of coffee, certain caffeine is going to be required to deal with whatever bullshit Callen is about to sling my way.

He looks up from the iPad in front of him, and I suck in a breath.

He looks awful.

"Did you sleep at all last night?" I reach out to run my fingers along his face, but Callen catches my hand in his, stopping me.

"I'm moving out, Caitlin." His voice is cold and scratched and utterly emotionless.

"What?" I gasp and drop my coffee to the table. "You can't be serious."

He lets go of my hand and wipes up my spilled coffee with his napkin like he didn't just take my heart and smash it into a million tiny, jagged pieces. "I'm taking over Cooper's old place. It's already furnished, so I'm going to take my stuff over there today."

"Callen . . . If you need to tell Maddox now, fine. Do it. You don't need to move out." I know I'm grasping at straws, but I've got to grasp at something.

He scrubs his face with his hands and shoves back from the table, scaring the shit out of me when he pulls away from me. "It's not him, Cait. It's us. It's this. We don't work. We shouldn't have happened."

"No," I snap through angry tears. "You promised. We're not a mistake, Callen."

His shoulders drop for a single second, and I think I might get an actual answer before his shields go right back up. "We are, Caitlin. This shouldn't have happened, and it can't happen again. This is what's best."

I shove his chest with all my strength. "Best for who?

Because it's not what's best for me, and I don't think it's best for you either."

He shutters his dark green eyes, hiding the anger that's staring back at me.

"Tell me what I did. Why are you mad?" I shove him again when he stays silent, and I scream for both of us. "Give me a goddamned answer, Callen. You owe me that."

When I lift my hand to shove him again, he catches my wrist. "You have an answer. You just don't like it. We were a mistake. We can't happen. I get it if you want to tell Maddox about us, and I'll take the fucking blame. But Cait . . . this *was* a mistake."

He drops my hand, and the look of utter contempt on his face scares me.

"You don't love me, Caitie. You love the idea of me. You deserve someone who loves you, and that's not me." He nails my coffin closed and picks up a bag from the floor I hadn't seen before, then walks out without another word.

I hurl my coffee cup across the room as a feral scream rips from my throat before I collapse on the floor, irrevocably broken.

SINCLAIR
81

Part II

The Philly Press

BEHIND CLOSED DOORS

Breaking News.

In a shocking, unprecedented move, Coach Joe Sinclair has officially stepped down as the head coach of the number one most winning team in NFL history. Rumors have been rumbling all season that this one was going to be his last, but Sinclair, Sr., has responded as always with, "No comment." Today, as we start week eleven of the regular season, with one week before our beloved Kings have a rematch on Thanksgiving with their Super Bowl rivals, the Nashville Fury, Scarlet Kingston-St. James announced the organization would forever be home to Sinclair before transitioning to how excited the team is with what his son Declan would bring to the table as the newly minted head coach.

Now the question on every Kings fan's mind is what is happening behind closed doors to make this coach step back. Was this a forced transition by the team owners? And if so, why? Our Kings are seven and three in a season rife with injuries. Why change things now?

Only time and this reporter will tell. Stay tuned, football fans.

#KroydonKronicles #BehindClosedDoors

"You want to talk about it?" Maddox asks from the other side of the bar in West End. Everyone and their brother saw the press conference earlier. It's a fucking miracle Dad managed to keep things quiet for as long as he did. But that's all going to change soon. The spotlight will be blinding now. Someone is going to find out.

"Nah, man. I'm good." Lies. All fucking lies.

I haven't been good in months.

The only thing good is my ability to lie.

I've perfected that.

"You should have stayed in Ellwyn longer. The whole scene was crazy." Maddox pushes the beer my way with a smirk as Killian agrees.

"Yeah. Maybe next time. You two shits already knew I had to fly home with the team. What was so special about it anyway?"

The league has been scheduling international games for us for the past few years in an effort to bring football to other countries. It's not my favorite thing, but it's not the worst. We played in Ellwyn three weeks ago, and apparently, since we won, we'll be playing there again next year.

Oh, yay . . .

"Yeah . . . been a crazy few weeks. But now it's time to get down to business," Killian announces like he's psyching himself up for the hell his life turns into when he's in training mode. "I'm gonna miss having a life."

Maddox lifts his beer and taps it to mine as Kill stares at us with a bottle of water in his hand. "Here's to missed chances," he toasts, and I choke on my drink.

"The fuck?" I cough.

"Come on, man," Killian shakes his head. "It's not like it's your first casual fuck. Just the first time it's with an actual princess."

I look between the two of them, relieved he's not talking about me but definitely not following whatever he's talking about. "What'd I miss?"

"Madman bagged himself a princess."

I blow out a long, low whistle. "Fuck, dude. An actual princess?"

"I don't want to talk about it," Maddox tells us, ending the conversation. At least he tries.

"Not like she's next in line for the throne or some shit. You could call her," Kill pushes a little harder, and the look Maddox gives him says it all.

He's not calling.

"Wasn't Lennon a princess?" I ask because it feels good to not hate myself at the moment.

It won't last, but it feels good.

"Fuck off. Technically, I don't think she had a title . . ." Maddox tries to take my beer away, but I pull it out of reach.

"Hi, boys," Bellamy bounces over and kisses the guys on

the cheek, then looks at me and curls her lip. "Missed you when you guys got in last night."

Killian wraps an arm around her shoulder. "Looking good, B. Got a hot date?"

"Not exactly." A coy smile plays on her lips, and she looks right at me. "Caitlin does though."

My stomach drops.

It's been three fucking months, and not a day has passed that I haven't regretted what I did. How I fucked it all up. Then I remember Sam's words and know I'd do it again if it meant keeping her safe.

Bellamy is the only one who knows, and I'm pretty sure if I still lived with them, she'd have cut my balls off in my sleep already because she only knows whatever Caitlin told her.

Cait can't ever know the rest.

She never said a word to Maddox, and neither did I, even if it makes me a shit friend most of the time. He's been traveling with Killian on and off more lately, so at least I haven't had to lie to his face. *Not much.* Not until now, when I have to keep my fucking mouth closed and act like Bellamy didn't just land a knockout blow.

"Who the fuck is the date with?" So much for keeping my mouth shut.

"Is Jude with her?" Maddox asks, and Killian laughs.

"Why would Jude be on a date? Everything okay?" I try *and fail* to sound casual about it.

"It's like the two of you have never seen her date before. She's a big girl." Killian tugs Bellamy against his side. "And you. Don't egg these assholes on. One of Dad's fighters needs a stylist, according to his agent. He was meeting with Caitlyn today. That's all it was."

"Dinner is a date." Bellamy pushes away from Killian and cocks her eyebrow my way. "When a man takes you out, it's a date. He opens a door, buys a meal, and if he's lucky, gets a goodnight kiss." Something catches her eye, and she smiles. "Speaking of which, I've got my own date. Don't wait up, fellas."

She walks away with an extra sway to her steps that screams *fuck you.*

And it's directed at me.

"You set my sister up with a fighter? *Who?*"

"I didn't set her up. I told her one of the guys needed a stylist. That's it. Who Cait fucks is on her, not me."

I see fucking red the second the words leave his mouth.

"Ahh, man. *Stop.* I don't want to think about that." Maddox nails Killian in the face with his dirty bar towel.

"Whatever," Kill mumbles. "If I gotta hear about my sister and her husband, you can hear about Cait going on a date."

I finish my beer and slam it on the bar. "I'm out."

"What the hell? What'd I say?"

I don't bother answering Killian.

I don't need to.

What I need is a bottle of tequila and an empty house.

Fuck you, Sam.

"**G**et up, asshole."

I drag a pillow over my head and flip Leo off from the couch.

"Go away," I groan, my head pounding in time to some kind of fucked up beat.

What the hell *is* that?

"No can do. It's Thanksgiving, remember?"

Shit. Wait . . . did I lose a whole week?

"And let's not forget whose fault it is either. You and Dad are the ones otherwise occupied on Thursday. You're the reason we're having dinner today instead of sleeping in. Some of us had games last night." He kicks my leg. "Dick."

"Fuck off, Leo. I'm up." I sit and rub my eyes as I work on moving. "My head hurts like a bitch."

"Just guessing, but it might have something to do with the empty bottle of Don Julio. Maybe if you'd get the fuck up and get showered, I wouldn't have to be a babysitter. *Seriously, man.* I don't know what's going on with you, but you look like dog shit." He sniffs me, and I consider head-butting him.

Kill two birds with one stone and all that shit.

If my head hurts from that, maybe the Don Julio will take a back seat.

"Dude, you smell worse than you look. Don't make me shove your ass in a cold shower."

Head-butt is looking pretty good.

I stand and stare at him. "I'd like to see you try, man."

"Leo," Cooper growls from the front door.

When did he get here?

"Head over to Grandpa's. I'll get Callen moving."

"Whatever you say, Uncle Coop. He's salty as shit today. Maybe you can figure out what the hell is going on with him. The rest of us gave up." Leo looks back at me as he walks out. "Take a fucking shower."

Cooper waits for Leo to leave before he picks up the empty bottle. "Leo's not wrong, Callen. Take a goddamned shower and meet me down here. I'll make the coffee."

When I don't move, he crosses his arms over his chest. "Mom's been cooking all day, Callen. Don't make her wait for you."

"She's not your mother," I mumble like a fucking child as I head to the stairs.

"She's more mom to me than mine has ever been, you little dick. She's also going through hell, and she wants her whole family together. That includes you. Men give a shit about making their mothers happy, Callen. Give a shit."

I ignore my brother as I move into the bathroom and step into an ice-cold shower.

I know I'm being a bitch.

But this is hell.

Three fucking months, and nothing's changed.

Strike that.

Nothing has gotten better.

Worse—yeah.

Treatment is kicking Dad's ass.

And Caitlin won't speak to me.

I know that's how it needs to be, but fuck me, the reality of it is hell.

Once I'm showered and dressed and feel half-human, I make my way back downstairs, where Coop's cleaned up my mess from last night.

He kicks one of the kitchen chairs away from the table. "Sit."

"I'm good," I answer and reach for the coffee before he gets in my way.

"It wasn't a question, Callen. Sit your ass down." My brothers are all at least twenty years older than me. And for the most part, I'm pretty sure I could take any of them in a fight. But right now, I'm thinking Cooper might be the exception.

I sit, and he hands me a cup of black coffee.

"Drink."

I look from the mug to him. "You gonna make speaking in single syllables a thing now?"

"You gonna grow the fuck up and talk to someone about whatever the hell is bothering you, smart-ass?" He drops into the seat across from me. "Sorry, I didn't hear that. In case you weren't sure, now's when you speak."

"I'm not one of your kids, Coop."

"You're right. My kids don't sulk for weeks, Callen. And I know this isn't about Dad, so don't try to say it is."

I groan, not sure how I got here.

"You ever feel like no matter what you do, you're fucked?" I ask, trying to figure this shit out.

"More times than you'll ever know. But I'm pretty damn good in those situations. So how about you let me help you. You've been angrier than I've ever seen you for weeks, little brother."

Anger is easier to deal with.

Anger I can use. Can channel.

Football is a great sport for angry men.

You get paid enough money for your children's children to never have to work a day in their lives just to hit someone on a field.

"It's not just the Dad stuff. That's not helping anything, but it's not that. There's other shit going on that I can't talk about."

"Does it have something to do with why you moved in?" He pushes like I knew he would.

"Coop, seriously, brother. Let it go." I blow out an aggravated breath and watch Coop's face change as something clicks.

"It wasn't Bellamy Wilder," he says slowly as he lifts his mug, waiting to gauge a response I won't give him. "It was Caitlin Beneventi, wasn't it?"

I school my face, not wanting to confirm anything.

"Tell me I'm wrong, Callen. Tell me you didn't fuck over Sam Beneventi's daughter."

I shake my head and clench my jaw so damn tight, I'm surprised my teeth don't shatter.

"I didn't fuck her over. I broke her."

Mozart composed his first symphony when he was five years old. He played in front of two imperial courts when he was six. I'm twenty-four, and I just stumbled over my coffee order.

—*Caitlin's Secret Thoughts*

"So . . . how was your date?" Bellamy asks as she stirs a pumpkin cream latte.

"I told you yesterday, it wasn't a date." I'm forced to inch away when the cinnamon smell hits me and turns my stomach.

Adelaide sits across from us with her head buried in whatever book she's writing this week. I can't keep up with her, and she never lets us read them before she's done. "I just had to dress him."

"Wait." She pops her head up from her minty-green MacBook. "He was undressed, and it wasn't a date?"

Bellamy pats the top of Addie's head like she's one of the dogs. "Maybe if you'd come out of the cave every once in a while, you too could undress a date instead of just writing about it."

"Listen." Addie rolls her pretty brown eyes. "Some of us work in a hospital. Others have a writing cave. You have surgeries, and I have a book due in three weeks that's not done. You know that makes me nuts." She spins her honey-blonde hair up into a bun and shoves a pen through it, locking it in place. "And I'd be happy to date if a single guy I meet is interesting enough to bother dating."

"I mean, standards do complicate things," Bellamy agrees, and my heart hurts again.

I know Jagger thought yesterday was a date. Killian tried to say he just needed a stylist when he introduced us, but Jagger was looking for more than clothes. He was good-looking with big muscles and gorgeous green eyes, but they weren't Callen's, and every time he got just a little too close, I was reminded of how much I wanted them to be.

He was just wrong.

Felt wrong.

Smelled wrong.

Looked wrong.

He wasn't Callen, and that made him wrong.

Callen, who I'll never forgive and may never recover from.

Fucking asshole.

"Cait . . ." Bellamy whispers my name, but I must not look up in time because the next thing I know, the bitch is kicking me under the table with the toe of her pointy black boot.

Like the adult I am, I kick her back. "What the hell?"

"Oh shit." Adelaide looks over the top of her screen, and her eyes triple in size. "Do not turn around."

Of course, I do the exact opposite of what I'm told because I despise authority and always have. I blame my parents for that. Only when I turn, my heart sinks.

There he is.

The dick who haunts my dreams with his eyes and pisses me off in my reality with his fucking existence. I've played nice. Nicer than he deserved.

I haven't told anyone what happened between us.

Okay. Maybe not, *not* anyone.

But Bellamy and Adelaide don't count.

They're my friends. Not his.

And I needed to talk to someone.

When Maddox and Killian got home from Vegas, I told them I was sick. The flu. I was contagious. Whatever it took to get them to leave me alone. And it worked. They're men. It's simple. Get nasty and they get the fuck out of Dodge.

Just like some other people I know.

Asshole.

He and Cooper walk over to the counter, and I turn around, keeping my back to him. He doesn't deserve to see me.

I hold my head high and straighten my shoulders, refusing to look back.

I've managed to avoid him for the most part. The one thing the son of a bitch was right about was that it's easier not having him down the damn hall. But at the same time, it's just another thing that breaks my heart.

"You okay, Caitlin? You're looking a little pale." Bellamy looks concerned as I close my eyes.

"I'm fine. My stomach has just been off today. The smell of your latte made it worse," I admit as I break off a piece of the scone in front of me, hoping maybe it will settle my stomach, but no such luck. Damn it. "I think I'm gonna go, guys. I'm not feeling so good."

"Cait. You really need to consider going to the doctor. You may have a food allergy or have developed a sensitivity to something. This keeps happening." My bestie is an incredible nurse. She's also got shit timing because right now, with Callen not ten feet behind me, I don't want to be lectured about the possibility that I'm allergic to gluten.

I grab my purse and force a smile. "Talk soon."

And then I'm gone before I can possibly run into Callen.

That doesn't mean I can't feel his eyes on me as I walk through the door.

Fuck you, Callen Sinclair.

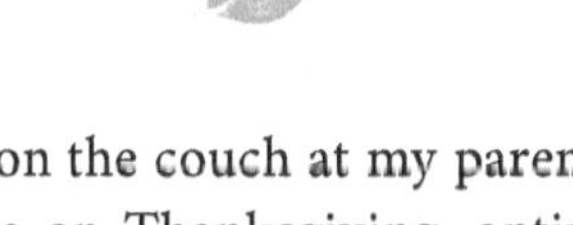

I curl up on the couch at my parents' house when I get there on Thanksgiving, opting to take a nap instead of helping to make the fresh ravioli Mom and Nonna make each year. I vaguely register my brothers coming in and out of the room and choose to ignore them when they turn on the Kings game. Because why wouldn't Callen haunt me here too?

"Move down, Cait," Lucky bitches as he sits by my feet, and maybe I kick him before I make room for him. Little brothers are dicks.

I pull the chunky red cable-knit blanket off the back of the couch and roll away from the television, not in the mood for this torture. Unfortunately, it only takes a few minutes and a ridiculous amount of yelling at the TV by all three of my brothers before I get up, deciding I need to find a quieter spot.

Like I said . . . dicks.

When I wander into the kitchen with the thick blanket wrapped around my shoulders, Nonna immediately stops stirring the sauce with her wooden spoon and presses her lips to my forehead. "You're not warm, principessa. Why do you look sick?"

"Thanks, Nonna. I didn't think I looked sick. Just tired. I'm fighting a bug I can't seem to shake."

"You should have your iron levels checked. They gave me a pill for that."

I kiss my great-grandmother's cheek and smile as she lifts the sauce spoon to my lips.

"Yumm. That's really good."

Mom walks into the kitchen, her dark hair pulled back, dressed in a black sweater and black leggings. If you didn't know she was in her fifties, you'd never believe it. She's as beautiful now as she's always been. Yay for good genes. "Of course it's good. It's my sauce."

She's cocky too.

"Are you sick, honey?" She looks me over and furrows her brow. "You look pale."

"She needs iron," Nonna tells her, and I shake my head.

Everyone thinks they're a doctor.

"I'm fine. Just tired. I can't shake how tired I am," I complain, not bothering to tell her it's been months since I've gotten a good night's sleep. That would only lead to questions I can't answer.

"Sit, principessa. Tell us about all the exciting things you're doing. In my day, you got married and you had babies. You didn't design dresses for singers and dress athletes for interviews. I was listening to that Lilah Ryan on the Alexa this morning. I like her music."

"Nonna . . ." I laugh. "You listen to Lilah?"

Nonna refuses to tell us her actual age, but we're pretty sure she's at least ninety, considering she's Dad's grandmother. According to her, age is a state of mind, and she refuses to admit she's any older than fifty, even if Dad is older than that. The idea of her listening to Lilah makes me smile.

"She wears your dresses, so I listen to her music. It's as

simple as that. And that brother of hers is so cute," she adds with a wink.

"It's the Sinclair genes," Mom agrees, and she's not wrong. "They all had gorgeous kids."

I'm pretty sure a growl slips past my lips before I can stop it, and judging by the looks on Mom and Nonna's faces, they heard it too. *Oopsie.*

"Caitlin . . ." Mom corners me the way only she can. "Your brother mentioned you seemed upset with Callen last month. Is everything okay? Or has a different Sinclair made you growl like that?"

"Maddox's friend?" Nonna asks as she drops fresh pasta into boiling water. "Why would he make you growl? That boy is so sweet."

To *her,* maybe.

"Oh, Nonna." Mom pulls the chicken Milanese out of the oven, and my stomach flip-flops. Not a good smell. "Don't you remember the way she used to follow him around and the way she'd stomp off when Maddox and Callen wouldn't let her play?"

I hold my hand up to my mouth until the nausea passes. "I was a kid."

"Some things don't change, Caitie."

Nonna smiles at Mom, then looks at me, and my stomach drops. "You look green."

"I don't feel so good . . ." I feel it happening in slow-motion as I turn and dash to the bathroom. I barely make it to my knees before I'm throwing up again, only there's nothing left to throw up since I haven't eaten today, and I'm left dry-heaving as my brothers yell in the background.

"Should have laid off the shots last night, Caitie."

Stupid fucking Rome.

Lucky chuckles as my body revolts, and tears stream down my face.

The boys are all decent pukers.

Not me.

Rome will actually gag himself to get it over with.

Just the thought brings on another round of dry heaves.

"Shut the door, Cait. I don't want to get sick," Lucky yells, and if I thought I could get up, I'd go back in the family room and puke on him. Dickhead.

"Here, honey." Mom gathers my hair in her hands and presses a damp, cool washcloth to the back of my neck. "How long have you had this bug, baby?"

"I don't know," I moan and thank God for Mom's obsessive need to clean as I lay my face against the toilet. "The smell of the Milanese turned my stomach."

"Amelia, do you remember the way Milanese used to make you sick when you were pregnant?" Nonna asks Mom, and my stomach flips like an upside-down roller coaster.

"I'd have to be having sex to be pregnant, Nonna," I moan.

"Shut the door," Maddox yells.

"It was so weird because you didn't get sick right away," Nonna continues, and Mom brushes the hair from my temple as my eyes close.

"This is the first time she's gotten sick," Mom defends me.

No. *No.* No. *No.* My. God. No.

"She's not pregnant, Nonna," Mom tells her, and I start doing the math in my head.

"I was sick this morning too," I croak. "And last week . . ."

We used condoms.

I'm not pregnant.

When was the last time I had my period?

Fuck.

I don't even get a regular period.

For fucks sake, they warned me it could be hard to get pregnant.

I can't actually *be* pregnant.

"Caitie . . ." Mom lifts my face and sees the concern. At least I think she does when she turns to Nonna. "Could you grab me my phone, Nonna?"

"What do you need your phone for? You're not taking a picture, are you?" I moan.

"No, principessa. I'm DoorDashing a pregnancy test."

Fuck my life.

One hour, two bottles of water, and four positive pregnancy tests later, I'm back in the fetal position on a bathroom floor. The difference is this one has radiant heating and is attached to Mom's master bedroom. And this door is closed and locked.

"I can't be pregnant," I sob. "I can't. This can't be happening."

Mom runs her fingers through my hair, trying to calm me down, but there is no calming down. Not now. Maybe not ever. What the hell am I supposed to do with a baby when some days I'm pretty sure I fail at taking care of myself? I had a bag of chips for dinner last night. You can't feed a baby a bag of chips.

"Ma . . ." Lucky bangs on the door. "I'm hungry. When are we going to eat?"

She kisses my forehead and gets up as primly as she can from the floor, then cracks open the door. "Luciano Beneventi, I swear on all that is holy if you do not get the fuck out of my room right this second, I will tell that trashy little tramp you snuck out of the house this morning that she's one of no less than three women you think I don't know you sneak in and out of your room. And after she's done clawing you apart with those daggers she calls nails, I will call the other two. And don't you think I don't know who they are or how to get hold of them. I've been your father's wife for nearly three decades. I know things. Now get downstairs and do not come back up."

When he doesn't move fast enough, she shoves him back with a push. "Go."

Under different circumstances, I'd laugh at the look on Lucky's face.

Under these circumstances, I may never laugh again.

Mom shuts the door and locks it. "Honey . . . I have a few questions."

"Yeah," I croak. "So do I."

Mom gets back down on the floor next to me and lays my head in her lap, then goes back to running her fingers through my hair. "Well, you know, kiddo. The time to ask may have been before you started having sex."

A hysterical laughter bubbles up my throat and past my lips.

One I can't control.

One I can't stop until I'm sobbing again.

"We used a condom," I protest.

"It only takes one time—"

"We used them every time." My heart cracks all over again, just thinking about *that* week.

"Oh . . ." Her hands stop. "*Every time.* There were a lot of times?"

"Mom . . ." I close my eyes. "There were apparently enough times."

"Was it good?"

"Oh. My. God. Mother." I never knew I'd one day wish the earth would open up and swallow me whole like some kind of bad sci-fi movie. But I'd take that over this any day.

"Honey, I just want to know that it was at least good sex. Trust me. Good sex can make a lot of things better." She says it so matter-of-factly that I realize I'm too shell-shocked to even care that she's talking about sex with my father.

"It was good sex. Really good sex. The kind of sex you never want to end because you know you're going to be changed on a molecular level when it's all over," I whisper, remembering what it was like to be held in that asshole's arms and wishing desperately that I was still there. That he was holding me now, making this all better.

She pushes up the sleeves of her sweater and fans her flushed face. "Damn, honey. I think I might need a cigarette after that."

"You don't smoke."

She ignores me. "And do I know this man, Caitlin?"

Forget cracking. What's left of my heart is shattered.

"It turns out, I'm not sure *I* even knew him."

"**A**nd then what happened?" Bellamy asks, lying next to me in my bed the next day after she gets off her double shift at the hospital.

"I made her promise I could have a few weeks before we talked to my dad. I need to wrap my head around this before I can handle the freak-out he's going to have." I shove my hands under my pillow and ignore the fact that I'm wearing Callen's shirt to bed.

Bellamy mirrors my position. "And Amelia's going to keep it from him?"

I nod. "But I have to call the doctor's office today and schedule an appointment. That was her one demand."

"I figured your mom and dad had that whole *you tell one, you tell both* thing going for them." Of course she did. Bellamy grew up in a normal house. With a schoolteacher for a mom and a fisherman for a dad. Secrets were probably never kept in her house.

"Secrets are part of my parents' lives. She wasn't happy, but I'm an adult, and she respects me. So she agreed." Thankfully. Because I can't imagine doing this without my mom, and the thought of telling my dad right now scares me almost as much as the idea of being responsible for keeping a human alive.

I've had plants die in less time than it takes me to pick out my clothes for work.

"So what are you going to do?" B asks after a few minutes. "You know you don't have to go through with this if you don't want to. It's your choice."

"I know in theory it is. But for me, there is no choice." Once I calmed down enough to think more clearly, I knew what I was doing. I wasn't excited about it. I'm still not. But my heart told me this was what's right for me. Of course, my heart also told me I loved Callen, so its judgment skills are somewhat lacking. "I'm going to have it. I'm probably going to fuck up its life the way I'm apparently excelling at fucking up my own though. So there's that to look forward to."

Maybe I should start a therapy fund instead of a college fund.

Do they have them?

"What about Callen?" she asks the question I haven't stopped asking myself since I climbed in bed last night. One I still don't have the answer to.

"What about him?"

She holds my glare for so long, I think she may have forgotten how to speak. "You've got to tell him, Cait,"

"I know," I answer softly. Aching. Wishing this was happening in a different time under different circumstances. One where he was here with me, and we were both happy about this surprise. "But I'm not even ready to talk about this with anyone else yet. I can't think about Callen's feelings now. I will. I promise. When I'm ready."

Bellamy slides one of her hands under my pillow and links her fingers with mine. "The longer you wait, the harder it's going to get."

"Pretty sure I've already hit that wall. I'm not sure how much harder it can get."

I know just how wrong I am before the last word even leaves my lips.

I thought *hard* hit the day Callen left, but it's gotten incrementally worse each day since.

And that was before I learned exactly how much my life was about to change.

FOOTBALL BLUE BALLS

Another lackluster showing from our Kings tonight has left this reporter almost as disappointed by their lack of performance as a virginal bride on her wedding night is with her husband. Even worse . . . another loss means another lost opportunity for our favorite ballers to show up and show off in force to celebrate. Ahh . . . the good old days when all it took was Callen Sinclair appearing at a bar and bam—we'd have ourselves a juicy headline.

This reporter isn't giving up hope though. With now twelve games behind us in the regular season, the Kings are leaving us desperate for two things: A chance at the taste of a post-season victory and a chance at a bite of some deliciously, decadent gossip.

#KroydonKronicles #TheGoodOldDays #FootballBlueBalls

"This seat taken?" Dad asks as he climbs the last few steps of the nosebleed seats and sits next to me in a now-empty Kings stadium. He zips his heavy jacket and kicks his feet out as he looks out at the empty field. "Looks different up here, doesn't it?"

"Sure does," I admit. "Kinda looks peaceful."

"Not something you often say about a football field, son."

I drop my elbows to my knees and lean forward, trying to block some of the wind from hitting him. "Not often you see it without sixty-five thousand people filling the seats, I guess."

I knew Dad was in the stadium tonight, even if no one else knew it. He was watching the game from Declan's office. He did the same thing last week at the Thanksgiving game. Managed to get in and out without anyone seeing him.

He hasn't been seen at a game since he stepped down. Didn't want to confuse the players, he said. Didn't want to fuel the press. Doesn't seem to be making a difference, though, and my shit performance tonight isn't gonna help that.

"You calmed down yet?"

Shame washes over me. "Not my best behavior. I get it."

"Do you?" He looks small sitting here in the dark cold night. And he's never looked small a day in his life. "You've spent the last few months turning into another player, Callen. One I don't recognize. One who's going to ruin everything you've worked so hard to achieve. Care to tell me what's going on with you?"

"Nothing, Dad. It's all good." Complete bullshit, but that's what I do now. I bullshit my way through it. My day. My game.

"Don't lie and tell me everything is fine. You've been a shit liar your whole life, and I didn't raise you to be a good liar."

A gust of frigid wind whips through the stadium and settles in my chest.

"Come on. Let's get back inside. It looks like it's going to snow," I tell him, pretty fucking sure my conscience can't handle it if he gets sicker.

"The passes you dropped tonight were cake passes you've been catching since pee-wees. You don't drop cake passes, son. You popped off to your offensive coordinator. You got in an argument with your quarterback. You argued with Declan. You would have never done that with me. None of this is like you, so don't tell me there's nothing wrong."

I lean back in the hard black, plastic-molded seat and cross my arms over my chest, staring at the field. "Kind of a lot of shit going on right now."

I leave my sentence vague. My plan wasn't to guilt my father over his diagnosis tonight or ever. I'm a grown man who's gonna what? Cry over his daddy not coaching him anymore?

Dad pulls a Kings knit beanie from his coat and yanks it on his head.

"This isn't about me. There's something else there. There has to be—because you know me better than this, Callen. I'm going to get through this. I'm a fighter. We're both fighters. And I've got way too much to live for to not win this fight."

"Don't make promises you can't keep, old man." I take my gloves from my pocket and hand them to him. He shouldn't be out here with a weakened immune system. "Come on. Let's get back inside. It's colder than a witch's tit out here."

Dad shakes his head and looks back out at the stadium he helped make great.

"You know something?" He asks, then waits me out like always.

"Know what?" I answer him, because he's more stubborn than I am most days, and the quiet moment I was looking for when I came up here after the game is already shot to shit.

"You were my second chance. Declan, Nat, and Cooper . . . they didn't have the childhood you did. They didn't get the same father you did. They didn't have two happy parents. *Your mother*—she made me a better man." He smiles like he's lost in a memory.

"She made me more present. I had a more stable job by the time you came around. I had a partner to balance all the things. Because of her, you got the best of me. And I'm not done watching you grow the fuck up yet, apparently, because you're acting like a child throwing a temper tantrum because his favorite toy was taken away. I know, unlike Declan, you actually wanted to play for the Kings. But I don't think I'm what's tying you up like this. So you're gonna sit here and tell me who or what is holding the goddamned rope, or I'm going to sit out here all night, and your mother is going to bitch us both out when she has to send one of your brothers to find us. The choice is yours, Callen."

"You know you're fucking stubborn, old man," I groan, pretty sure I don't have a fucking choice in the matter. Nothing like being nearly thirty and fucking shit up so badly your sick dad has to solve your problems. "But you're not the only one."

"That I am. But don't think for a minute I can't wait you out, kid. I've done it before. And I'll do it again. You never made anything easy. You always had to learn everything the hard way. I've waited you out a time or two before, and I'll do it again."

I look at him.

Really look.

His skin has a gray tint to it already, and he's only a few weeks into the more aggressive treatment they decided to switch to, but the fire is still there. You hear men talk about what it's like growing up in the shadow of a legend, but they rarely mention what it's like watching that legend deteriorate in front of your eyes.

"Callen, it's fucking cold. Speak, son."

"There was a girl . . ."

"There always is." Dad's laugh turns into a cough. "Was she the right girl?"

That's his first easy question.

"Yeah . . . she was."

"Didn't she feel the same?" he asks, probably trying to figure out what the hell happened, since I'm not exactly being forthcoming.

I think about the pain on her face the day I left.

The look in her eye the other day at the bakery.

"The thing is, the timing was shit, and I'm not sure if it's ever going to line up." I don't offer more. The less people who know more, the better for Caitlin.

After a beat, I turn and look at him. "Don't go stoic on me now, old man."

"Guess I'm just surprised. I didn't realize I raised a quitter."

Fuck.

Dad never raised a hand to me, but he just landed a hard hit.

"I didn't have a choice," I argue, with her crystal-blue eyes pooling with tears at the front of my mind. "I did what I had to do."

He looks skeptical. "If you can live with that, then live with it. Stop this shit. But I know you, son. And I'm pretty sure you can't live with it."

Me living isn't what matters.

Caitlin living is.

LEO

Dude. Thought you were gonna get in a fight on the sidelines last night, Uncle.

MADDOX

Nah, man. Not his style.

KILLIAN

I'm with Leo. The whole world saw the picture of you screaming at Declan.

HENDRIX

He's not his brother during a game. He's his coach. You shut off the family shit. You have to. How else would I kick Nixon and Leo's ass every time?

NIXON

Not how I remember it.

CALLEN

Listen. I was pissed. I'm not now. It's over. Emotions run high during the game. That's all it was.

LEO

Still looked like you were gonna hit Dad though.

NIXON

Shut up, Leo. Kenzie's on call at the hospital tonight. I've got the house to myself, and Monday Night Football is on in ten minutes. If you're coming. Bring food or beer. Up to you, assholes.

KILLIAN

I miss food.

MADDOX

You eat.

KILLIAN

Yeah. Chicken and rice is what we feed the dogs.

LEO

I like chicken and rice.

HENDRIX

I heard you like raman since Nixon moved out. You ever heard of a meal service?

LEO

Sorry. Mommy didn't set that up for me when I moved out. Must be nice being the baby.

HENDRIX

You said it. Not me.

NIXON

Nine minutes.

My doorbell rings ten minutes later, and I curse Nixon. I wouldn't put it past him to have walked to my place to drag my ass back to his. Some days, this town is too damn small. I could just ignore the fucker, but he's persistent. Always trying to do the right thing. Leo would let me starve to death, then let the dogs in to lick my bones if he thought it would be fun to watch.

The bell rings again, and I grumble as I make my way to the front door. "Dude, I just played last night. I'm not in the mood—" I swing it open and find Maddox on the other side. Not Nixon.

"You were saying?" he asks as he walks around me into the house and into my kitchen. He opens the fridge, tosses me a beer, then cracks one for himself.

"Apparently, I was saying help yourself to my beer," I tell him as I open the bottle and toss the lid into the trash from across the room. "He shoots. He scores."

"Certainly weren't doing much of that last night." Maddox leans against the counter and watches for my reaction, but I don't react. "Come on, man. We lived together for nine years, including college. What the fuck was up with that shit last night?"

"I already did the whole therapy thing with my old man. I'm good. How about you? You still acting like you're not hung up on the princess?" When all else fails, the best defense is a good offfense.

"Kill's got a big mouth. I'm not hung up on anyone. Between the bar, the gym, and a few things I've got going on with my dad, I don't have time to focus on anything else."

"Oh yeah . . ." I know I shouldn't ask. It's an unwritten rule. You don't ask Maddox about Sam or his business. None of us do. But I'm dying for something, anything that might give me information because I haven't heard from Sam since that night. "How's the stuff going with your dad?"

"I don't know. He's been a moody son of a bitch lately. Not as moody as you. But moody."

"Gee, thanks." I crack a smile, managing to forget for a minute how much Maddox is going to hate me if he ever finds out what happened.

"He worked through most of Thanksgiving. At least until Caitlin got sick. Mom made him get his ass to the table while she stayed with Cait."

My head spins. "Sick? Like bad sick? What was wrong?"

"Dude. She got a stomach bug or something. Probably ate too much raw cookie dough. She's been baking so much, you'd think her job was to stock Sweet Temptations with cookies. Who knows? She seems better this week." Madman finishes his beer and tosses it in the trash. "Come on, man. Let's go watch the game with the guys."

I fucking hate this.

All of it.

Including myself.

My ducks may not be in a row now, but you can bet your sweet ass my ducks are having more fun than yours are. Your ducks probably hate you and your anal-retentive self for making them line up like that. #FREETHEDUCKS

—*Caitlin's Secret Thoughts*

I stare at the phone burning a hole in my hand as I try to work up the nerve to message Callen. I promised myself I'd talk to him after my ob-gyn appointment this afternoon, and I'm afraid if I don't schedule him in now, I'll chicken out later.

Chicken out or decide I hate him too much to see him.

There's a fifty-fifty chance it can go either way.

Adelaide always writes *a fuck it* moment in her books.

Why can't my *fuck it* moment be as much fun as hers are? Ugh. *Fuck it.*

CAITLIN

I need to talk to you.

The stupid little dots start and stop at least three separate times before he finally answers with one stupid word.

CALLEN

Why?

Are you okay?

Okay. Maybe he redeemed himself with the second text. *Douche canoe.*

CAITLIN

Just be home after work today, Callen. You owe me that.

CALLEN

I don't know if that's a good idea, Cait.

CAITLIN

Nothing about you is a good idea. But sometimes we have to be adults.

Be a fucking adult and be home after five, Callen.

Men suck.

I sit in my gynecologist's office, pissed at the world in an uncomfortable pink paper gown and what equates to an outdoor tablecloth covering my legs.

Someone should design better paper gowns.

My feet dangle off the table, and I'm freezing.

I didn't think to wear socks today, and it's cold as hell in here.

What's with that phrase anyway?

Cold as hell?

Hell is supposed to be hot, not cold.

How can it be *burn in hell* and *cold as hell*?

It doesn't make sense.

"You doing okay, Caitlin?" Bellamy asks as I start spiraling. She stands next to me like a guard ready to take down anyone who looks at me wrong, not that anyone is going to do that here. At least I hope not. We should all have a Bellamy in our lives.

"No. I'm cold, and I want socks," I whine because this is awful.

I don't tell her I want Callen too.

I'll take that one to the grave.

"Knock, knock," my cousin Kenzie says from the other side of the door.

Kenzie came home after her residency and joined our aunt's practice.

I've always gone to our Aunt Wren, but I felt more comfortable scheduling with Kenz, now that she's home. I guess I didn't want to see the possible disappointment in Wren's eyes.

"Are you decent?" she asks as she cracks the door.

"Listen, Dr. Hayes. I'm very much not decent. These gowns suck. Now come in," I snap back, and she opens the door laughing.

Evil.

"Hi, ladies." She seems stunned to see Bellamy in here with me. "Cait, I was surprised to see your name on my sheet today."

"Lucky, I guess." Not that I feel lucky. Not now.

She reads over her tablet, and her entire face changes. "Okay,"

"Guess somebody didn't do her homework," I stage-whisper to Bellamy.

Oh my God. What's wrong with me?

My nerves are shot.

My anxiety is through the roof.

And I'm a human incubator, just like the kind we had for the baby ducks when Mom went through her farm animals phase. Chickens, ducks, and a baby goat. They lasted a year.

"Reel in the crazy, Cait. I think you're scaring her." Bellamy leans her hip against the table and links her pinky with mine as Kenzie sits on her little round stool on wheels by the counter.

"Not scaring me. Just catching me a little off guard. That's all. Nothing to worry about. That doesn't happen often." She scrolls down a page or two on the tablet, then lays it on her lap. "So, how about you tell me why you're here today, Caitlin."

"I'm pretty sure you just read that I'm pregnant, Kenz," I snap, then immediately feel like shit for snapping. "Sorry. It's been a rough few weeks."

Suddenly tears pool in my eyes without my permission, and Kenzie hands me a tissue.

"How are you feeling?"

"Like my world is crashing in around me. Like I'm four months pregnant and somehow didn't find out until last week," I admit quietly. "Kinda like this is a sick joke."

She nods and goes into doctor mode. "It says here conception was mid-August."

"Yes," I shake my head and force myself to pull it together.

"Could it have been later?"

I chew my bottom lip, wishing things were different but knowing they're not. "No. I haven't had sex since then."

"Okay." She enters something on her screen. "And how have you been feeling?"

"I guess I've been fine for the most part. A little nauseous but nothing major. I threw up a few times around Thanksgiving, but I thought morning sickness happened when you first got pregnant. Not later on." I've tried doing the whole Google search, but all I managed to do was order a few books that make me cry every time I pick them up. "Why wouldn't it start until I was almost three months pregnant?"

"We're going to talk about that time frame in a few minutes." She nods and adds another note to her screen. "And your period?"

"My periods have never been regular. I have irregular periods. Wren put me on the pill for it a few years ago, but the hormones made me crazy, and it wasn't like I was having sex, so I went off it. I mean I've used condoms. Not that they worked, apparently." I force myself to shut up for a hot second and gather some sense of composure. "Maybe I should have made the appointment with Wren."

Kenzie rolls her little ass over and squeezes my hand. "I'm happy to ask her to come in, if that's what you want. But Caitlin, I don't want you to feel embarrassed talking to me. My only concern is keeping you healthy and delivering a healthy baby. You could tell me anything, and I'd bet you I'd heard it before. And I can't utter a word of it outside of this room."

"Well, that's good because my father doesn't know yet."

"Oh," she says a little less sure as she scrolls further down her little checklist. "It looks like you left the father's information blank."

"Do I have to have that?" I ask as my teeth chatter, unsure if it's from the cold or the nerves.

"No. It just helps give us a more well-rounded medical history."

"And you can't repeat anything I tell you, right?" Fuck. I sound like a child scared she's about to get in trouble.

Kenzie looks at Bellamy, then me. "No. I'm the only person in this room who can't say a word, according to HIPAA."

I close my eyes and take a few deep breaths.

I forgot about how close Callen and she are. Or that she's engaged to Nixon Sinclair. Maybe I didn't think this through. I should have gone to a damn clinic where no one knew me. And I would have if Kenzie's office wasn't around the corner from Everly Wilder Designs. Getting in here without Jude noticing wasn't the hardest thing I've ever done.

"It's Callen," I blurt out and wait for the fallout. But she doesn't move a muscle. "I haven't told him yet. I wanted to see you first. But I'm going to. I swear."

She nods and lays the tablet on the counter. "Okay. Well, once he's aware I'd ask you to have him fill in his part of the intake form. But let's not worry about that now. How about you lie back and relax."

"Pretty sure that's what got me into this mess," I murmur, and Bellamy chokes on her laugh.

"What is wrong with you?"

I look at my best friend. "Everything."

My head is threatening to explode like an atom bomb as Bellamy and I walk out of Kenzie's office, trying to wrap my head around everything. "Seriously? Is this new math? Can you explain to me how I'm seventeen weeks pregnant? Because it doesn't make sense to me, at all."

She links her arm through mine. "Wait . . . do you actually want me to answer you? Because I'm going to say the same thing Kenzie did."

I hold up the string of three ultrasound pictures Kenzie printed out for me of my little pomegranate. "Seriously . . . the size of a pomegranate? Not even a cute fruit? It's shaped more like a bean to me."

"Healthy, Cait. Your baby is healthy. You're healthy. And you get to find out the sex at your next appointment. It's okay to smile."

The last time I was happy, I got my heart broken.

I'm scared to death to leave myself open to that again.

But if anything was ever going to be worth it, I guess my little pomegranate would be that thing. I smile and carefully put the sonogram in my purse.

"Pomegranate Beneventi would be an awful name, right?" I turn back to ask Bellamy—right before she screams.

The Philly Press

MOMMY OR MOMMIES

Breaking News.

Two of Kroydon Hills lesser-known socialites were spotted walking out of a doctor's office on Main Street this afternoon, with one holding what looked to be a sonogram. Now, I'm not sure about you, but even this reporter could get on board with Caitlin Beneventi and Bellamy Wilder switching teams to play with each other. However, it seems someone may have had a differing opinion. Sources are reporting that a black SUV hopped the curb, barely missing the mommies-to-be. Everyone seemed shaken but okay as the reckless driver sped off. Now the question stands—is there more to the story? Could this be a jealous ex? Possibly the baby-daddy? Or was it just another case of someone texting and driving? Guess we'll have to do some digging to find out.

#KroydonKronicles #MommyOrMommies

I walk out of the shower and over to my locker, feeling better about my practice than I've felt in a while. Things were clicking. We were hitting our marks.

"Good practice out there today, Sinclair."

"Thanks, man." With a chin tip to my QB, I toss my towel in the basket and pull my sweats on, then grab my phone as it vibrates in my bag.

Looks like Coop's been blowing it up.

COOPER

Call me when you get this.

COOPER

Callen—Call me back.

COOPER

Looks like you're at practice. Call me.

I throw a hoodie on and hit Coop's number as I head to Declan's office.

Don't let this be bad news about Dad.

"You need something, Callen?" Dec closes his laptop as I walk in, waiting for Cooper to pick up the damn phone.

"Is Dad okay?" I ask as I shut the door and switch my phone to speaker. "Cooper blew up my phone during practice."

Declan grabs his own phone, then tosses it back down. "I've got nothing."

"Callen," Coop finally answers.

"Coop, you're on speaker. I'm in Declan's office. Is Dad okay?" Declan and I both hold our breath for the split-second it takes Cooper to answer.

"Dad's fine. It's not Dad."

Declan rounds the desk and takes my phone out of my hand. "Then who the fuck is it, Coop?"

"Give the phone back to Callen, Dec, and give him your office," Coop orders, his voice void of all emotion, and the hair on the back of my neck stands on end.

"Fuck you, it's my office," Declan snaps back as emotions run high between him and me in direct contrast to Coop.

"Stop," I yell, not willing to waste another second when something is obviously going down. "It's fine, Coop. Just tell us what's going on."

"I just sent you a *Kroydon Kronicles* article. I saw it an hour ago but wanted to see what I could find out before I called you."

"Whatever it is, ignore it. They're desperate for a story, and I haven't given them one, so they're probably making shit up." The *Kronicles* have been trash for years.

"Not this time, brother. Caitlin was walking out of a doctor's office and was nearly hit by an SUV—"

My vision sharpens to a single pinpoint as a woosh rolls through my ears.

No.

This isn't happening.

"Tell me she's fine and the article was wrong, man." I'm not sure when I moved, but suddenly, I'm in front of my locker, grabbing my keys and trying to get Declan to move the hell out of my way. "Fucking move, Declan, or I'll move you."

The only thing I care about is getting to Caitlin.

"You don't even know where you're going yet, Callen." He blocks me again. "Where is she, Coop?"

"She's at her parent's house. She's okay. She was released from the hospital a few hours ago. It was her and Bellamy. Both girls are fine."

The adrenaline letdown is fierce as it rushes through my body.

She's alive.

She's okay.

Holy. Shit.

I drop down on my bench and feel my stomach roll.

"Callen . . . there's more," Cooper's voice is loud in the emptying locker room. "She's pregnant."

"What?" I had to hear him wrong.

There's no way . . .

Declan holds his phone out to me with the *Kroydon Kronicles* article pulled up. "It says one of the girls might be pregnant. It doesn't confirm anything," Dec argues as I rip his phone out of his hands and skim the article.

"I have better sources than the *Kronicles*, guys." Cooper leaves little room for argument. "You need to go to your girl, Callen."

Declan looks from my phone in one hand to his in my other. "Your girl? Caitlin?"

Without stopping to answer, I toss him back his phone and run out the door. "She's at her parents' house?"

"Yeah, man. Sounds like she's shaken up but fine. You gotta calm down before you drive anywhere, brother."

"The fuck I will." I yank my truck door open, and Declan rips my key fob out of my hand.

I hadn't even realized he followed me.

He pushes me toward the front of the truck. "Get in. I'm driving."

It's then that the weight of everything hits me like a ten-ton anvil on my chest.

"She's all right," I whisper, not sure which way is up, just that I'm fucking drowning.

I could have lost her today, and she wouldn't have even known . . .

It would have all been for nothing.

She still wasn't safe.

Fuck this.

I jog around to the passenger door and jump in.

"Drive carefully and call me later," Coop tells us before he hangs up.

"Breathe, brother." The wheels squeal as Declan peels out of the parking lot on what feels like two tires instead of four. "We'll be there in fifteen minutes. You need to get your shit together before then."

"Fuck," I yell and punch my dashboard.

Anger is easier to deal with than fear.

Anger I know how to control.

Fear is paralyzing.

"Get it out, man."

It takes a minute before I can breathe again without fire in my lungs.

"Okay, good," Declan tells me while we're stopped at a red light that I'd really wish he'd run. "Now you want to tell me what the hell is going on? And when exactly you started seeing Caitlin Beneventi?"

"August." I don't bother denying it because Sam can suck a dick for all I care. I'm never denying it again. Fuck him, if he can't keep her safe.

"Want to tell me what happened?" he asks.

"No. But you might not want to come inside. It's not going to be pretty," I warn him.

And when we pull up to the gate ten minutes later and the guard lets us through, I turn to my brother. "Call your wife. Tell her to come get you because I don't know what I'm walking into, Dec."

"What the hell, Callen? What's that supposed to mean?"

"It means if I have my way, I'm not leaving here without Caitlin, and I don't want you here for this shit. Sam's your friend, but he's not mine."

But that woman inside that house—the one who's carrying my baby—she's mine.

*D*eclan doesn't listen.

He follows me to the front door and smiles sweetly when Amelia opens it for us.

"Where is she?" I ask, not giving a shit what kind of an ass I sound like.

"Caitlin?" Amelia steps back, letting Declan and me inside. She kisses his cheek, seemingly confused.

Until she isn't.

Her eyes narrow on me, and a hard glint takes shape in her icy blues. Eyes the same color as her daughter's. Her entire attitude changes in an instant. Where a second ago, she was confused and open, she's now closed off and furious. "Why are you here, Callen?"

"Amelia—" Declan starts, but Amelia holds up her hand, stopping him.

"This doesn't involve you, Declan," she snaps, and I get a glimpse of the woman everyone likes to warn you about. The one who killed another woman to save Declan's wife's life. "Your brother took something that didn't belong to him, and instead of treating it like the precious gift it was, he tried to destroy it."

Every word . . . Every syllable . . . They're laced with a deadly venom directed at me. "So, I'm going to ask this one more time before I have you escorted out of my house, Callen. Why. Are. You. Here?"

"Callen?" Maddox comes out of the kitchen with Lucky and Rome next to him. "You here to see Cait?"

"He's leaving," Amelia announces.

"I'm not," I move around her until Rome blocks me.

"Hey, man." He widens his stance. "Not sure what's going on, but you heard Mom. Sounds like it's time for you to leave."

Maddox stays back, watching. "What the hell is going on?"

"Why don't you ask your friend, Maddox," Amelia challenges, like she thinks I'm going to back down.

Maddox watches me.

He looks from me to his mother, then back to me again.

He stiffens and balls his fists by his sides.

"You've got to be fucking kidding me," Maddox's voice booms through the three-story foyer as the pieces click together. "My sister?"

"It's not like that, man." I try to get around Rome, but he mirrors every step I take. "I'll tell you everything *after* I see Caitlin."

I don't even care if she doesn't want to talk to me.

I just need to know she's okay.

I need to see it for myself.

I need to know it's not too late.

Rome blocks me with his whole body, shoving me back.

"My fucking sister?" Maddox moves, but Declan blocks him.

He grits his teeth, seething, like I knew he fucking would if he found out this way. "This isn't your fight, Declan."

"Move, Declan," I tell my brother, not wanting him involved in this.

"We're leaving, Callen," Declan tries to force my hand, but he's out of his fucking mind if he thinks I'm leaving without seeing Caitlin.

"I love her," I tell anyone who gives a shit to hear it in the room.

Three words I should have given her months ago.

Maddox charges me like we're on a football field.

Bad fucking move.

We both fly back through the round wooden table in the center of the foyer. It splinters as it gives out beneath the weight of us, shattering a crystal vase that shoots in every direction around the room, pinging off the travertine tile floor.

We wrestle for a minute before I manage to hold him back, wrapping my arms around his upper body until I've got him locked down with no move left. "You wanna hit me?"

Fuck. I didn't want this to happen, but it's clear that's what he wants.

Because in Maddox's mind, I betrayed him.

"I wanna fucking kill you. I can't believe you'd do this to her. To me."

I shove him off, and we both jump to our feet.

"It wasn't like that, man . . . I fucking love her. I've loved her for years."

"You've got a funny way of showing it, you fucking piece of shit."

I see the punch coming before it connects, but I don't dodge it.

I take the hit and spit out the blood.

I deserve it.

This was always how it was going to end.

I was always going to choose Caitlin over Maddox.

It was always going to be her, and my friendship with him was always going to be the price I paid.

"I'll give you that one." I flex my jaw. "But that's your only shot. You got yours. Now I'm walking up the stairs. Don't bother trying to stop me."

"Why now, asshole? You knock her up and leave her alone, and now all of a sudden, you want back in?" he yells, and everyone else ceases to exist.

It's just me and him in the room.

All those years of friendship, and he thinks I'd do that to her.

"How about you ask your father," I tell him in a tone so calm . . . so quiet . . . so in control when everything is spiraling out around me, that it only magnifies the rage.

"What?" Amelia interrupts from the other side of the room where she made no attempt to stop the fight.

"Ask Sam why," I tell her as I look around the chaos and see the most powerful man in Philadelphia standing in the doorway. "I did what I was told I had to do to keep her safe."

My words are directed to Amelia, but my eyes are locked on Sam.

"You said I'd get her hurt. Could get her killed. You told me I'd be the reason." I take a step forward, and no one else moves. "I broke her fucking heart so she'd be okay. Is she okay now, Sam?"

"What's he talking about, Sam?" Amelia asks, but Sam doesn't answer.

"Daddy . . ." comes a quiet voice from the top of the grand staircase, and the vice that's been squeezing my heart, making it impossible to breathe since Cooper's call, finally loosens the first little bit.

My girl is standing there, wrapped in a bright red blanket. A giant bruise covers one side of her beautiful face, but she's okay.

She's breathing. And she's right here. "Is it true?"

"Go back to bed, Caitlin." They're the first words Sam's spoken, and every person in the room seems to be holding their breath from the fallout.

Everyone but me.

**My parents didn't raise me to ask to be loved.
Not by them. Not by anyone.
Love needs to be given freely.
No exceptions.**

—*Caitlin's Secret Thoughts*

I broke her fucking heart so she'd be okay. Is she okay now, Sam?

I can't get Callen's words out of my head in the suddenly deafeningly quiet house as I walk down the stairs, careful not to trip on my unsteady legs. My bruised body aches from the near miss of the accident earlier.

A shiver rolls down my skin, just thinking about it.

One minute, we were talking, and the next, Bellamy was screaming as we both dove.

It all happened fast—so fast, it's a blur in my mind.

The smell of rubber as the tires burned the asphalt before the car peeled away.

The way Kenzie and Wren ran out of the office, shouting instructions.

Everly's hysterical voice as she called nine-one-one.

Mom holding my hand after she flew out of the bakery and never letting go.

Not even in the ambulance.

I was given every test imaginable, but none of them calmed me down until they hooked me up to the fetal monitor and let me hear the heartbeat.

My baby's heartbeat.

Fast and strong and still there.

Still. There.

That sound and everything it represented scared me to death in Kenzie's office.

The whole thing. The pregnancy. The baby. The lack of Callen. All of it.

But my God, barely an hour later, it wasn't until the minute that beautiful little galloping beat came through the machine that I knew I was okay. Everything was going to be okay. I can figure this out, and I'll never complain about this pregnancy again because my little pomegranate is okay.

I may not have planned it, but I want this baby.

Even if it took me nearly losing it to realize that.

I hadn't been at my parents' house long when I heard Callen's voice.

I thought I was dreaming at first. As much as I hate to admit it, I just wanted Callen all day today. At Kenzie's. At the hospital. I wanted him there with me. With us. But the dream of him may have been easier than this . . . whatever *this* is.

"Daddy?" I ask again with a shaking voice to match my shaking body. "What's he talking about?"

My mother meets me at the bottom of the stairs before Callen can get to me, but his eyes carry the weight of the world with them as they look over every inch of me. They settle on the scrapes and bruises on my face, and I watch him physically break, wishing it didn't bother me.

Mom blocks Callen. "Are you feeling okay?"

I nod and glance at my father, who's standing silently across the room, before stepping in front of Callen. I don't need to be protected. Not from him. If I survived him leaving, I can survive whatever the hell he's doing here. "What do you mean you broke me so I'd be okay?"

He raises his hands toward my face, and I jerk away. "No. You don't get to touch me."

A bruise is blooming on his chin, and I want to kill my brother.

No matter how angry I am, I don't want to see him hurt. Not by Maddox.

"Caitie . . ." Callen's voice . . . *that voice*. God, how I've wanted to hear my name on his lips for months.

But not now and not like this.

"Will one of you answer me?" I channel all the anger and fear I've been holding on to. "Now."

My mother wraps her arm around my waist, as if carrying my weight for me. "I think that's a really good idea." She looks at my father in a way I've never seen before. "Care to fill in the blanks?"

The room stays silent for far too long before he clears his throat.

"I did what was best for you, principessa."

It's like a bubble pops and sucks all the oxygen from the room.

"What did you do, Sam?" Mom's voice is so calm, it's frightening. She's never questioned my father before. Not in front of me and my brothers. Not once.

Dad crosses the room, careful not to step on the shards of crystal and wood, and stops in front of me, and I know the look on his face. I know the stress in his eyes. This is all business-related. This wasn't about Callen. This was about me. "I did what was best for you. I did what I had to do. What I've always done. And to keep you safe, I'd do it again."

"Oh, Sam." Mom stiffens beside me. "Tell me you didn't."

"Didn't what?" I demand while my brothers stand silently watching as if there were a ping-pong ball volleying back and forth between us.

Dad's jaw sets in an angry clench I'm also all too familiar with. "I've never discussed my business with you, and we're not starting today."

I try to get my fuzzy brain to make sense of all of this, but it doesn't.

I'm not sure if it's a protection mechanism or if I hit my head harder than I thought when I went down.

"Cait . . ."

I turn around and look at Callen. Declan stands behind him, quietly having his brother's back. But Callen . . . he's heartbroken, and it makes me want to scream. I'm so angry. At him. At my father. At my brother.

"You told me you loved me, and then you were gone," I remind Callen. Anger and heartache mixes with mental exhaustion and physical pain. "You said you were wrong. That we were *wrong*, and you left. Moved out. You made me think I was crazy. That there was never anything there. That there was nothing between us."

"Fucking coward," Maddox growls, and I expect Callen to lose his mind over his best friend calling him that, but it's as if he's dismissed Maddox entirely.

The opposite of love isn't hate.

Everyone thinks it is, but it's not.

It's indifference.

Callen ignores Maddox and keeps his focus solely on me.

"I would have done anything to keep you safe. To keep you whole and breathing. I thought I had to—"

"Wait . . ." I turn slowly back to my dad. "You told him my life was at stake? You told him what? That he made me *unsafe*? But you never told me? My life, Dad. My. Life. How could you not tell me?"

My father has the decency to hold my rage-fueled glare and not look away, but he doesn't answer.

"Did you tell him he had to break it off too? Was that you? Tell me it wasn't," I beg, but he doesn't budge. He doesn't need to say a word. I already know.

"You did," I gasp as my head throbs with the realization that all of this . . . the heartache. The pain. The devastation. It was avoidable. "It was your fault. I've been miserable for months, and it was because of you."

It starts to make some kind of warped sense.

Why Callen moved out so quickly.

Why this man who spent a lifetime protecting me destroyed me in one conversation.

"I could have had everything I ever wanted, and you stopped it without giving me a choice. I will never forgive you for that."

"Caitlin—" my father pleads in a tone I've never heard from him before, but I move on, unable to look at him.

"And you." I spin on Callen. "Did it even occur to you to talk to me? That maybe I deserved a say in how I lived *my* own life? Because I would have chosen you. You were worth it to me, even if I wasn't worth it to you. We could have figured it out together. But instead, you unilaterally decided you knew best for me. Like I'm a child who needs to be saved. Shame on you."

"You hating me was a small price to pay to keep you safe, Caitlin. It might not have been the right thing to do, but it was the only fucking option. You were all that mattered." He looks so sure. So confident. And yet so pissed.

You can hear a pin drop as I turn away, unable to look at him one second longer.

I take in the destruction around me.

The bruise on Callen's jaw.

The antique table Mom and I found at a flea market a few years ago, flattened and broken on the floor.

The crushed roses and Nonna's favorite crystal vase, shattered.

Then I look at my brother, the one Callen tried so hard not to hurt, and I'm utterly disgusted with him and his part in all of this.

"Let's not forget about you." I take a step toward Maddox, and Lucky and Rome both take a step back. It would almost be funny, if it wasn't. "God, I looked up to you. For years, I looked up to you. You had this circle of friends that I would have given anything to be a part of. You held those girls up on pedestals. Hell, you still do. Our cousins. The twins. You respected the hell out of them. *I watched.* For years I watched, and I was jealous."

I pull the blanket tighter, as if it can protect me from the pain.

The pain the men in this room caused.

"But you never let me in that circle, did you, Maddox? You hold your friends up to such high standards and in such high regards. There's only one problem with that—the higher you hold someone, the harder they fall." I laugh. "I should know. But God forbid one of those friends is interested in me. I mean, it's not like he's worthy of my love. Right, big brother?" My voice grows incrementally louder with each new thought, but Maddox stays quiet. Guess he's taking a page out of Dad's book.

I really wish he wouldn't.

I'm hungry for a fight.

I want a bad guy.

I want something or someone to focus all this anger on.

"He's good enough to be your best friend, but not good enough for me?" I shove Maddox's chest, but he doesn't budge. "That's rich, asshole. Do you know he didn't want to let anything happen because of you. I fucking loved him, and he made me promise we wouldn't lie to *you*. Because he respected you and me."

"He's not good enough for you, Caitlin," Maddox yells back, and his anger is visceral. It's a living, breathing thing. "He's fucked every woman he's ever met. Callen's a whore. You deserve better."

"It's not like you're a saint, big brother." Disdain floods my words. "None of us are. Here's the thing though—you called this man your best friend. But have you been paying attention? Because I have, and he's never—and I do mean *not ever*—brought a woman back to the condo since the day I moved in. Not once. He wasn't whoring around. Not at the bar. Not at the house. I saw it. *I felt it.* For four fucking years," I scream at the top of my lungs, hysterical. "Four years, he wouldn't make a move. It wasn't until I pushed him that he finally caved." My mother moves behind me, laying a hand on my back. "Four. Years. Maddox."

"Caitlin," Mom says coolly. "You've got to calm down. It's not good for the baby. They told you to relax. This isn't taking it easy."

I shake my head, never taking my eyes off Maddox or the way he stands his ground.

"You fucked up," I hiss. "You fucked up with him, and you fucked up with me."

Maddox finally breaks. He seethes, but there's a change in his eyes.

There's a pain that wasn't there a minute ago.

The mask falls.

"How could you, Cait? He's Callen," Maddox yells at me,

and Rome moves between us. Maybe to protect me—or maybe to protect Maddox from me.

Tears burn the backs of my eyes as a sob bubbles up my throat, and I throw his words back in his face. "How could *you*? He's Callen." I let that jab hit as hard as it was intended. "He's the boy you grew up with. The man you've roomed with. The one you trusted with your life. The one who spent a lifetime earning that trust. The only man I've ever loved. And you just hit him."

Maddox rocks on his feet.

"He's Callen," I sob, suffocating, and step back, looking around until I find Callen, needing him to save me one more time, even if I hate myself a little for it. "I still hate you, but I've got nowhere else to go. Can I go home with you?"

He holds his hand out without a word, but I move around him to the front door, refusing to take it.

"Are you sure you want to go with him?" Mom asks as Declan quietly goes outside, but Callen stands here, holding the door for me.

"I love you, Mom, but I can't stay here, and I don't want to go home where Maddox will be."

"Caitlin," Dad interrupts. "We don't know what happened today. I don't think you should leave. This house is safe."

"We have two very different definitions of *safe*, Daddy."

This must be what shock feels like—because I don't feel a thing as I walk away.

She is both hellfire and holy water.
Which side you get depends on one thing.
You.

—*Caitlin's Secret Thoughts*

We sit in silence as Callen drives into the city to drop Declan off at his car.

No one dares to speak until we park next to Declan's car.

He leans forward from the back seat and gently rubs my arm. "You're going to be okay, Caitie. I know it doesn't seem like it, but you will be. And if you need anything at all, you know Annabelle and I will always be here for you."

He presses a quick kiss to my head, this man who's been an honorary uncle to me my whole life. "Anything, Caitie."

I nod quickly. I have no words left to speak, and my emotions are all bubbling right there at the edge of my sanity. If I crack now, I'm not sure when or if I'll stop.

"Thank you," I manage to push past my lips almost inaudibly.

Callen waits for Declan to get in his car and pull away before he turns to me.

The car reeks of devastation.

It's rolling off us both in waves.

"Do you need anything from the condo? I can call Killian and ask him to make sure no one is there." I don't know if I appreciate the kind gesture or if it pisses me off because I'm not ready to be anything other than mad.

"No. Can we just go to your house, please? I don't want to see anyone." The words whispered speak so much truth.

Ones I can't even begin to understand the full extent of.

I don't want to see a single soul.

Not even Callen.

I close my eyes, pull up the chunky blanket wrapped around me and turn away.

"Caitlin . . . we're home." His words are soft, but they hurt just the same.

This isn't my home.

I can't go home.

Not to where I've lived for the past four years and not to where I grew up.

Not now.

Callen helps me down from the truck, and I can't help but pull away the second my feet hit the ground. "This was a bad idea."

"Just come inside, Caitlin. We can talk or you can sleep. The decision is yours."

I hate that I don't *hate* him.

I can't. But I want to.

It's a weird thing . . . stepping into his space, but nothing about it screams Callen.

Whites and pale blues dominate the space with touches of navy and emerald. It's soft and serene and completely unlike him, but it somehow fits. I stand in the center of the family room that's open and airy and connected to the beautiful kitchen, and I'm suddenly clinging to my fury. "You really made this place your own, didn't you?"

"We going with sarcasm instead of substance? I can do that, if it's what you need. But I'm pretty fucking sure neither of us is going to sleep until we talk."

What I need, not what I want.

Callen always knew the difference.

"I don't think I can do this tonight, Callen. Me being here doesn't mean we're back together. It means I have nowhere else to go."

Everything hurts.

My mind.

My heart.

My body.

My fucking soul.

"That's not good enough, Caitie." He steps into my space, careful not to touch me. Respectful. Always respectful. And I hate him. "Is it true?"

"What?" I snap but stand my ground. "Is what true?"

Why do his eyes have to be so expressive?

Why can I see his pain as if he sliced himself open and showed it to me from the inside?

"Are you pregnant?"

I move to one of two deep navy and white pinstriped chairs and ottomans sitting next to floor-to-ceiling windows overlooking the lake and the falls and sit, staring out into the darkness before I work up the nerve to look at him. "Yes."

"Fuck, Cait. When were you going to tell me?" he growls at me, and I manage not to claw his eyes out.

I nod my head slowly . . . not calmly.

"How do you know it's yours?" Maybe I want him to hurt as badly as he's hurt me.

Maybe I'm no better than my brother.

He leans over the chair, resting his hands on either arm, caging me in. "Because I know you, kitten. You didn't go hop on some casual fuck. You love me."

"Loved. Past tense." I straighten, not wanting him to know he's affecting me.

His fingers gently move my hair off my shoulders. "We'll see about that."

"Whatever, you cocky asshole. Of course it's yours. But I only just found out on Thanksgiving. Today was my first appointment. That's why I wanted to talk to you. I wasn't going to hide it from you. I just needed to know it was real before I put myself through the hell of talking to you."

He straightens and shoves his hands in the pocket of his hoodie. His eyes lock on mine, and that same energy crackles in the air like it always does. "Are you okay? Is the baby?

"Yes," I answer immediately because I don't hate him enough to put him through that kind of hell. I'm not that cruel. "I'm due May first."

The smile that stretches across his handsome face does me in. "Callen . . . I can't do this. Not tonight. Maybe not ever. I appreciate you letting me stay here until I figure something out."

"Glad you appreciate it because you're not going anywhere until we find out whether someone was trying to kill you today. Whether you want to hear it or not, the only reason I broke your heart was because I was told your life was in danger, and it was the only fucking way to protect you. I loved you then. I love you now. You and this baby are my responsibility, Cait. Let me take care of you."

"Fuck you, Callen. I'm no one's responsibility."

"That's all you heard?" he groans and paces the room.

I don't tell him I heard everything, even if I wish I hadn't. "If I stay here, we have rules."

"I'm listening . . ."

"Number one. This doesn't mean we're together. It doesn't mean I like you. And it certainly doesn't mean I forgive you," I point out what I think is the obvious first. "Number two . . ." Shit. What the hell is number two?

"Number two," Callen adds with a fucking smirk. "I want to go to every doctor's appointment. You tell me everything."

"Pertaining to the baby," I clarify. "And I agree to the doctor's appointments. Kenzie is my doctor."

"Number three," I point at him, feeling my fight drain from my body as I get sleepy. "Keep your declarations of love to yourself. There is no us. You broke that, not me. And right now, I'm focused on our pomegranate, not on fixing what you broke."

"Pomegranate?"

I lean into the corner of the chair and pull my feet up under the blanket my mother is never getting back. "There's a website that tells you all about the baby's development, and it tells you what size it is each week. We're seventeen weeks pregnant, and our baby is the size of a pomegranate."

His brows lift. "The hard-shell thing or one of the seeds from inside?"

"Of course you know what a pomegranate is. Ugly, stupid fruit," I mutter. "The hard-shell thing. And our next appointment is the week before Christmas. We can find out the sex of the baby then, if you want."

Even I'm not so coldhearted that I'd keep him out of our baby's life.

Callen drops to his knees in front of me and very slowly reaches out, probably waiting for me to smack his hand away. I don't. I give him this one thing because I owe it to our little red fruit and take his hand and rest it on my still-flat stomach.

"Our baby . . . Christ, Caitie. We're going to have a baby."

The tears are back, and this time, they don't stop.

No matter how hard I try.

"Test run, Callen. I make no promises on how long I stay."

I can't give him more than that.

My heart can't take another break.

It wouldn't ever recover.

Not again.

SINCLAIR

81

Part III

NATTIE

Is today the day?

MURPHY

That Brady realizes you're fucking nuts?

CARYS

Be nice, Murph.

MURPHY

Listen, I'm still cleaning green glitter out of my car from Thanksgiving.

NATTIE

You deserved that.

DECLAN

What day?

CARYS

Do you live under a rock, Dec?

DECLAN

Sorry. I have a job, Carys. A kinda important one.

NATTIE

Ohh. Did you hear that? He's important.

DECLAN

Whatever. What did I miss? Did they change Dad's treatment?

NATTIE

No. It's Callen and Caitlin's appointment. She's twenty weeks, so Callen said they're going to find out the sex of the baby.

CARYS

Cooper and Callen are on a run this morning. I'll ask him what time the appointment is when they get in and let you know.

I jog into Cooper's kitchen as he chants the theme song from *Rocky*.

"Dude, it wasn't a race." I laugh as Carys shakes her head from across the island and slides a tray of sugar cookies in the oven. The house smells like Christmas on crack.

"Dude," Coop mocks me. "Sounds like something a loser would say."

"Ignore him, Callen. He's old and has to prove his masculinity." She smiles, and Coop smacks her ass.

"Pretty sure I already proved that this morning."

Carys blushes and tucks her hair behind her ear, and I look away.

"Come on, guys . . . I'm good. I don't need to see it." I groan and raid their fridge for a bottle of water.

"Sorry, little brother." Carys pulls away from Cooper and

takes her tea over to the kitchen table. "Today's the big day, right?"

"Yeah. In about two hours," I tell her, equal parts excited and freaked the fuck out. The family has taken the news well. They're happy for us, but in typical fashion for my family, they want to be overly involved. Mom's ready to buy baby clothes already. Carys needed to tell her no. I think Dad already ordered a Kings jersey. "So, you want to tell me what it's going to be like?"

Lines pinch Carys's forehead as confusion sets in. "Being a parent?"

"No, the doctor's visit," I admit sheepishly. I'm not even thinking about when the baby gets here. I'm not sure it's possible for me to think that far ahead when I'm struggling to get through the day-to-day with Caitlin. Being so close to her and somehow being as far apart as we've ever been is fucking killing me. I guess that's why I've been trying to read everything I can about the pregnancy. When all else fails, I prepare. Study. Learn everything I can. Whether it's watching tapes or apparently, reading every baby book I can get my hands on. "I mean, I've read a few of the books." Lies. I've read them all. "But I figured you did this all with Nattie when she was doing the whole surrogate thing for you, right? You were at all the appointments. Does it hurt? The sonogram? What am I supposed to do for her?"

"Callen . . ." She lays her hand on my arm and squeezes. "Haven't you talked to Caitlin about it?"

My heart sinks.

I knew I'd have my work cut out for me, but I guess I didn't think it would be this bad.

"Yeah." Cooper sucks air in through his teeth. "Our boy isn't exactly talking to his baby mama."

"Asshole." I flip the cap of the water bottle at him, but the fucker catches it like Mr. Miyagi catching a fly. I already told him Caitlin and I are struggling to find a new normal. Less her and more me. She seems fine with being pissed. I'm the one trying to fix it. To fix us. Because there's no way this is how it's supposed to be. Supposed to end. We don't end. I refuse to accept anything else.

"Maybe. But I'm not wrong. How the hell are you living together but not talking?" He tosses me back the cap. "I know you can talk to girls. I've watched you do it."

Carys looks at Coop like he's stupid. "But this isn't any girl. It's *his* girl." She sighs with a dreamy look in her eyes, like she thinks this is some kind of fairytale. And that right there . . . that *my girl*, that's what I keep thinking. She's mine. She always was. I just have to get her to remember that. "Why aren't you talking to her?"

"Other way around." Cooper makes a motion with his hands, so I do the same, only I flip him the fuck off instead of making a turning motion.

Brothers are dicks.

"Mom . . . I need lunch money on my card," my niece Lexy yells as she races into the kitchen and grabs her keys off the wall. "Hurry up, guys."

She turns to look at us and lights up when she sees me. "Uncle Callen," she squeals and throws her arms around my neck before the twins follow her down. Lincoln and Lochlan saunter in, in Christmas pajama bottoms with Cousin Eddie from *National Lampoon* all over them and Kroydon Hills football hoodies.

Oh, to be the big-shit senior in high school again.

Damn things were easier back then.

"Pajamas?" I ask as I hug both boys.

Lexie's smile could light up the whole damn town when she looks at her brothers. "Last day of school before the holiday break. It's always pajama day."

She opens her puffer coat and shows me her red and

white candy-cane leggings, and I keep my mouth shut. These kids have gotten so old. They chat with their parents for a hot second before all three rush through the door, and my head spins a little. "Man. You've got six months left before graduation. That's nuts."

"Enjoy all these firsts, Callen. One day, you're holding a newborn. The next, they're eighteen and looking at colleges. Trust us. It's rough," Cooper takes the seat between me and Carys. "Now, what are you going to do about getting Caitlin to talk to you?"

I shrug, fucking frustrated. With myself. With Caitlin. With the whole situation.

"I'm going to wait her out, I guess. We barely speak most days. Not that she's really speaking to anyone besides her mom, Bellamy, and one or two friends. And I get it. I do. I hurt her. But how do you get the most stubborn woman you've ever met to forgive you when she won't acknowledge you're in the room?"

"Ask your sister." Cooper tugs Carys closer. "I mean, if you want the most stubborn woman I know to tell you what would work for her."

She smiles like he's not wrong. "Okay . . . So she hasn't forgiven Sam yet either, right?" Carys sounds like she's watching a soap opera, not listening to my life. She's enjoying it all a little too much.

"No. Not him or Maddox. Most days, she's pissed at Rome and Lucky just for the hell of it. She's always pissed at me." I know I'm fucked up because when I think about the way she'll walk by me without saying a word or making eye contact, I smile. She's cute as hell when she's pissed, but I'm pretty sure she doesn't want to hear that now. "Wanna give me some girl advice?"

She pauses with her mug halfway to her mouth. "Let me think on it."

"What did you get her for Christmas?" Cooper asks, and I look away, fucking pissed I didn't even think of that.

"Christmas is in four days, Callen." Carys's green eyes narrow, and she smacks the table in front of me as her oven beeps. "Please tell me you're not that dense."

"Think again," Coop warns her, and I keep my mouth shut because he's not wrong.

"I'm not even going to be home for Christmas, guys. We fly out to Arizona in two days and won't be back until after midnight on the 25th. Christmas will be over," I'm not sure why I'm bothering to defend myself—my sister obviously thinks I'm stupid. She's probably right.

"She's the mother of your unborn child, Callen. Have you seen the size of the Sinclair babies' heads? She's literally going to push a watermelon out of her vagina." My face contorts as a mental picture flashes before my eyes, and I shiver.

"Nice visual, Carys," I bitch as she pulls a tray of cookies out of the oven.

"Buy her a Christmas present and kiss her ass, Callen. You broke her heart. Ignoring each other isn't going to fix it. You have to prove to her that you're in this. That you only did it because you thought you had no choice."

I finish my water and toss it in the trash, then drop a kiss on the top of Carys's head. "I'm trying."

"Words are weak, little brother. Try harder." She points a red and green spatula at me. "You've got four months left before the baby is born, and they're going to be over before you know it. Fix this before you miss this window and you're both too exhausted from lack of sleep and diaper blowouts to even think about romance. Romance her." She smacks my knuckles as I steal a cookie. "Now go and send the chat a pic as soon as you find out if I'm getting a niece or nephew."

Cooper grips my shoulder. "And make sure Caitlin knows

I'm five minutes away if she needs anything while you're gone."

"Thanks, man. Her dad still has Jude on her, but I'll make sure she knows."

"Hope the kid doesn't talk as much as his mom," Cooper smiles at Carys.

"Stop it, Cooper. Chloe doesn't talk that much," she defends her business partner and Jude's mother.

"Pretty sure he takes after his dad more than his mom," I tell them both. "I mean, he's built like Dean. And quiet like most of the Beneventis, even if he looks like Chloe. So there's that. Gotta go, guys. Wish me luck."

"Luck . . ." Carys calls back as I walk out of the house, fairly fucking sure I just heard Cooper smack her ass and tell her to strip.

My family is a bunch of horny motherfuckers.

Caitlin

BELLAMY

It's the big day. You ready?

CAITLIN

God, yes. I'm tired of referring to my baby as a weird little assortment of fruits.

BELLAMY

What's it this week? A kumquat?

CAITLIN

A what?

BELLAMY

I don't know. It's just a fun word. Is Callen going with you to the appointment?

CAITLIN

Yes. I'm tempted to make Jude drive me so I'm not stuck in a car with Callen.

BELLAMY

Try to enjoy the appointment, Cait. This is exciting.

CAITLIN

I know. I'm going to try. I've just been extra hormonal this week, and I don't think Christmas is helping any. I've never not spent it without my family.

BELLAMY

Is your mom still making your dad sleep on the couch in the office?

CAITLIN

As of last week, yes.

BELLAMY

Are you doing the big Christmas dinner with the Kingstons?

CAITLIN

I don't think I feel like it this year. Addie and I were talking about spending it volunteering at the soup kitchen instead with her sister.

BELLAMY

Oh, I didn't realize Coraline was home. Wish I could do that with you. I've got to be at the hospital at ten, so I'm house-hopping between Cross and Ares's houses to see the kids, then heading in. Are we still doing a girls' Christmas Eve?"

CAITLIN

Absolutely.

BELLAMY

Perfect. Good luck at your appointment.

CAITLIN

XOXO

I stuff my phone in my pocket as I look around at Callen's very un-Christmasy house and want to cry. I want to be happy today. It's a big day. But instead of being excited, I've been fighting tears all morning. Everly closed the showroom and offices until after the new year, so I'm stuck *here* in hell with the Grinch.

And just like that, the green bastard with a tiny little heart appears. Damn it. If he was actually green and ugly, it might make all this easier. But of course he's not. He's Callen. No man on the planet looks better in sweats and a hoodie than this man does, and instead of turning me on, it pisses me off.

Okay. So that's a lie.

It turns me on too—because lately, when I'm not ready to cry, I'm ready to scream in frustration. *Sexual frustration.* There's a reason you should be in a relationship when you're pregnant. Sure, it'd be nice to have a partner to help with the baby. But it would be even nicer to have a partner to help with the orgasms. I can't look at Callen without first thinking about how much I want to kill him, then deciding I'd rather fuck him.

Occasionally, I think it in the other order.

Either way, I'm not going there.

Not again.

So I ignore him instead. But not today. Today is our first appointment together with Kenzie. Because that's not going to be uncomfortable at all. My cousin and one of his best friends checking out my vagina. It should be a regular party. *Yay!* Not.

Fuck. And now I want to cry again.

"Hey, kitten," Callen stops in front of me and pulls a bunch of bananas from behind his back. "I got you something."

I look from them to him, confused. "I'm sure you're trying to tell me something, but I have absolutely no idea what, so I'm just going to say no. We need to leave in an hour."

I brush past him, and he grabs my arm, sending an electric current coursing through my body, and if looks could actually kill, he'd be dead on the floor where he stands. But this brave man doesn't let go.

"Did you know the baby is the size of a banana today?"

And just like that, the tears are back.

Fuck you, Callen Sinclair.

I swallow down the emotion. At least I try. "You're not going to eat them, right? Because that would be weird."

His smile stretches across his entire face, and the first teeny, tiny shard of my heart feels like it might have just slid back into place. "No. I'm not going to eat them. I just thought today was the last time we'd probably refer to our baby as a fruit and wanted to commemorate it."

He hands me the bananas, and this time, I take them.

"I was hoping we could get lunch after the appointment. We need to talk," he tells me without ever taking his hand off me, and I swear, it's making it hard to think.

I absolutely despise from the depths of my soul that he's right. We do need to talk. But it'll be on my terms. Not his.

"I want a Christmas tree."

Callen looks confused at first. Then the fucker looks

cocky, and damn him for it looking so good. "Lunch first, then we get you whatever tree you want, kitten."

I yank my arm away before I jump his stupid, annoying bones.

"Tree first, then takeout. I'm not sitting in public with you," I counter.

He steps into my space, and my traitorous heart skips a beat. "Tree first, then lunch at The Busy Bee, and I'll buy you whatever decorations you want for the tree."

"Fine," I agree but refuse to let him have the last word. Partly because I'm not ready to give in, but mostly because demanding, commanding Callen is really . . . really hot. Not that I'm going to be telling him that any time soon. Wait. Any time *period*. Not soon. Not later. Stupid, traitorous hormones. "I want the whole house decorated if I have to go to lunch. All of it, Callen. Not just the tree. I want lights outside. I want garland on the fireplace. I want a stocking for Cupcake. If you're going to try to buy my forgiveness, which isn't going to happen, I'm going to bankrupt you."

I walk away and drop the bananas off in the kitchen as Callen laughs.

"You can try," he laughs, and it sounds so good.

Too good.

I try to ignore him as I pretty much stomp my way upstairs to the guest room I've claimed as mine—because there was no way I was going to share a room with Callen—while a familiar mantra repeats in my mind.

I will not kill Callen Sinclair.

Only now, it should probably be *you cannot kill your baby's daddy.*

Most girls want roses and romance.
I want honesty and someone who will fight for me.
Is that too much to ask?

—*Caitlin's Secret Thoughts*

I glare as Callen looks at the medical instruments attached to the ultrasound set up and wait for the smart remark.

Three. Two. One.

"What the fuck is that thing? It looks like a dildo." He turns around to me with a stupid grin. Sexy but stupid.

"It's a transvaginal ultrasound wand." Callen's eyes double in size. "Stop," I warn him. "Kenzie had to tell me what it was last time before she used it. Get your mind out of the gutter."

If someone had told me six months ago, I'd be lying in an ugly paper gown—*yes I'm still stuck on this*—basically naked from the waist down on an exam table with Callen Sinclair next to me . . . well first, I'd have probably been confused, then I'd have wondered if we were getting kinky in a doctor's office. And that would still be easier to believe than our actual reality.

"Knock, knock," Kenzie announces from the other side of the door, and Callen immediately moves next to me with his arms crossed over his chest. He looks protective. Always protective. Damn him.

"Come in, Kenz," I tell her and lock eyes with him. "Breathe, Callen."

"Aren't I supposed to be telling you that, Cait?"

Kenzie smiles when she sees Callen before masking her surprise and going back into professional mode. "How are we feeling today?"

"Pretty good," I tell her, a little nervous. "The nausea is gone, but I'm still exhausted."

Kenzie's mask slips again, and she looks between Callen and me. "That's not abnormal, and you've had a lot going on, Caitlin. Stress can do crazy things to a body. I want you to listen to what yours is telling you. If you're tired, sleep. If you don't feel up to doing something, don't do it."

Callen drops his hand to my shoulder and squeezes once before he slides it down my back for support, and I hate how much I want to lean into his touch.

"Your blood pressure looks good, and your urine was fine. No issues with sugar. We'll schedule you for a gestational diabetes test at your next visit."

"Why? Is something wrong?" Callen asks as he moves closer.

"Not a thing. These tests are standard procedure. Nothing to worry about. We'll do plenty of testing over the next few months, and your job is to not worry unless I tell you to." Kenzie sounds perfectly clinical as she eases Callen's nerves.

It seems to work, and he slides his hand back up to that spot between my shoulder and neck and squeezes. It's unfair just how right his hands feel on me and just how much comfort he can still give.

It doesn't go unnoticed by Kenzie either. "Now... Let me just do a quick internal to make sure everything looks good. Pop your feet up here," she tells me, and I get to experience the lovely humiliation of having an internal exam in front of Callen, before she pulls her gloves off and smiles. "All good. Are you ready to see your baby?"

The energy in the room turns on a dime, and when I look up at him, I don't see the man I hate. I see the boy I loved. "You ready to see our baby?"

He opens his mouth, but no words come out, and he closes it and nods again. His eyes stay locked on mine, and when I lie back, he takes my hand in his . . . and I let him.

"Now this is going to be a little cool," Kenzie tells me as she squeezes jelly on my belly, then presses down with the wand, and I watch tears pool in Callen's eyes as he hears our baby's heartbeat for the first time.

"That's a strong heartbeat," Kenzie tells us, and Callen drops down into the chair next to the exam table and rests his elbows next to me so he can hold my hand in both of his. He presses his lips to my fingers.

"That's our baby's heartbeat, Caitie."

I manage to nod, which is good because there are no words for this moment.

Kenzie takes a few images, then she points at the screen. "Do you see that? They're sucking their thumb."

"Oh wow," I gasp. "Look at their face. Those lips."

"Those are your lips," Callen whispers, awed.

"Do you want to know the sex of your baby?" Kenzie asks, and Callen and I have a silent conversation between us. A shared history after a lifetime of being in each other's orbits, and it only takes one look for us to be on the same page.

"Yes," I tell her. "Please. I need to stop saying *it*."

She pauses the screen again and takes another shot. "Congratulations. You're going to have a daughter."

Callen presses his forehead to mine as tears stream down my face. "A girl, Caitie. We're having a girl."

I close my eyes and focus on the beauty of the moment instead of the pain. "We're having a girl."

"What about Persephone?" I ask as I steal one of Callen's fries later that afternoon. We've gotten a tree and basically bought out every decoration Target had left, which wasn't much, this close to Christmas. My Amazon cart is going to get a workout tonight. And as promised, now we're at The Busy Bee having lunch. Sometimes I forget how good their strawberry shakes are. I could see these being a pregnancy craving, for sure.

Can I send Callen on strawberry shake runs if we're not together but we're living together? I'm going to need to put a pin in this and get the general consensus of the girls later.

Callen drags his fry through a disgusting amount of ketchup and pops it in his mouth. "Persephone Sinclair is gonna be hell on a little kid learning how to spell their name."

"First." I hold up a finger and steal another fry. "Who said Sinclair? Beneventi is a great last name. And second, I had to learn Caitlin Beneventi. What's the difference?"

He pushes the rest of the fries my way, and I smile triumphantly. "Persephone is a longer name than Caitlin, and why wouldn't it be Sinclair?"

I add an extra shake of salt and pepper and feel no regrets as I make fast work of his fries. If I have to carry his baby and look at his stupidly handsome, annoying face every day, the least he can do is feed me.

"Why would it be Sinclair? We're not married. You don't have to do any of the work. I have to carry her. I have to get fat. And I have to have my body ripped open to give birth. Why should she get your last name?" I'm only half-serious, but that half matters. The other half is a traditionalist at heart and wants our daughter to have her father's name. He's going to be a great father, and she's going to love him. But I'm not ready to tell him any of that.

Callen tries to take his fries back, but I slap his hand. "No backsies, Sinclair."

He looks torn. "I guess I just always figured we'd be married when we had kids, and you'd all have my last name."

My hand stops midway to my mouth as I stare in absolute shock. "Excuse me?"

"I'm vetoing Persephone," he evades. "We can deal with the last name thing later, but I'm not naming our daughter Persephone. What the heck would her nickname be? Percy?"

"Why does she need a nickname?" I push, and he might as well smack my forehead with the look he gives me. "Okay, so our families are nickname people. Forget I said that. What about Serefina? Her nickname could be Sera."

"Sera Sinclair?" He looks less than impressed.

"Sera Beneventi," I argue, and we basically end up in a stare-off until I break first and laugh.

"I missed this, Cait."

It feels good.

Until it doesn't.

"Maybe you should have thought about that before you broke my heart, Callen." Some days, I wonder how we're going to manage co-parenting when I can barely manage being in the same room with him most of the time. Then other days, I want nothing more than to hear him say he's sorry one more time so I can tell him I love him and forgive him and to please never let go.

But how can I do that when I can't trust him with my heart?

My life? Yes. He's proven that.

But my heart . . .? How many times am I supposed to let one man break it?

Today has been an incredible day, but it's not that day. Not yet. Maybe not ever.

"I'm never going to stop apologizing for that. I know I hurt you, and I'm so fucking sorry." All teasing is gone from his voice. Pain is there in its place, clinging to every word. I want to say, *good, join the damn club*. But I can't. Because as mad as I am at him, I still hate seeing him hurting. "Please, Cait . . . put yourself in my shoes. If someone told you if you stayed with me, you'd be putting me at risk, can you honestly tell me you wouldn't have done the same damn thing?"

A million smart-ass answers are sitting on the tip of my tongue, but I can't force any of them out. Because I can't say I'd do anything all that different. But Callen doesn't deserve to know that because the one different thing I'd do is talk to him first.

"You should have talked to me. You could have saved us both so much pain." I throw my napkin on the table and signal the waitress for the bill. "We could have been happy, Callen. We lost our chance. We lost the life we deserved." I grab my purse and get up.

"Where are you going?" He asks, frustrated.

"To the bathroom. Pay the bill. I want to go home . . . Oh wait. I almost forgot. I don't have one of them anymore."

CALLEN

Are any of you available?

KILLIAN

I'm around.

LEO

Me too.

NIXON

Like right now? Give me an hour. We've got a day off and Kenzie should be home for lunch any minute.

LEO

So what? You're going to cook her lunch?

NIXON

No, asshat. I'm going to eat her for lunch.

CALLEN

Does anyone have a ladder?

"**W**here did you say Caitlin is?" Killian asks from the bottom of the ladder as he hands me the next string of white icicle lights Cait picked out to be strung along the edge of the roof.

"Her friend Addie lives around the corner in the old Winbury bed and breakfast. Jude drove her there. I'm surprised she even told me where she was going," I admit, frustrated. Who'd have thought hanging lights would be hard.

"I thought the old lady that owned that place died," Nixon asks.

"All I know is Cait's friend lives there now. She's barely talking to me. So it's not like I'm getting a full story." Fuck. I almost staple my finger to the shingles.

"Can somebody tell me why we're doing this again?" Leo hangs green garland strung with white lights along the porch railing. "Pretty sure this isn't getting you laid, Uncle."

He's not wrong.

There's no chance of that happening. But I'm not trying to get laid. I'm trying to earn back her trust so I can win back her heart.

"Because it's what she wanted, and it's Christmas. Or how about because I'm leaving her alone while I play a game on the other side of the damn country that day, and I'm pretty sure she's skipping her family's Christmas, in case I didn't already feel like a big enough asshole." I groan and look at the still half-empty roof. Who knew this shit took this long to do?

"Just saying, but I'm pretty sure you not being here is the best present you could give her."

Fucking Leo.

"Dude. Do you ever hear the shit you spew?" Nix gets the wreath hung on the door, then moves to help Leo with the garland. "Do you have ribbons or something she wants with this?"

"What the hell do you know about ribbons, Nixon?" Killian questions as he unravels the next strand for me.

"More than you three, since Kenzie had me do this shit the day after Thanksgiving. Apparently, ribbons are important. And according to Kenzie, they should be red or gold. And if they're red, there are only a few acceptable shades." He has the next string of garland up in half the time it was taking Leo. "My girl gave me a dissertation on the importance of it all as we got this shit set up."

"Was it worth it?" Killian eggs him on, but Nixon doesn't give a shit.

"Let's just say there are a lot of uses for ribbons," Nix answers, and Kill whistles.

"Okay. I hear ya." Leo laughs. "Dude, do you have ribbons?"

Fuck. That might have been the only thing Caitlin didn't buy today. "I don't think so."

"Kenzie got hers from that place right off Main Street. You think they're still open?" Nix straightens the wreath and looks at us all like we should know the answer to that.

Leo holds up his phone. "For another hour."

"Let's roll, men." Killian pulls out his keys.

Two hours, a shit ton of ribbon, lights, and green garland later, and the house looks like something out of one of those Hallmark Christmas movies my mom likes to watch. Minus the bows. We got the ribbons, and they're tied in something, but I wouldn't exactly call them bows. Apparently, four athletes who all have to tie skates, or cleats, or wrestling shoes, can't tie a bow to save our fucking lives. They're tied but they look like ass. Well-intentioned ass. But ass all the same.

And if I've learned anything since this woman moved in,

it's that intention doesn't matter to her. Action does. Guess we'll see how this goes.

Caitlin

"And then what?" Adelaide's sister, Coraline, asks from the other end of the softest couch I've ever sat on, a glass of wine in one hand and a chocolate chip cookie in the other— because baking fixes everything.

"And then nothing. I left and came here. I've been here since."

"And then she baked. Where do you think the cookies came from?" Addie answers as she dumps leftover chocolate chips in her warm bowl of popcorn, and Coraline almost spits out her wine.

"Not from you. That's for sure. These are actually good." She studies the cookie like it holds the answers to the world's greatest mysteries in its ingredients, then pops the rest in her mouth. "Your mom owns the bakery in town, right?"

I nod and dip my cookie in my milk—because no wine for me.

Another thing that's Callen's fault.

He's just racking them up now.

Addie tosses popcorn in her mouth, then licks the melted chocolate from her fingertips. "Her family owns everything in town. You'll get used to it."

"Do you guys own The Busy Bee? I put in an application there today. They legit have the best strawberry shake I've ever had."

"Right? They really do. And no, well not exactly. My uncle's wife's grandfather owns it, but someone else runs it for him now." I eye Addie's popcorn and decide I'm craving salt more than sweet right now. Which leads me back to my earlier pin from lunch at The Busy Bee. "I need your opinions, ladies. Am I allowed to send Callen out on cravings runs?"

"Why wouldn't you be?" Coraline asks as she sips her wine, confused, and Addie throws popcorn at her head.

"Try to keep up and try to slow down on the wine. You're not twenty-one yet." She swings her own glass between her and me and delves into my dysfunction, trying to break it down for Coraline, who's only been in town a few days. "She loves him. He loves her. It's been years in the making. Totally epic love kind of shit. He fucked up. Like big-time fucked up. Kinda the biggest. Now she's pregnant with his baby, and he's kissing her ass because it turns out, it's really all her big, scary, DILF-y dad's fault." Adelaide giggles. "Oh, and don't forget her hot-as-fuck brother is his best friend, and they got in a fight over her." She looks at me and smiles. "That about sum it up?"

I rub my temples, unsure whether to be bothered or impressed by all of that.

"Seriously, Caitlin. If I wrote this in a book, my readers would tell me it wasn't believable," she muses, and Coraline laughs . . . hard.

"Your readers wouldn't care as long as the sex was good." She taps her glass to her sister's, and I whimper internally. I miss wine. "Was the sex good?"

My entire body heats at the thought. "The sex was incredible. Just short-lived."

"Oh, I'm sorry. Two pump chumps ruin it for everyone." Coraline looks completely heartbroken for me, and Addie spits her wine out all over the coffee table.

"Oh my God . . ." She laughs uncontrollably while she

wipes up her mess with a napkin. "She said it was incredible. Would it be incredible if he had a stamina issue?"

I roll my eyes. This might be the first time I've ever seen Adelaide buzzed, and she's a funny drunk. "He didn't have a stamina issue. There were no chumps. He had a timing issue. *Literally.* We were only together a few days when everything fell apart."

Good lord, what I wouldn't give to have his hands on my body again.

"So use him," Coraline offers like it's the most completely logical conclusion.

"Shit. Did I say that out loud?" I ask, mortified. My sex-starved brain needs to shut up. "Nobody tells you how horny you are when you're pregnant."

"They kinda do." Addie snorts. "Haven't you ever watched TV or read a romance novel? Everybody talks about how horny you get while you're pregnant."

"Yeah," Coraline agrees. "And how good the sex is."

I guess it can get worse.

"How would you know?" Addie glares at her sister.

"Chill out, lightweight. I've never been pregnant. I just read your books and watch movies. Way too much Netflix."

Addie seems satisfied with that answer and points at me. "You live with him. You can't get more pregnant. Just have sex with him."

It's his fault I'm pregnant in the first place.

Which does technically make it his fault I can't stop thinking about sex . . . and orgasms. And kissing. My God, I miss his lips.

"Do you have a picture? I need to see this man." Coraline stares at me. Her big, doe eyes framed by mile-long lashes blink up at me, demanding to see.

I pull up a selfie I took of us at West End on my birthday

and hand it to Coraline, and she immediately jumps up from the couch. "Shut up."

"Oh please, dear God, I promise I will never say anything bad about anyone ever again if you do not tell me that you slept with Callen Sinclair," I beg.

I don't think I could handle it if the first real friend I have outside of Bellamy has a sister who slept with Callen. *My Callen*. Well, not exactly mine. But completely mine.

This is just cruel.

"Trust me. If I had slept with that man, I don't think I'd ever let him out of bed. He looks like he knows exactly what he's doing. Please tell me he can find a clit," Coraline begs, and I say a silent prayer of thanks to whoever the hell was listening to me.

"Oh . . . he can find a G-spot and a clit." I open my mouth to shut Addie up, but she keeps going, "with his mouth and his tongue."

"Adelaide—"

"Sorry." She shrugs and puts down her glass. Mental note —be careful what I tell Adelaide. She's got loose lips when she's drunk. "I think I may have had too much wine."

"Ya think?" I ask while Coraline laughs.

"I say use him. You live with a man who looks like a sexy beast of a race car." When Addie and I both get confused, Coraline rolls her eyes. "High-performance with sleek lines and lots of muscle. Follow along here, ladies. And he already knocked you up. Hop on and take him for a ride."

Addie raises her hand. "I second that vote. Then tell us all about it. I could use some inspiration for my new book hero. Porn is getting old, and Callen *is* hot."

My mouth hangs open for a hot minute. "Porn?"

Addie shrugs and apparently gives up on the glass when she goes straight for the bottle of wine. I guess the holidays could suck worse. I could be the James sisters, who've lost both parents and their grandmother in the past two years. I think my friend may be trying to dull the pain today.

Could I actually do that?

Separate my emotions from sex and basically use Callen to scratch an itch?

Coraline hands me back my phone, and I stare at Callen on the screen.

Damn it. They're both right. He is hot. He's also talented with his mouth, his hands, and his beautifully thick cock. Even just thinking about it makes me needy.

Needier.

Maybe I can do this.

Or maybe this is the worst idea I've ever had.

Guess there's only one way to find out.

I slide into the front seat of my cousin's black Escalade and ignore the glare he throws at me. "Seriously, Jude. Can you protect me more from the back seat than you can from the front?"

Jude is two months younger than me, but he's trained under Killian's father, Cade, his entire life. He's also been part of my father's world, I suspect, since we were in high school. But I can't be sure, and he'd never tell.

He's gorgeous and confident and supremely quiet, unlike the rest of the men in my life lately. To the rest of the world, those men are quiet. But to me . . . to me, they're constantly the loudest voices in my head.

He's been part of my security team since I went to college, and Dad moved him into the main position once I graduated.

"Don't you ever wish you were doing something other than watching me?"

"You're the job, principessa."

I wait for more, but it doesn't come.

Alrighty then.

"Can I ask you something?" He side-eyes me as we turn off Adelaide's street. "Am I safe?"

I hadn't planned on asking that, it just sort of slips out without thought.

Damn.

"I mean—"

"Your father has increased your security since the accident. You may not notice it, but that just means we're doing our jobs. Everyone is aware of how much you hate having a team. Your mother does too. But whether you want to be or not, you were born high-profile, Caitlin. You're a Kingston and a Beneventi. You're a billionaire heiress with mob connections, even if no one mentions that second part. Ignoring it doesn't make it less true. You shouldn't have snuck into the doctor's office that day. All you had to do was tell me where you were going. I don't crowd you. I never have. I know you fucking hate this, but it's my fucking job to make sure you're safe, and I can't do that if you don't help me."

Holy shit.

That might be the most consecutive words my cousin has ever said to me.

And they make me feel like shit.

"I'm sorry, Jude. I didn't think about it that way," I admit quietly as a light dusting of fluffy snow begins to fall.

"Well, start thinking about it that way. You've got a lot of people who love you and care about your safety. Stop being a brat and start looking at it from their perspective. Keeping you safe is the top priority, principessa. Everything else comes second. It has to."

He turns onto Callen's street, and his words ring out like a war cry, loud and booming in my head. Damn him. "Are you talking about my father, my brothers, or Callen?"

Jude cocks an eyebrow as Callen's house comes into view. *Oh wow.*

"I'm talking about all of them." He turns down the driveway and parks the car. "Especially the one who did all this, I'm guessing for you, in the few hours you've been gone."

Beautiful white lights are strung from the lines of the roof and wrapped around evergreen garland draping from the porch banisters. The wreaths are hung on the door, and as Jude opens the car door for me, I see the dark-red bows tied on each post. *Callen . . ..*

Jude walks me to the door, but presses his hand flat against it, blocking me from opening it. "Forgiveness is a choice, Cait."

I stare at him, shocked this is coming from Jude but somehow not surprised either.

"I'm working on it. But it's not that easy," I whisper in the cold night.

"Try harder. Forgive. Forget. Do something that means you're moving on. Because being miserable is a shitty way to go through life. Now go inside, lock the damn door, and go to bed. I'm going home. Text me in the morning if your plans change for tomorrow, okay?"

He drops his hand and walks away without waiting for a response.

When I step inside, I'm met with the smell of the fresh Christmas tree we picked out earlier. Callen set it up in the center of the family room. The boxes of unopened ornaments sit on the coffee table, and Cupcake's stocking is hanging on the mantle while she sleeps in her new red, green, and pink holiday doggy bed in the corner of the room.

"Do you like it?"

I look over to where Callen stands at the bottom of the steps in black sleep pants, shirtless. His toned skin pulled tight over corded muscle covered in beautiful ink. It's too much.

"You're not fighting fair, Sinclair," I murmur, dazed. It's too much.

The beautiful decorations and the beautiful man.

He must see the waver in my eyes because I swear he stalks across the room like a lion stalking his prey, sensing the weakness. "I'm fighting to win, kitten. Nobody said I had to fight fair."

I give up the first inch of the battle when I lean into him . . . unable to stop myself. "The house looks great." I lick my lips and try to slow my breathing. "Thank you."

"You like it?" he asks as he slowly brings his hands up to cup my face, like he's waiting for me to lash out. And I want to. I really do. But I just can't. Not tonight. Not right now.

I close my eyes and relax into his touch as a traitorous tear slips past my lid.

He thumbs it away. "Forgive me, Caitlin. Forgive me because I love you, and I did it for you."

"Tell me you'd do it differently," I challenge him, knowing his answer. "Actually . . . don't answer that."

He tips my chin up and locks his green eyes on mine.

"I don't forgive you, Callen. But I want you to make me forget. Make me forget tonight, and tomorrow I'll go back to hating you." I drag my hands up the smooth skin of his back and sink my nails into his shoulders as he lifts me from the floor and wraps my legs around his waist.

His mouth crashes over mine, and agony and ecstasy war with each other at the first touch of his tongue to mine.

"You don't hate me, Caitlin. You can't. You're mine, and I'm going to show you what you already know but refuse to admit."

"Jesus Christ. Shut up and make me come."

"Fuck, Caitie," I groan as she presses her warm lips to my skin. *Jesus.* "Are you sure?"

She clings to me, desperate, like she's a waning fire, waiting either for that last breath of oxygen to give her life or to put her out. And I know without a doubt, she's going to burn us both down in the process, but I can't stop it. I couldn't even if I wanted to.

"Have I ever been unsure, Callen?"

Her lips drag along my shoulder, and her heels dig into my ass. "For years, I wanted you, and I was sure."

Her teeth bite into my skin as she tries to take what she needs before I'm willing to give it. "Now, I want you, but just for tonight. I need your body. I want your cock, Callen. I want to feel you inside me. I want you in my mouth. In my hands. In my pussy."

"Caitie," I groan, unable to hide the need heavy in my voice. "Be sure, because I can't say no to you."

"You did it before," she snaps, then covers my mouth with hers as her palms slide between us and over my chest. "Don't say no, Callen. Not tonight. Please, give me what I need, even if it's not what I want. *Please.*"

I crush my mouth against hers, fueling the fire until it flames higher and higher.

Tik. Tik. Boom.

"You're going to want to kill me for this tomorrow." I bite at her lip.

"But what a worthy death it'll be." Her nails score my skin as our tongues tangle, fighting for control.

I want her more than I've ever wanted anything or anyone.

I want to own her. Her wants. Her needs. Her love and her fucking hate.

I want it all, and I want it to stop and start with me.

I want her to feel me between her creamy thighs for weeks.

Electricity soars between us, frenzied and uncontrolled.

Feeding the fire.

Demanding more.

"You've fucked hundreds of women, Callen. Now shut up and fuck me."

I spin us around and slam her against the wall, shaking one of the stupid wreaths we hung inside earlier before it falls to the floor.

"I've only ever loved one woman, Caitie, and that's you."

I press a hand against the wall and wrap the other around her head, deepening our kiss. Controlling her. Running my tongue over her lips, then swallowing her breath and giving her mine.

Needing her. Wanting fucking everything. To fix us. To fuck her. To undo the pain I've caused. Desperate to put it all behind us. To fuck it away. Dying for a taste of my woman.

To remind her she's mine.

"Callen," she cries out as I slide a hand down her body and

squeeze her ass. "Enough playing." She pulls her mouth away and grinds down on my cock. She grabs my face and bites my lip before she drags her tongue down my throat and shoves me back until I put her down.

"I want to taste your cock, Callen," she demands as she slides down to her knees. Her long, dark lashes kiss her cheeks before she looks up at me, and a devilish smile graces those beautiful full, pouty, pink lips.

Her tongue darts out to wet them before she digs her nails into my hips and drags my pants and boxers down.

My cock bounces up, and Caitlin's blue eyes darken with desire before she leans forward and traces the top of my dick with the tip of her tongue.

"Your cock wants to fuck me, Callen." She tries to wrap her hand around me, and her eyes widen when she can't.

"Fucking right, baby. You sure you're ready for me?" I challenge as I gather her soft, dark hair in my hand and wrap it around my fist, then tug as I hang onto my control by a fraying thread. "You got me where you want me now. You gonna suck my cock, kitten, or do you talk a big game?" I ask, loving to see her claws come out.

She stiffens before those lashes flutter again, and her blue eyes sparkle with challenge.

"Challenge accepted, asshole." Caitlin squeezes me before she drags her tongue along my balls and up the length of my shaft.

She looks up at me and holds my eyes as her tongue swirls over the precum pooling at the tip.

Fuck me . . .

"You look so goddamn pretty on your knees for me, Caitie."

A chord tugs at the base of my spine when she wraps those pouty, pink lips around my cock and takes me down her throat.

Her blue eyes water as she gags, and goddamn, she's a fucking vision.

"Fuck . . ." I growl when she swallows, and my cock hits the back of her throat. "Cait . . ."

I look down at her just as she slides her hand inside her jeans.

"You think you're gonna get yourself off while you suck me off, kitten?" I cup her face in my hands and steel my spine with an iron fucking grip on control.

She doesn't answer me, just swallows again and unzips her jeans, and I see red.

I pull back, and Caitlin's lips slide off my cock with a pop.

"The fuck you are. Your orgasms are mine."

Caitlin

*B*efore I can respond, Callen runs a thumb over my swollen lips. "You come when I say you can come."

My eyes double in size as I sit on my knees, disgusted with myself because holy fucking hell, I'm so turned-on, my body is humming.

"Fuck you, Callen," I curse him, as my pussy pulses in time with my heartbeat, fucking desperate for his dick.

I want to tell him he doesn't own me.

He had his chance.

But that's a lie.

He'll always own my heart.

Even if he'll never have it again.

"Oh, you're gonna fuck me, baby. You're gonna ride my

cock until you're screaming so loud, every house on this lake hears you. But you're gonna ride my face first, kitten."

Why do I have to love a fucking asshole?

Anticipation coats every single inch of my skin as Callen reaches down and lifts me to my feet.

He pulls my sweater over my head and stares in awe at my breasts.

My body may not have changed much yet, but my boobs have definitely gotten bigger.

Callen drags a rough thumb over one nipple and watches as it pushes back against the lace. He covers it with his mouth, and I moan.

Fuck. I think I could come from this.

His hot tongue against the soft lace creates the sweetest sting against my sensitive skin.

It's too much.

It's not enough.

"Callen," I whimper, trembling and ready to cry with need as he rips my bra from my body and sucks in a hot breath.

"My God, Caitlin. You are—"

"Shut up and fuck me, Callen," I demand, and the bastard smiles.

His hand slides down my stomach and cups my sex over my jeans.

He doesn't say anything.

He doesn't need to.

That cocky fucking smirk says it all.

Callen drags my jeans and my panties slowly down each leg, then buries his face in my pussy and inhales.

I should probably be mortified, but one word keeps booming like a drum corps over and over in my head . . . And it's not *no.*

Fuck.

Callen rises and steps back, inches from me, but not touching.

Leaving me absolutely aching for him.

For his body. His cock. His tongue.

For so much more than I absolutely refuse to put into words.

And the confident fucker knows it.

"Tell me you're mine, Caitlin. Tell me who's pussy this is. Tell me," he demands, and I want to cry because he's not wrong, but I absolutely refuse to let him be right either.

"Please, Callen. You owe me this. I can't give you those words, but I'm standing in front of you, naked and pregnant, with a broken fucking heart. Give me this tonight."

"You're going to love me again, Caitlin," he tells me as he lifts me in his arms.

There's a fire in his green eyes that I've loved seeing, but tonight, it makes me turn away.

He carries me to the dining room table and lays me out like he's going to feast for days.

My body vibrates with anticipation, and he brushes his lips over mine, bruising them hard.

He knows what I need.

Callen pushes my body down until my back is against the cool table, the hard wood unforgiving, and drags his finger along my collar bone and over my breasts before his mouth makes the same trail.

He bends one of my knees and plants my foot flat on the table before he swirls his tongue in my belly button. "Gonna fuck you soon, Cait. Tell me I can."

His finger plays with the lips of my sex. Up and down but never in, and I whimper.

"Tell me, Cait. Tell me I won't hurt the baby," he growls, and my God, I want to give in to everything he wants.

Why . . . why does he have to be so fucking perfect every time but when it mattered most?

My body hums with needy anticipation.

"You won't hurt the baby, Callen. Now I'm begging you, please fuck me."

In a move so fucking hot I lean up on my elbows to watch him, Callen drops to his knees and throws one of my legs over his shoulder, pressing the other one out further and opening me completely to him. And my God, he looks vicious and gorgeous—and maybe as damaged and broken as I am.

My body comes to life as his firm lips press against each hip bone, then skims down my sex. Teasing me like we've got all day.

Like I'm not dying more and more with each touch.

Until finally, he buries his face against my hot sex, and I see stars.

My back arches, and my hips raise from the table until Callen grips my hips and holds them in place.

"Your orgasms are mine, Caitlin."

"Callen," I plead and try to force myself free, dying to move. To force him where I want him, and the fucker chuckles and slaps my pussy in a move that tops the last one for the hottest moment of my life.

Of course, this asshole is a sex god too.

"More," I sob, and he drags his tongue up my pussy before he pulls back and slaps me again . . . and again . . . And holy-fucking-shit . . .

My clit throbs.

My body zings.

My brain practically blacks out as I scream over and over.

Callen buries his tongue inside me before dragging it back up to my clit and scrapes his teeth over the hypersensitive bundle of nerves.

I squeeze my breasts between my hands, dying for relief, and this golden fucking god between my legs groans against me.

"That's a good girl, kitten. Tell me, are you ready to come?"

"Callen . . ." I whimper.

"Words, Caitlin. I want your fucking words."

"Please, God. Make me come," I scream, and he stuffs three fingers inside me and works me over and over, bringing me to the edge of my orgasm before backing off.

Again and *again*.

Until my vision darkens and my hearing tightens.

Until I feel tears burning behind my eyes.

When he finally curls his fingers and bites my clit, growling into my pussy, I come, shaking and moaning and fucking his face.

My eyes focus on one thing.

And it's the sexiest sight I've ever seen.

Callen Sinclair between my legs.

My juices coat his lips and face as he kisses his way up my body and pushes his tongue in my mouth, only to pull away again.

"No, Callen . . . What—"

"I need to get a condom, Caitie," he tells me between heavy breaths.

"You don't," I beg. "I'm already pregnant, and I'm clean," I plead, desperate to feel him now. All of him.

"I've never gone bare, Caitlin. Are you sure?"

"I might not be able to trust you with my heart. But I know I can trust you with my body. Please just fuck me."

The fight is right there under the surface of his eyes, but with the first snap of Callen's hips against mine, we both hiss at the sheer perfection, and I cling to him as he fucks us both into oblivion.

BUMP WATCH

Bump watch alert.

Caitlin Beneventi was spotted leaving her doctor's office with Kroydon Hills' favorite baller, Callen Sinclair, by her side. Can the rumors be true? Did C plus C make three? Are Caitlin and Callen the newest *IT* couple to watch? And if so, how have they managed to keep it quiet for so long? We here at the *Kronicles* gave you the original scoop on what's sure to be a genetically blessed baby three months ago. It's not like Sinclair to manage a low-profile, but somehow, he's managed to stay out of the spotlight . . . Until today that is. *New year, new leaf?* We're not sure, but there's been no comment from either camp. When asked, our sources confirmed these two beautiful people have been living together and are expecting a late-spring delivery. Let the bump watch commence.

#KroydonKronicles #BumpWatch #BallersBaby

"I can't tell you how much I appreciate you fitting me in today. This outfit is fierce. Really, it's perfect, Caitlin." Lilah holds the black garment bag up as I walk to Callen's front door.

"I'm happy to do it. The clothes are already starting to not fit me, so at least one of us can get some use out of them." I sigh, already longing to fit in my jeans again. I've only gained five pounds, but it's definitely in my hips and belly. A tiny little bump, but there's no way I'm buttoning them all the same.

"Come on, you don't look like you've gained any weight at all."

I lift my oversized cashmere sweater and turn sideways to show off the tiny little bump hiding under my black leggings.

Lilah's face melts in the sweetest way. I guess she's a baby person. The kind who goes all gooey every time they see an adorable baby. I wouldn't exactly call myself a baby person. I fully expect to melt for my baby, and I love my friends and family's babies. But I'm not going to stop someone on a plane to tell them their kid is cute. Lilah seems like she'd be a plane stalker.

"I still can't believe you and Callen are having a baby. It's so exciting."

You and me both, sister.

You and me both.

"You're coming to the game tonight, right?" When I don't answer, she pops her hand on her slim hips. *Ugh. I used to have slim hips too.* "You're coming. You have to. Today was Grandpa's last treatment, and it's the first game he's going to since he announced his retirement. We're all going to be there supporting him. Plus, it's the playoffs," she pleads. "If they win tonight, we're going back to the Super Bowl. Don't you want to tell little baby Beneventi-Sinclair they were there to watch their daddy cinch the Super Bowl bid?"

I hate that I can't argue with anything she's saying, so instead, I go with the easy mark. "You mean Sinclair-Beneventi?"

"Come on, Cait. At least come watch me sing in this outfit. I mean, you could wear a matching Sinclair jersey if you really wanted to," she teases . . . at least, I think she's teasing.

"Umm . . . No. I won't be doing that. One of us wearing Callen's jersey is enough. And it's only acceptable because he's your cousin, and it's your grandfather's former number too." I've worn Callen's jersey to the Kings' games for years. A few of my cousins who are close with him and I have all worn his while the twins wore their dad's. But it feels like me wearing it tonight would be different. It would mean something different.

"Think about it," she adds, and I open the door, bracing for the cold.

"I'll think about it," I placate her with no intention of doing it. "I'll see about the game. If I'm not there, I'll be watching it on TV, cheering you on." I hug Lilah and watch her walk to her car. But it's not her car that has my attention. It's my brother's car pulling up next to hers that's making me hesitate.

What the fuck?

I haven't spoken to Maddox in months.

He tried at Christmas, but I never called him back.

And I don't want to speak to him now.

I consider closing the door and locking it, but if he really wants in, the asshole will just pick the lock. Damn it.

I wait until he's halfway to the door, then step outside in the cold. "Stop."

"Get back inside, Cait. It's fucking freezing out, and you don't even have a coat on." High-handed asshole.

He's not wrong. It's bitterly cold outside. But I will make Elsa look like a summer Sunday at the beach before I admit I'm cold. "What do you want, Maddox?"

"I want you to go inside and hear me out." He blows on his hands, and I watch the cold air float off him before he shoves them into his peacoat. "Don't be stubborn, Cait."

"Don't be a dick, Maddox." I will outlast him if it's the last damn thing I do. He hurt me. He hurt Callen. He could have been upset and handled it like an adult instead of throwing a temper tantrum. Yeah . . . I'm holding on to this grudge. "What do you want?"

"Fine. You want to do this out here?" He walks up the steps until we're standing toe-to-toe on the porch. "We'll do it out here. What do I need to do to fix this shit?"

"Not that," I snap and go inside, letting the door slam shut behind me. But the asshole follows me in anyway. "I didn't say you could come in."

"Didn't say I couldn't either . . . What do you want to hear me say, Cait? That I'm sorry? I'm fucking sorry. Is that better?"

"No." I spin on him, ready to scream, but that's when I see it.

And damn him for letting me see it. He's hurting too. Fucking asshole men.

I don't yell. I take a few calming breaths and walk closer to the fireplace I've been loving this winter and control my voice. "It's not better because you don't mean it. For sorry to mean anything, you have to mean it. And you don't think you did anything wrong."

"No. I don't. I think I was protecting my sister—"

"Fuck you, Maddox. I don't need protecting. Everyone assumes I'm some weak damsel in distress, but I was raised in the same house as you by the same parents. If you'd stop treating me like glass, you might realize I'm not as breakable as you think." I close my eyes and try very, *very*, very fucking hard to take a calming breath. "What did you think you were protecting me from? Callen?"

Maddox's shoulders tighten, and his jaw clenches.

Oh yeah, that's it.

Callen.

"You're my kid sister, Cait. The first memory I have of you is Dad telling me it was my job as your big brother to take care of you." Maddox impressively manages not to raise his voice either. Look at us, acting like adults. *Still an asshole.* He pounds his fist against his chest. "My job."

I hate this.

I hate everything about this.

Everything.

"I was never not safe, Maddox. The only person in the world I ever thought I could be safe with outside of our family was Callen." I rub my side, and Maddox's eyes catch the move.

"Was?"

My brother never misses a thing.

Damn him.

"It still is, smart-ass," and I hate him a little for making me admit that. "It's more complicated now, but I still know I'm safe with him."

My heart might not be safe, but my life is.

"I'm sorry if I hurt you, Cait." And this time when he says it, I believe him.

But it's still too little, too late.

"He was your best friend, Maddox," I argue because he might be sorry for how he treated me, but it's not enough. "He's Callen, and he was going through hell. And you hit him."

"Caitie—"

"No." I shake my head. "Don't you dare *Caitie* me. He deserved better than that, Maddox. Shame on you for not thinking more of Callen. Shame on you for not trusting him. For thinking he'd do something like fuck your sister like she was trash."

"Caitlin," he bites out, angry again.

"No, Maddox. You came here to make it better. Well, I'm telling you what you need to do to make it better," I yell, no longer giving a shit that my voice is raised. "I need you to hear me, big brother. To really listen to what I'm telling you because, honest to God, it matters."

"Fine. What are you telling me?" He looks annoyed, but he knows he's lost the high ground here. I'm pregnant and stubborn, and I'm winning this battle. "Spell it out for me."

"I'm telling you that if you want to fix anything with me . . . if you want to be involved in your niece's life, you're going to make things right with Callen. Because until you do that, there is no relationship between you and me to save." *Shit.* That felt good. Empowering.

"You've got to be kidding me . . ." He shoves his hand through his hair, and I manage not to laugh in his face because this asshole is so mad at Callen, but I swear to God, they're two sides of the same coin.

"Nope. Fix it. Apologize for being an insensitive prick who didn't trust his best friend. Because that man respected you and me. If he'd had his way, he would have called you the very first day we got together. It's only because I begged him to wait until you came home that he even considered waiting." I hate that I'm defending Callen almost as much as I hate the idea of Maddox thinking he has a right to be mad at him. "Callen didn't do anything wrong. If you fix it with him, then it'll be fixed with me."

The most annoying smile I've ever laid eyes on slides in place on Maddox's face. "Then how come I hear you're still barely talking to him?"

"Check your sources. We're talking." I don't share that we're *barely* talking. He doesn't need to know that.

"I don't care what he says or what you say. It was wrong, Cait. We're going to have to agree to disagree. Could I have handled it better? *Maybe*. But do you even remember the rest of the hell of that day? You almost died. We could have lost you and the baby, and we had only just found out about her. You threw us all for a fucking loop."

Maddox's dark eyes beg me to listen to him, and it pisses me off to think I actually understand what he's saying. I don't want any piece of him to be even in the vicinity of being right.

It's easier to be indignant when you think you have the higher ground.

If he has a point, I lose that ground.

"I can't believe I'm going to say this, but seriously, Caitlin, put yourself in his shoes. If Dad tells you being with someone is dangerous for that person . . . If *Dad* said you being with someone was going to put their life at risk, wouldn't you do anything to keep them safe?"

"I don't know. If it meant breaking someone's heart—"

"Don't even try to finish that sentence, Cait. You'd do the same thing he did. He didn't have a choice. We've grown up with Dad, and neither of us has ever stood up to him until that day. We've never had to because he's always been the one in control." He doesn't look remotely happy about it, but my brother stands here, defending Callen's motives even though they haven't spoken in months.

"There's more to it than that," I try to tell him.

"There's not. If that's why you're putting him through hell —*Mom's words, not mine*— then there really isn't. Maybe try taking a spoonful of your own medicine, little sister." He raises his brow and waits for my answer.

One he's not getting. He doesn't deserve it. Hasn't earned it.

"There's more to it than that," I try to tell him.

And I hate that he's not wrong.

I've lived in Sam Beneventi's world for twenty-four years.

I know not to ask questions and not to expect answers.

I know how intimidating my father can be, just by opening his mouth.

But I still hate what Callen did, no matter how much I wish I didn't.

The weird flutter comes back again, and I push my hand against my stomach.

"Are you okay?" Maddox moves toward me, and I take a step back, not wanting his hands on me. Not now. Not when I'm all up in my stupid, hormonal feelings.

"I'm fine." I shoo him away. "I'm just tired, and I want to take a nap before the game tonight."

"You're going?" he asks as his eyes stay zeroed in on my hand.

"Well, I guess so."

But I'm still not wearing his jersey.

The Sinclairs have never watched a Kings game from our family's suite. Coach has always been on the sidelines, and Katherine is typically with the rest of their family in their own suite. But tonight, they're both in our family's suite, waiting for the national anthem and kickoff. It's a strategic media move to show that Coach has the Kingston family's full support. He already knew he did. He's been like family for as long as I can remember. But now the media will know it too.

I guess I shouldn't be surprised when he stands next to me at one of the high-top tables and wraps his arm around me. "Hey, kiddo, how are you feeling?"

I'm not a hugger, but something about seeing him here, knowing what the past six months have been like for him, has me stepping into his hug.

"I'm okay, Coach. How are you? I heard today was your last treatment." I pull back and am immediately struck by the shadows under his eyes. "How are *you* feeling?"

"Treatment day is never the bad day. It's the day after that isn't the best. But I'm done. Now it's wait and see. I get another scan in a few weeks. But enough about that. You want to tell me how my grandbaby is doing?" His eyes soften and warm at the mention of the baby. "Have you guys settled on a name yet?"

"No." I smile. "Not even close. Callen keeps shooting down every one I like."

Coach grins at the mention of Callen. "He's always been stubborn. Gets it from his mother."

"I'm sure he does," I laugh. "Has Callen shown you the ultrasound yet? We had an appointment yesterday, and they did one of those 4-D ones." I open my purse and pull out the copy I kept in there. "She's got his big head."

I hand him the image and hold back my own tears as I watch his pool in his blue eyes. "Oh wow, Caitie. She might have his big head, but she's beautiful. I'll bet she looks just like you."

He runs a finger over the scan. "I'm not going to pretend I know what's going on between the two of you, and I hope I'm not overstepping when I say this, but I hope you guys can work this out. Not for the sake of the baby. You're two mature adults. If it's not meant to be, this beautiful baby girl will be better off with two happy parents who aren't together than she ever will be with two unhappy parents who stayed together for her sake. But if you guys care about each other as much as I think you do . . . as much as you need to get through the ups and downs of life, I hope you both put in the work to fix it. There's nothing greater in this world than having a partner who's willing to stand by your side and fight your fight when you're too tired to do it yourself. I didn't have that with my first wife. I have it with Katherine. It makes all the difference, Caitie."

My words get caught in my throat.

Strangled by the pain.

"What if I'm not sure whether we have that, Coach? I don't know if he'll stay and fight. He left last time," I finally admit, hoping no one is close enough to hear.

"Sweetheart, did you ever consider that walking away when you love someone is the hardest thing he could have ever done? If he was strong enough to not be selfish and stay, maybe he's the guy who will fight your fights with you."

He kisses my forehead the same way his son does, and I somehow manage to keep it together until we get a warning that the cameras are going to zoom in on Coach.

I step back, and Katherine walks into his arms, but he holds onto the sonogram as he waves.

And he looks at me and winks.

That's when my first tear falls.

The snow starts to fall as I look up at the jumbotron where my parents stand in the Kingston's suite, smiling out at the field, and fuck if I'm not pretty damn sure my dad is holding our sonogram picture in his hand. And there, behind him, is my girl, wearing *my* Kings hoodie.

Not that anyone else would know. But I know, and that's enough for me.

Mine.

My whole fucking world right there.

Her and the baby.

My soul screams it in a cadence for my heart.

I'm pulled out of my thoughts when Lilah walks out onto the fifty-yard line and belts out the opening of the national anthem. I'll never get tired of hearing her sing it at our games, something she's done since we were kids.

For most men, this game is a sport.

For some it's a way of life.

For me . . . it's a family legacy.

Something we share on so many levels in so many ways.

And today, it's my turn to step it up.

As I walk out with my co-captains for the coin toss, and the snow dusts the turf, I know without a shadow of a doubt, it's going to be a nasty game.

A physical game.

The best kind of game.

And we're going to win.

It's 20–14, and the Wolves are winning with less than a minute to go in the fourth quarter.

It's been a battle. A war of attrition. The only way to win this kind of monster game is to be flawless. Every play counts. Every move counts. And every penalty glaringly counts.

We need a touchdown and the extra point to put this bitch to bed.

I stand to the right of my quarterback in what could be our last huddle of the season—*the fucking hardest season of my life*—and look around at these ten other men.

Fuck. I'm not ready for this season to end this way.

"All right, boys," Mason, our QB, tries to get us pumped. "It's been a long fucking game. I'm tired, sore, and freezing my balls off. Let's get our shit together and put these motherfuckers away, so we can go home, get warm, and get laid."

Some days, it's harder than others to get the guys worked up for the last few plays.

Today isn't one of those days.

You can see it in their eyes.

We need this win.

Mason turns to me and smacks my helmet. "Sinclair—

you're going to be the workhorse we ride to the finish. So fucking buck up and get ready. The ball's coming to you."

He looks around the huddle with a thunderous clap. "Ready . . . Break."

And it's on.

I move into slot position, second in from the end of the line, ready to run through this shit-talking fucker across from me.

Let him talk shit. This ball is mine, and he's never gonna touch me.

Mason and I are in sync, like two kids playing catch in the backyard, dreaming of a future in the NFL. A future most men never have the opportunity to enjoy. One I fucking love. And maybe this game just reminded me why.

Out of the corner of my eye, I see our center snap the ball, and I take off out of the blocks like an Olympic sprinter straight down the field.

I'm twenty yards down before I look over my shoulder and see the beautiful fucking spiral arcing into my hands.

The defensive back pulling my jersey tries to intercept.

He's got no chance.

I'm taller. I'm faster. I'm stronger. And I'm fucking better.

In a move so beautiful, it's gonna be on everyone's recap tomorrow, I catch the ball and beat his ass another thirty yards down the field, dragging him across the goal line as the clock runs out, and we tie up the game.

Mason points at me from where he's been tackled to the turf, and I point back.

We fucking did it.

We've got one play left, and the guys and I are on the sidelines looking through what's turned into a whiteout of snow as our field goal kicker takes his stance for the extra point.

We all hold our breath until the ball goes through the uprights.

"The rookie from Tennessee sets up for the extra point." The announcers call out, and we all hold our breath as the kid kicks. "The ball is up . . . and the point is good. The Kings win the game. The Kings win the game. The Philadelphia Kings are the NFC East Conference Champions, and they're going back to the Super Bowl. In a season muddled with injury and leadership changes, our Philadelphia Kings have managed to pull it together once again and show us why they're the team to beat every time we doubt them."

This game is the greatest goddamned game in the world.

And I'm a fucking king.

Thank fuck, Declan doesn't make me do the press conference. We're all well aware of what the questions would be if they put me in there and how salty the press would get with me when I refuse to discuss my father or my relationship status with Caitlin.

Not an option. No matter how much people want to know.

Fuck them.

Instead, I shower, change, and text Caitlin.

CALLEN

Hey do you need anything? I'm on my way home.

KITTEN

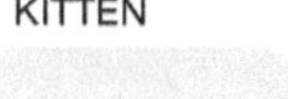

Her dots start and stop a few times before the message finally appears.

KITTEN

No. Just drive carefully, please. The roads are a mess.

CALLEN

Be home soon.

I think that was the nicest thing she's said to me in a while, and hey, I'll take it.

Beggars can't be choosers and all that shit.

It takes longer to get home than usual because she's right, the roads are a shit show, and traffic getting out of the stadium is at a standstill. By the time I walk through the door, my muscles ache, the ankle I rolled during the first quarter is sore as shit, and my fingers are still tingling from playing four quarters of football in a snowstorm.

I'm ready for a few days off before the shit show of Super Bowl prep and pregame media ensues.

The lights are off, and the house is quiet when I get home. At least, until Cupcake meets me in my bedroom. She whines as I change into my sweats and refuses to stop until I grab a treat for her from the extra stash I keep in here.

She's trained me well.

"Hey, girl. You want a treat?" I make her sit before she can have it.

"You're mean . . ." Cait whispers from the other side of the door, and I watch as she squats down, and Cupcake shakes her fat little ass as she trots over to her, forgetting who just gave her a cookie.

Cait squishes Cupcake's face and kisses her nose, and it's official—I'm jealous of a dog.

When she stands up, I get my first good look at her and swallow my damn tongue.

"Is that my shirt, kitten?" I ask, even though I know the answer.

That's the shirt I made her sleep in on her birthday. The one I dressed her in after she drunkenly stripped. And just like that night, she's beautiful and looks completely naked under it.

A beautiful flush washes over her gorgeous face. "I don't know what you're talking about, Sinclair."

"Did you give my dad a copy of the sonogram?" I ask, wanting her so damn bad, my hands are practically shaking with my need to touch her skin. To taste her. To fucking claim her. To make her mine. Permanently.

A nervous smile, one I don't see often on this woman, tugs at her lips. "Yeah. He was really sweet about it. You should consider taking advice from him on how to treat women." Her lips tip up as excitement sparks in her eyes. "Give me your hand."

"What?" I ask like an asshole before thinking better of it and giving her my hand.

We've barely touched since that night last month.

We've talked a bit more. But not much. Barely more than *Hey, can you get me a strawberry shake from The Busy Bee?* Maybe more if it's about the baby, but that's about it.

As far as Caitlin was concerned, we went back to our new norm.

Her hating me. And me trying to earn back her trust.

But I'd be fucking lying if I denied how much I want her.

In my life. In my bed.

All of her. Everywhere.

She presses my hand against her flat stomach and pushes down. "Do you feel that?"

"Feel what?" I ask, confused. "Are you okay?"

Her pale-blue eyes shine in the dark as she slides my hand under her shirt and rests it flat against her creamy skin. "Talk to her," she whispers softly, and I drop my hand.

So fucking slowly, I grip the hem of her shirt in my hands, giving her plenty of time to resist of she wants to. When she doesn't, I lift it over her head and toss it to the bed. She's perfect.

What I thought was a still perfectly flat stomach is rounded ever so slightly, like the beginnings of a tiny basketball of a bump. Cheeky pink panties emphasize the barely there bump, and a pink lace bra pushes up boobs that are definitely a full cup fuller.

I drop to my knees in front of her and gently place my hands on her stomach. "Hey, baby girl," I whisper as I brush my lips against her soft skin, and a shudder rolls over Caitlin's body. "You being good for your momma?"

Caitlin takes my hand in hers and moves its positioning more to the side before she presses down again. This time, I feel the tiniest pressure pressing back against my hand. "Holy shit," I whisper, awed. "Was that her?"

When I look up into Caitlin's eyes, they're full of happiness and unshed tears as she nods, unable to speak.

The tiny kicking stops, and I kiss her stomach again, wanting more, but just like her mother, it's going to be on her time. Not mine. The women in my life are all destined to be stubborn.

I pepper kisses along her ribs. "I loved seeing you there tonight, kitten. You, in my clothes. Pregnant with *my baby.* There at *my game. My family.* So fucking hot."

She's torn.

It's clear the way every muscle in her body is strung tight.

Hesitant. But not pulling away.

I get the feeling it's now or never.

That this moment, right now, matters more than any other ever will.

This is where I win the real game.

"You hold all the power here. Only you can put us out of our misery. Please, baby, you've got to forgive me. " I wrap my arms around her waist and rest my cheek against her bump. "I'm so fucking sorry for putting you through hell. I swear to you I'll never do it again. Give us this chance."

"You're my life, Cait." She cups my cheeks in her delicate hands and tilts my face up to her. "It's you and me. In every life, in every fucking way, I'll choose us every time. I'm so fucking sorry I made you doubt that, kitten. Give me one more chance, and I'll never let you doubt it again."

In this life . . . In every life . . . I choose you every time.

—*Caitlin's Secret Thoughts*

"Stand up, Callen." My words are muffled, like they're being said under water, and I have to strain to hear them myself as my heartbeat thrums so loudly in my ears, it drowns out everything else around us, leaving just Callen and me.

He stands and runs his hand over the back of my head, anchoring me to him. But it's not enough. "Callen—"

I'm not even sure what I'm trying to say, but he waits for me to gather my thoughts. Doesn't push. That's not his way. *Never his way . . .*

I let my eyes soak him in. The golden-tanned skin and beautiful ink covering this beautiful man. This man I don't doubt would give his life for mine. This sometime annoyingly incredible man who's refused to stop trying to regain my trust, and a sob bubbles up from deep in my throat.

"You hurt me, Callen, and I don't think I'll ever recover if I let you in again and you break my heart *again*. I'm holding it together now with tape and hope," I admit, knowing I've lost the fight. I don't have the strength to keep fighting this. I'm not sure I'd even want to fight it anymore if I could.

Not with Callen standing in front of me with so much love shining in his eyes.

He bends his knees, bringing eye to eye, and brushes his lips over mine. "I've never belonged to anyone but you. Please, baby. I'm so fucking sorry."

"*Callen . . .*" I sob.

"Please, baby. I will love you every day of this life and the next, Caitlin. There's no way this is the first life we've found each other, and it won't be the last. You're mine. You've always been mine. My heart. *My home.* It's you. They're not yours to take. They're just you. They've always been you."

"Show me, Callen."

Callen

"**A**lways, kitten." I press my mouth to hers, swallowing her beautiful moan with the first taste of her.

She's warm and soft and clinging to me as I carry her to the bed I plan on keeping her in for fucking days, if I have my way.

The reflection of the snow off the lake filters into the room, bathing her in an ethereal pale light as I lay her down and stare at this beautiful woman. My fucking woman. Mine.

"I love you, Caitie." I press a kiss to her shoulder and drag the straps of her bra down her arms, slowly. Leisurely. Taking my time. Imprinting it forever on every strand of my DNA.

"Show me, Callen." She slips her arms out of the straps and runs the tips of her fingers up and down my chest.

She's magnificent, splayed out on the bed, her creamy pale skin glowing in the moonlight against her bra and panties. Pretty pink nipples push against the pink lace bra, and my mouth fucking waters at the sight before me.

She's everything I'll never take for granted. Every filthy fucking fantasy I've ever had come to life, and I'm going to cherish her. Worship her. Protect her.

Mine repeats in my mind like an old school anthem.

The kind that hypes you up to take on the world.

"Christ, kitten . . ." I take her breast in my mouth and suck her through the lace, loving the way Cait's back arches off the bed. She tugs at my sweats, forcing them down my body.

"I need you, Callen."

I'll never be able to deny her anything.

"You're gonna have me, kitten. But first, I've got to get you ready." I fist my cock through my sweats, and she presses a bare foot flat against my chest with the most devious smile spreading on her face.

"You're in front of me in no shirt and those damn sweatpants, Callen. How about you take off my panties and find out just how ready I already am?"

"Oh yeah," I tease her, fucking dying over her confidence. So fucking hot for her.

"Your wish is my command, kitten." I press my face to her hot cunt and lick right through the scrap of lace blocking me. "Fuck, you're soaked for me, Caitie."

I flatten my tongue and drag it up her sex until I can't take it anymore and shove her panties to the side, needing in her.

"God, yes," she moans and lifts her hips.

With each long stroke of my tongue, I tease her with my rough finger, and Caitlin squirms against me until I throw her legs over my shoulders and cup her perfect ass in my hands, dragging her to me.

Caitlin moans as she grinds her pussy against my face, chasing what she needs.

What I want to give her.

"That's it." I drag my teeth over her clit, and her scream echoes loud in the quiet room.

She sinks her fingers into my hair and fucks my face, her body vibrating with need. "I'm so close, Callen."

"Take it, kitten," I growl against her hot core. "Take what you need like a good girl." I eat her like a dying fucking man until she gives me what I fucking need.

She comes on a sharp, keening, shaking cry, as she tugs my hair, and I inhale her pussy. Fuck air. I'll die a happy man with my face right here.

I push closer and bury my tongue in her hot, tight cunt, licking and sucking, *fucking feasting*, until I've wrung every last tremor from her body. "Fucking take it, Cait. Give me what I want."

She screams again, and I feel like I could come right now from that sound alone.

I don't wait for her to come down from her orgasm high before I pull back and rip her panties and bra from her body. Needing all of her bared to me. Needing to see her. To see the way her body has changed. "Swear to God, Cait, you've never been more beautiful."

A red flush crests over her skin as she smiles, and I flip her onto her knees. Her long dark hair kisses the middle of her back as she looks over her shoulder with a sex-dazed smile. "Are you going to fuck me now, Callen? We've got time to make up for."

"There's nothing in the world that could stop me." I kiss her lips. Her shoulders. Drag my lips down her spine and settle myself behind her.

Her ass is a fucking masterpiece in my hands.

Caitie pushes back against me as a needy little sound slips from her lips.

"Please, Callen."

Fuck. What those words do to me.

I drag the head of my cock through her drenched sex. "Never again, Cait. You and me. That's it. Never want to be without you again."

Her head drops to the bed as she whimpers, and I push inside her.

"Fuck, Callen. Don't be gentle. I need you . . . I want it all."

Caitlin

Oh God.

Callen pushes inside me slowly. So fucking slowly, I could cry . . . with relief. With want. With anticipation. It's everything. We both moan at the first feel of my body stretching around his cock. And holy fuck, does it stretch.

Every nerve ending lights up like never before.

I feel like I could cry or scream or come again already, and he hasn't moved yet.

I fight to catch my breath as I clench around him, needier than I've ever been.

"Please, please, please," I chant, unable to think further than this.

To feel anything but want and hot throbbing need.

"I know what you need, kitten." He drags out every slow thrust. Slower than I ever thought possible. Each decadent grind against my clit. *In and out*. Over and over. Building me up. Keeping me there. Kissing that spot that only Callen's ever known, only to quickly pull back, teasing me until he does it again . . . *and again*. Until I think I'm going to die if I don't come.

I scream out his name when his hips snap against mine.

So good it's nearly painful.

"Is this what you want, Cait? What you need?" he growls as his hands bite into my hips with each hard thrust deeper than the last.

In and out.

Over and over.

I close my eyes and grip the sheets beneath my hands as my entire body purrs and screams with mind-numbing, soul-scorching pleasure.

He drives into me relentlessly.

Each thrust deeper than the last.

Harder.

Better.

Until I'm screaming through my second orgasm, my pussy throbbing and aching, and still somehow, Callen demands more.

He wraps a hand around my throat, dragging his thumb along my jaw, and pulls my back up against his chest. "So fucking pretty, baby." His cock sits thick and hard inside me as aftershocks vibrate through my body. His tongue traces my ear, and his teeth tease my lobe before he scrapes them along my neck. His hand slides down and tightens around my throat, and my world comes into hyperfocus. He growls, "Breathe, Caitlin."

Oh fuck.

I close my eyes and lean back against him.

Trusting him.

Unable to do anything but beg for more.

Callen's hips slow as we move together in sync. As if

timing each movement, each shallow breath that slips through my lips.

My God, it's like every sense is amplified.

Every nerve ending ripped open, raw and hot, and pulsing in time with the beat of our hearts. And this man . . . My man . . . My world. The one I waited for. Begged to love me. Who's owned my heart my entire life. Fuck. He's everything.

It's his. I'm his. And he's controlling my body as if it were his own.

Each movement. Each push and pull and clench and thrust.

Controlling my movements. My pleasure. My sounds and words.

They're all his, and I've given them over completely.

Given myself over completely.

Trusting him with my body and my soul.

Pleasure runs thick in my veins as Callen growls behind me, so fucking sexy.

"You need to come again, don't you, kitten?"

"God, yes," I whisper quietly, unable to speak as I drag my arm back and throw it around Callen's neck, turning my face and taking his mouth.

He sucks my tongue in time with each thrust, and our bodies move together. Desperate for more. Raw and aching.

One hand slides down to my clit and pinches, and a scream rips from my lips.

I hold his hand to me. Moving with him as Callen sucks the sweet spot where my neck and shoulder meet. Until there's nothing between us. Two bodies moving as one. Sweaty and sticky. My wetness dripping down my legs.

He fucks me until I can't possibly last another second and then tightens his grip on my throat, and his hot breath tickles my ear. "Come on my cock, kitten. Take it all and show me who owns this pretty cunt."

A scorching-hot intense heat covers my skin as I shatter in his arms.

Colors explode behind my eyes like fireworks on New Year's Eve.

Callen fucks me through my third orgasm until I'm in tears, it's just too much.

Every inch of my skin is red-hot and hypersensitive.

One giant, raw, exposed nerve.

The hand on my throat slides down my body and cups my breast, palming it in his deliciously rough skin. "These have gotten bigger, baby. Are they more sensitive too?"

He pinches my nipple, and I scream again as he fucks me over and over. Never stopping until I'm sobbing in his arms. One orgasm rolls into another, and I lose count.

My throat rough and raw and my voice hoarse.

Until I can't possibly scream more.

Can't think. Can't speak. Can't breathe.

Until I'm limp in his arms and Callen is the only thing holding me together.

Until I'm promising to never leave him again. To forgive him. To love him.

Until I'm no longer broken, and he's put the jagged, shattered pieces of my heart back together.

Until a raw, primal sound is ripped from somewhere deep inside his chest, and my name is shouted out into the room.

We fall to the bed tangled in each other. Unable to move. Unwilling to care.

And it's not until hours later, when I know neither of us has slept, just stayed safe in each other's arms, that I turn and place my face inches from his. "I never stopped loving you, Callen Sinclair. I never will. But don't hurt me again because

I don't know how much trust I can keep giving you if you keep breaking me."

"Never again, Caitie. You're it. You and our daughter. Everyone else in the universe can fuck off. I don't care about any of them as long as I have the two of you."

My tired eyes search his face for any kind of insincerity. But I come up lacking.

I ghost my lips over his. "Promise me we'll show this baby a healthy love."

"I promise."

Those two words manage to somehow give me the peace I've been searching for, and I close my eyes. "I love you, Callen."

"I'll always love you, Caitlin. I promise."

Callen

Chapter 26

DAD

Your mom wants to have everyone over for a party this weekend.

NATTIE

Everything okay?

MURPHY

He said to celebrate, Nat.

COOPER

They just won the Super Bowl. Pretty sure it's safe to celebrate, Nat.

CARYS

I mean, it was three weeks ago.

DECLAN

You have the attention spans of an ant.

DAD

Our house. Sunday night. Think you can make it?

NATTIE

We're in.

MURPHY

Us too.

CARYS

We should be good.

DECLAN

I'll see if Nix and Leo have a game that night and let the rest of the kids know.

CALLEN

I'll check with Caitlin. But I think that should work.

DAD

Glad you got your head out of your ass, son.

MURPHY

Yeah. Now it can be lodged permanently up her ass.

CARYS

Aiden Murphy!

NATTIE

Eww, Murph.

COOPER

At least she's got a great ass.

CALLEN

Stop looking at my woman's ass, Coop.

COOPER

Make her your wife and I will.

"Thanks, Amelia. I owe you one." I stand in front of the counter in Sweet Temptations with a box of Caitlin's favorite chocolate chip cookies in one hand and a stupid fucking smile on my face. "I would have never gotten a single thing right if I had to pick it out myself. I appreciate your help."

"You're welcome, and I'll save that favor for later." Amelia folds her arms over her chest with a knowing smile, and I remind myself that I didn't make a deal with the devil, but I did just make one with his wife.

Not like he's an actual devil . . . But I'm sure there are some people in this town who think so.

Cait still isn't speaking to her father or Maddox, but Amelia has been at the house helping Caitlin get everything together for the baby. Hard to believe we've only got ten weeks left until we meet our baby girl.

"She's pregnant and probably changes her mind more than any woman you'll ever meet, Callen. Don't beat yourself up." She cocks her brow and smiles. "You know her coffee and cookie order. That's a love language for Caitlin. The rest will come eventually. Nonna and I will be over at the end of the week to help her get things set up."

She looks past me and takes a deep breath. "Do not fight in my shop."

With that warning setting off alarms in my head, I turn in time to see Maddox walking up to the counter and groan.

"Let's not do this today, man." It's been a good day, and I'd like to keep it that way.

Maddox shoves his hands in the pocket of his peacoat. "I didn't come here to fight."

"Out of my shop, Maddox. I don't want this here, and neither of you want it anywhere anyone can hear you." The look she gives him speaks volumes. Enough that Maddox shakes his head and looks at me. "I heard Cait's out of town. Want to take this to your place?"

"Sorry, man. You're not my type." I push past him until Amelia calls out my name.

"Callen . . ." She looks between her oldest son and me. "This is my favor. Talk to him. You can use my office."

I shake my head, and she smiles, knowing she won.

I'm not sure she and Caitlin have ever looked more alike than they do in this moment.

It's eerie, and I smile, hoping my daughter looks just like her mother.

When I said I owed Amelia one, I didn't know today would be the day or this would be the one.

Fuck me.

"Fine." I fucking glare at Maddox. "But let's make this quick. I've got shit to do before Cait and the girls get back from their spa day."

I follow him into Amelia's office and am immediately flooded with memories of us doing our homework back here in elementary school while Amelia brought us cookies and chocolate milk. I manage to push it out of my mind as I turn and face my former best friend with no clue how this is going to play out. "If you've got something to say, say it. I've got shit to do."

Probably should have just paid someone to put together the furniture that's waiting for me back at the house, but I convinced myself it would mean more to Caitlin if I did it.

Probably not my best decision.

"How is she?" Maddox asks as he eyes a picture of him, her, Rome and Lucky hanging on the wall. Matching devilish grins, covered in cupcake icing, stare back.

"You're going to have to ask her. If she wants you to know, she'll tell you." I hold tight to my anger, even though it's dulled over the three months since our fight.

"Has she forgiven you?" He pushes, and I don't bother answering. I don't think he actually expects me to, so he changes tactics. "You should have told me."

Now we're getting to it.

"You're right." I shock the piss out of him with my admission, but I never thought I was faultless in this whole fucking mess. "And I was going to. Would have if I hadn't talked to your dad first. Madman, you gotta understand if I hadn't promised you a fucking lifetime ago that I'd stay away from her, I'd have been with Caitlin for years by now. The only reason I wasn't was you."

"You had a funny way of showing it, man. You weren't lacking the ladies' attention," he snipes back.

Fuck.

"You wanna hear you're right? Fine. You're right. I wasn't a fucking saint before her. But I've been loyal since the minute I touched her. Christ, I've basically been loyal since the day you moved her into our condo. You didn't ask. You just did it. You put the one person I wanted under my nose for years, and I still stayed away out of respect for you. And you know what? I hurt her in the process. So fuck you. I'm sorry I didn't tell you, but your dad dicked us both over when he told me to stay away and keep this shit to myself."

Shit.

That felt better than I expected.

Maddox and I have never been feelings friends. He's been my brother. We helped each other through shit, but it's never been shit that's built up between us before.

"You're right," he agrees, and my head spins. "I told her it wasn't fair to be pissed because you did what Dad told you needed to be done. Most of us would have done the same thing. Maybe not Rome, because let's face it, he's a fucking psycho who loves drama, but the rest of us . . . We would have done it too. Fuck, man. My sister. You wanted my fucking sister for years?"

Maddox drops down on the mint-green couch along the wall and rests his elbows on his knees. "Do you love her?"

"I've loved her for a long damn time, man," I tell him without hesitation. "She's it for me. She's everything. She and the baby are my world."

He tilts his head and looks up at me with tired eyes. "You gonna marry her?"

"Yeah." I smile. "She doesn't know it yet though. So keep that to yourself."

Maddox grabs the box of cookies from my hand and steals one, like he's an alcoholic dying for a drop of whiskey instead of a chocolate chip cookie. "You think you can get her to talk to our dad?"

"You asking me or telling me?" I push back, tired of being told what to do when it comes to Caitlin.

"Asking. Help her the way she helped me." He breaks off a piece of the giant cookie and pops it in his mouth. "And while you're at it, can you tell her we fixed our shit?"

"How did she help you?" I know she hasn't forgiven Maddox. What I don't know is what he's talking about. "And when did we fix our shit?" I look around the room to make sure I'm not missing something, then wait.

"I came to her last month, wanting to make things right. But she wasn't willing to do that until I made things right with you first." He blows out a breath. "So I guess I'm sorry for being a dick. I should have trusted you, and I shouldn't have said what I did. Caitlin was right. And you should have trusted me. Man to man, if you tell me you love my sister and you're not going to hurt her, then I'll admit I was wrong. You're a good man. Treat her right and don't fuck up my niece."

"I'll accept your apology on one condition," I tell him and

hold out my free hand to help him up from the ancient couch.

"What's the condition?" Maddox asks, careful not to agree to something crazy.

"Come back to the house and help me put together baby furniture. I need to get it done before the girls get home from the spa."

"What the fuck, man? Can't you hire someone to do this shit? You've got one of the biggest contracts in the NFL."

I shrug a shoulder. "But think how great it will be to tell my daughter that Daddy and Uncle Maddox put her furniture together."

"Dude, you're gonna have a daughter . . . That's fucking nuts."

"I know," I agree as my heart beats faster, just thinking about it.

"You know we can never let her date, right?"

"Fuck, man . . . What the hell? Don't make me think about that shit yet." I grab the cookies back and shove him forward. "Shut the fuck up and help me put together the furniture."

At least I wore pants today . . .

—Caitlin's Secret Thoughts

"Do you want me to go inside with you?" Bellamy asks as we sit parked in Callen's driveway, looking from Maddox's car, to Rome's motorcycle, to the house, and back.

"What do you think they're doing here?" I ask her as I gather my bags, struggling to bend over to get them. The spa was heavenly and so were the little boutiques we stopped at on the way home, but now I'm back to exhausted, and I just want to be snuggled up on the couch with Callen and Cupcake, watching the latest episode of my favorite Food Network show.

Less than two months to go. And my little girl already has a better wardrobe than most grown women could ever hope to have. Problems of a stylist's kid.

Bellamy gets out of the car and waits for me. "I guess there's only one way to find out why they're here."

I get out of the car and stand there, pouting.

"What the hell? I was relaxed, B. I don't want to go in there and listen to my brothers and my baby daddy arguing." If I wasn't so tired and my limbs didn't still feel like jelly, I'd consider stomping my foot for effect.

"Girl, you've got to stop calling him that," she laughs and starts for the door.

Fuck. Guess I'm doing this.

"Fine. But it's not any worse than boyfriend," I grumble.

I feel like I'm sixteen years old when I say *boyfriend*. And sixteen and pregnant isn't the look I'm going for.

Bellamy takes a few bags from my hands and walks in first. "Honey . . . I'm home," she calls out.

My best friend, ladies and gentlemen. She's crazy, and she's all mine.

Those crazy-ass Instagram reels of little old ladies doing crazy shit when they're eighty . . . that's going to be us.

Lucky saunters down the stairs, the sleeves of his shirt pushed up and showing off his newest ink. "Hey, baby. Why don't you come give Daddy some sugar?"

"Oh gross," Bellamy gags. "I think I just threw up in my mouth a little."

I laugh out loud. "What the hell is wrong with you, Lucky?"

He peeks inside my bag, probably seeing it's baby clothes and not food, and loses interest, then kisses my cheek before he waggles his eyebrows at Bellamy. "She wants me."

"*She*," Bellamy cackles, "is five years older than you and not at all interested in teaching a little boy how to please a woman."

Lucky acts like he just took a shot to the heart when he covers it with both hands.

"You're gonna have to find someone else to be your Mrs. Robinson, Lucky."

"Your loss, B." He keeps his eyes locked on her until Callen walks into the room and shoves him away.

"You're freaking her the fuck out, kid." He wraps an arm around my back and rests the other on my basketball bump as he drops a kiss to the top of my head. "Did you have fun, kitten?"

And I absolutely melt in his arms.

I wasn't sure how I'd be able to let go of my anger after holding on to it for so long, but with him, it's harder to hold on to the anger than it is to let go.

Scary as hell. But Callen Sinclair is worth it.

"Dude, *you're* freaking me the fuck out. That's just weird shit. Does she purr too?"

Before Callen or I can laugh at my brother's stupidity, Bellamy interrupts, "And . . . thank you for proving my point. If you can't make a woman purr, you don't know what you're doing in bed, little Beneventi."

"The fuck? Little? I'm bigger than Rome and Maddox," Lucky argues as my other brothers both walk into the room, and I stand frozen in place.

Maddox *is* here. I know his car is here, but the last time we were all in one place, fists were thrown, and words were thrown. I'm not even sure what to think when Rome grabs his junk and laughs at Lucky. "Keep dreaming."

Moron.

Maddox ignores the comment and slaps him on the back. "Come on. Let's leave them alone." He smiles at me, then looks at Callen. "I'll see you at Crucible."

Callen gives him a chin tip, and my brothers leave as Bellamy laughs. "I expect to be updated tomorrow."

She drops packages on the couch and waves as she turns to leave, and Callen turns my face to his and brushes his lips over mine. "Did you have a nice time?"

"Umm . . ." I lick my lips, ready to jump his bones but

know I need answers first. "Don't bury the lead, Sinclair. Want to tell me what the hell my brothers were doing here and if you and Maddox broke any furniture before he left?"

He rubs his hand gently over my belly, and our daughter kicks him, hard. Which means she also kicks me hard. Callen smiles, and I wince. Men have it so easy.

"How about you come with me so I can show you the furniture we didn't break?" He takes my hand in his, and I lean my head on his shoulder, so damn tired.

He walks me past his room. I guess it's now *our* room. It's the room I've been sleeping in for the past month. But I haven't moved my clothes out of the one across the hall just yet. Maybe I'll just use that one as my closet. Again, stylist and designer. I see nothing wrong with having an entire room as a closet. Callen stops me in front of the closed door next to his room and turns to face me, and he's obviously nervous. "If you don't like this, anything can be changed, okay?"

"Should I be scared?" I giggle. Callen isn't usually one for dramatics, but as he pushes the door open behind him and keeps his eyes locked on me, I get it. And oh my goodness . . .

"Callen . . . You did all this?" I ask in awe. "You did the whole nursery?"

I step into the beautiful space he created for our daughter. Pale pinks and rose golds mix with the elegant white furniture I've been looking at for months. "How did you know?" I gasp.

"Do you like it?" He wraps a hand around the back of my neck and presses his lips to my forehead as I nod. "Your mom helped me pick out the furniture, and Everly may have told me about the chandelier you'd been looking at. And your brothers helped me put everything together."

I walk over to the crib and pick up the stuffed dinosaur

wearing the Kings football jersey and smile. "A little touch from your family. I love it."

Before I know it, I'm crying, and I can't stop. "Callen . . . I don't have the words. This is incredible. And my brothers . . . how did that happen?"

He moves me over to the pale-pink velvet Queen Ann chair and sits me down, then picks up my feet and puts them on the matching ottoman before he pulls off my ballet flats and massages my fat, swollen feet. Holy hell. This is heaven.

"Maddox showed up at Sweet Temptations today. He wanted to talk. He may have mentioned that you refused to talk to him until he made things right with me."

He digs his knuckles into my arch, and I moan and basically forget my own name.

"You blow me away, Caitlin. Your confidence. Your loyalty. You. I am constantly in awe of you." He puts one foot down and picks up the other and starts again.

"I'm sorry. I guess I should have told you . . ."

"No, Cait. I get it, and I appreciate it. Thank you." He leans over, lifts my shirt and kisses my belly. "I love you."

"Promise, Callen?"

"Promise."

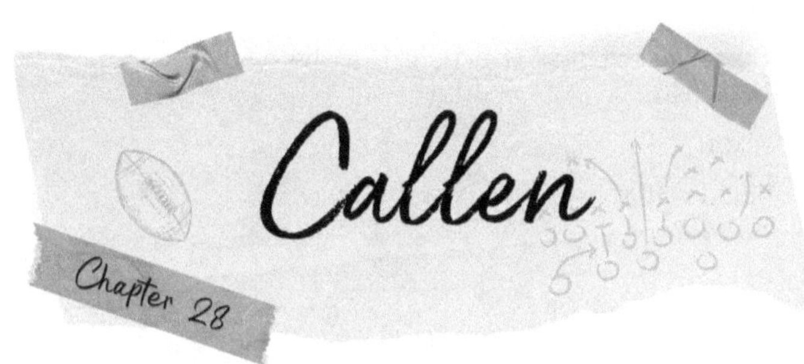

LEO

Bitches be crazy.

NIXON

That's because they don't like being called bitches, asshole.

LEO

Nah . . . they were crazy before that.

MADDOX

You know you're a fucking idiot, right?

CALLEN

I've been saying this for years.

KILLIAN

They're not all nuts.

LEO

I beg to differ.

MADDOX

Someone help him. They don't like when you beg, man.

NIXON

You don't tell people you're my brother, do you?

CALLEN

I've been acting like we're not related for years.

KILLIAN

Can't help you.

LEO

You can all go eat a dick.

*M*y sisters, brothers, and I sit around Mom and Dad's dining room table with everyone's significant other by their side, including Caitlin, and I guess I'm more old-fashioned than I ever realized because having her here by my side tonight only solidifies my earlier decision.

"Dad." Nattie grabs Brady's hand in hers and looks between us all. "What's going on?"

The rest of us sit silently and let her talk because she doesn't know how to be quiet.

He picks up Mom's hand in his, and Murphy groans. "You're not gonna tell us you're pregnant again, are you?"

"Aiden . . ." Mom chastises him, and just about everyone laughs.

Everyone but Cooper and Dad.

Shit.

I take Caitlin's hand in mine under the table and hold it

against her leg. Needing to feel her. Needing her to help ground me as I prepare for the worst.

"No." Dad looks at me and smiles. "The only baby Sinclair being born soon belongs to Callen and Caitlin." He looks between us and winks at Cait. "Sorry. Sinclair-Beneventi."

She rubs her belly. "We settled on Sinclair."

And okay, yeah. I'm pretty fucking happy she came to that conclusion on her own, but if I have to say anything about it, she's going to be a Sinclair too, very soon.

"Really?" Mom asks with excitement shining back at us, and I nod and look at Caitlin.

"Yes," Cait confirms. "Anastasia Sinclair."

Annabelle gasps, "After your mom. Oh my . . ."

Caitlin leans in to me as the table quiets, and all eyes go back to Mom and Dad. "I had my ninety-day scan last week, and we got the results back."

He looks at each of us, and my stomach sinks.

"It's not gone. But it will never be gone. We knew that. I'm living with cancer. And before any of you get upset, I need you to look at it this way. How lucky are we that I get to live with cancer when so many people don't? I'll have to stay on a strict treatment plan. But I get to live. I get to have a life with all of you." He lifts Mom's hand to his lips and kisses her knuckles.

"A long life," Mom adds. "There's no reason to think we don't have years and years of living left between us."

"Exactly," Dad agrees. "And in light of that, we've made a few decisions. We're going to spend the next year traveling to all the places we've always dreamed of going. We considered selling the house but couldn't bring ourselves to do it. We have too many amazing memories locked in these walls. So if any of you or any of your children want to live here, let us know. They can take care of it for us. And who knows, maybe one day we'll want something smaller. But right now, we want to enjoy this next part of our lives."

I've never been in a room with my family as quiet as this.

It's like I'm in a vacuum, and all the oxygen has been sucked from the room.

Fuck . . . I'm so happy for him and for Mom. Happy they're getting this time. Happy we're not losing him. But I guess I'm a little heartbroken, too, to know that they won't be ten minutes away like they've always been.

"Guys, this is good news," Dad reminds us all. And it is. But it's also heartbreaking.

"Daddy," Nattie finally breaks the silence as she lets go of the grip she has on Brady and moves to Dad. "We love you."

"You kids are everything to us. And I can't tell you all how grateful we are for the life we have and the family you've all given us," Dad tells us as he pats Nat's back.

"And we'll be back all the time between adventures," Mom adds. "But like your father said, we're thinking about getting something easier to maintain. Smaller."

She locks her eyes with mine. "Raising you has all been the greatest adventure of our lives. But like Dad said, the adventure isn't over."

I wrap an arm around Caitlin and pull her to me, trying to be happy for my parents while I'm also sad my kids won't get the same experience with them my brothers and sisters' kids got. But I know I need to be grateful they'll have them at all. Not everyone is so lucky.

"So does this mean I'm stuck with Declan again next season too?" I ask, trying to lighten the mood. Because we knew going into this thing, the odds weren't good, and no matter how sad it makes all of us to think of them not in Kroydon Hills, this was really great news tonight.

Best-case-scenario kind of news.

"Because seriously, I've invested well. Maybe I should just

come with you guys," I add, joking, and Caitlin kisses my cheek.

"We could raise the baby in Europe and teach her what real football is," she says as she looks up at me adoringly, knowing exactly what I was doing.

Every man at the table groans, and Murphy throws his napkin. "Say it with me, Caitlin. Soc-cer. *Soc-cer*. It will never be real football."

I look around the table and catch Dad smiling at the way I'm holding Cait's hand and shake my head.

Yeah . . . Not everyone gets to be this lucky. But we are.

*A*fter dinner, I grab Coop and pull him aside. "Hey, man. You still good to go with me tomorrow?"

"Where you going?" Murphy asks as he walks around the corner with a drink in his hand and a curious look on his face.

"Keep it down, asshole. I'm picking out Caitlin's engagement ring." I look around to see if anyone else is about to surprise us. Thankfully, no one is.

"No shit," Murph laughs and squeezes me in a big bear hug. "Look at you."

"Shut up, Murph. She doesn't know." I shove him away as Declan joins us. And *fuck*. I know Murphy's about to tell him.

"Dude, Callen's gonna propose to Caitlin tomorrow."

"What?" Declan asks, confused, and I shake my head.

"You're a moron, brother. I'm getting the ring tomorrow, not proposing tomorrow. Way to keep your mouth shut," I lecture Murphy, not at all surprised, before I fill the guys in on my plan.

"You're going to ask Sam for his permission, right?"

Declan pushes, and I know he's right. I just haven't been ready to think about it yet. "I know you don't need it. I know she's her own woman. But as a father of daughters to you, little brother, who's about to have a daughter of his own, I'm telling you, it means something when they ask. You might hate him right now. Hell, *she* might hate him right now. But one day, it'll be fixed, and he'll still be her father. Ask."

I guess when you put it that way, I don't have much choice.

Especially when I realize I haven't even met my daughter yet, and when her future husband asks, I'm telling him no.

MADDOX

You sure you don't want me to come
with you?

CALLEN

Thanks, man. But I'm good.

MADDOX

If you survive, do I get to be the best man?

CALLEN

You're a dick.

MADDOX

Yeah. And . . . ?

I should still be the best man. I mean, there
was that one hit. But in over twenty-five
years of friendship, I'm pretty sure that's not
bad. I mean, seriously. I broke Rome's arm
once.

CALLEN

We were ten, and you pushed him off the roof of the garage. You're lucky that's all he broke.

MADDOX

He was gonna jump anyway.

CALLEN

Fine. You can be my best man. Now I've got to go jump off a roof.

—Text from Maddox to Callen.

I wait for Jude to drive Caitlin over to Adelaide's house for book club before I head over to Sam and Amelia's house with Cait's engagement ring burning a hole in my pocket. With only six weeks left before her due date, I've put off talking to Sam as long as I can. Time to man the fuck up and get this shit over with.

Hopefully, he doesn't shoot me.

When Lucky answers the door with a smart-ass look plastered on his face, I fucking cringe. "Hey Ma—" he calls out. "Better put away the crystal. Callen's here."

"Always gotta be a little dick," I grumble, and this crazy fucker grins bigger.

"Big dick, Sinclair. I'm a big dick with a big dick."

Amelia moves behind him and slaps the back of his head. "If a man has to brag, he's overcompensating, dear. Try to keep that in mind when you decide to remember how to behave one day. Now get out of here."

"Ma—"

"Luciano, I said go." And the look she gives me when I laugh says it all.

It also says *shut the fuck up*, so I do.

"Callen . . . is my daughter with you?" I know she wants me to help her bring Caitlin and Sam back together, but Cait hasn't been willing to even discuss it. I've tried.

I can't imagine going four months without speaking to my father, but I understand where she's coming from. Pain is a bitch. It's hard to fight and harder to forget. And in my girl's eyes, the pain started with him.

"No. She's with Adelaide and Bellamy for book club. I wanted to see if I could speak with Sam." I tell her as she opens the door wider and invites me in.

Amelia's eyes narrow, and she bites down on her lips. "You can. But be warned, Cade and Becket are here. They're in the back playing poker."

Fuck me.

"Want to change your mind, Callen?" she challenges with a smile.

"No, ma'am." I mean, I could have hoped for better timing, but why would anything about us be easy. I shouldn't have expected it to start now.

She tugs me in for a quick hug and wipes her eye. "Be good to my baby, Callen."

Guess I know where Caitlin gets her awareness from. Amelia Beneventi can read a room.

When she walks me into the den, Sam, Killian's father, Cade, and Kenzi's surrogate dad, Becket, all look up. It's like the start of a bad joke.

A mafia boss, an MMA champ, and a US Senator walk into a bar . . .

"Callen would like a minute, Sam." I look at Amelia, who's practically giddy, and I wonder if it's because she knows I'm asking Caitlin to marry me or if it's because she's having fun throwing me to the fucking wolves.

"Don't kill him, Sam. Scarlet has a lot of money invested

in next year's team," Cade tells him. Seriously? The Kings' GM's husband doesn't want me dead because I make his wife a lot of money. Good to know.

"I can make him disappear if you do it," Becket smiles, and I take it. I've known these men my whole fucking life. I know how close they are, and I know what they're like. I also know I've protected each and every one of their daughters at one time or another, and whether they want to admit it or not, they respect me. So bring it on.

"I can do this here, or we can take it somewhere else," I tell Sam, cocky as hell, because with or without his permission, I'm marrying his daughter. "It's up to you."

Sam bares his teeth, and the others laugh.

"Welcome to hell, prince." Becket sits back with his hands behind his head and gets comfortable, while Cade gets up.

"Where do you think you're going?" Becket asks.

Cade grabs a bottle of scotch that costs more than my first car—and it was a decent car— and holds it up. "We need more alcohol for this."

"Why?" Becket laughs. "It's not like he can knock her up more."

"Assholes," Sam cuts them both a glare.

These are his people.

The guys he could always be himself with.

That was always Maddox and their daughters for me.

But they're not my people.

"Watch it," I growl, not liking anyone referring to Caitlin as knocked-up.

They sit up and take notice, and I'm officially over this. "I'd like your permission to marry your daughter."

"Oh shit . . ." Tweedledee and Tweedledumb sit back and take notice.

"Excuse me?" Sam doesn't bother to stand—he just turns

to face me. He doesn't need a position of power to be powerful, and he knows it.

"I'm going to marry Caitlin. I'd like to do it with your blessing. But I'm going to do it either way. I love her. She's going to be the mother of my baby. They're mine to take care of. Mine to protect. They already are. But I'd like to do it right."

"Might have wanted to wait to knock her up until after you had a ring on her finger, Sinclair," Becket warns, and I have my hand wrapped around his throat so fast he doesn't see it coming.

"Say it again, Senator. I dare you. Talk about her like that one more time," I warn him, and Sam grabs my shoulders and pulls me back.

"Let go, Callen," he says very calmly, and I drop my hands, seeing fucking red and completely over this bullshit.

I never loose my cool, but when it comes to my woman, I go from zero to *you're going to fucking die* real quick.

"This was a bad idea. Listen, I'm marrying your daughter. It would be really nice if you could make things right with her so you could be in her life. As someone who came close to losing his father this year, I would hate for Cait to lose you. And for the baby not to have you. But that's up to you. Fix it with her or don't. Your call, Sam."

I turn to leave but see Amelia standing in the doorway, glaring.

Pretty sure she's not glaring at me.

"Callen, stop." Sam crosses the room until he's standing in front of me. "You'd marry her without my blessing or my permission?"

I look him in the eye and refuse to back down. "I'd marry her tonight if she'd let me."

"Good . . . To keep her safe from this world, you're going to need that kind of strength," Sam tells me.

"And those bigass balls too, kid," Becket adds. "You know that was a federal offense, right?"

"No, it was not, Becket," Amelia scolds her brother. "Stop being a little baby, and don't make me hurt you for saying Caitlin is knocked-up again. Have a little class."

"I was just playing," Becket mumbles, while Sam and I stare at each other.

"I've tried to talk to her, you know. She won't call me back," Sam looks from his wife to me, obviously uncomfortable with all of this. "I love my daughter and my family, and I was trying to protect them the only way I know how."

Amelia wraps her arm around my shoulders and squeezes me like I'm one of her boys. "Try harder, Sam. I will not miss out on one single second of my first grandbaby's life because of you and your business."

"So, do I have your permission?"

"You don't need my permission, Callen. But you have my blessing. Keep her safe." He offers me his hand.

"And maybe try not to assault any more US Senators," Becket adds.

"Time to shut up, man," Cade tells him, and I decide it's time for me to go.

I've got better things to do tonight.

I once read that in the hands of the right man, a woman can be a hundred different versions of herself, limited only by his willingness to make her feel loved and safe. I feel loved and safe. So when do I get to be the version of myself who can see my feet again? Because I miss being able to bend to shave my legs in the shower.

—*Caitlin's Secret Thoughts*

*B*ook club is different when one of your friends is a romance author. You talk about the spice in the book, and she points out the plot holes. I mean . . . it was still hot, even if I now realize it wasn't very good. It also made me appreciate Callen and his big, beautiful dick because listening to Bellamy, Adelaide, and Coraline talk about the lackluster sex they've either had before or are having now—yeah, even nearly nine full months pregnant—I can't relate.

My sex is great.

We've had to get a little more creative as my bump gets bigger and more in the way, but I'm pretty sure Callen has taken that as a personal challenge he's determined to best. And I've got to say, my man loves a challenge.

Pregnancy got so much better once I started getting orgasms whenever I want them.

Which is exactly what I think I want when I walk in the house that night. An orgasm . . . or three. What can I say? Callen's a giver, and I will happily be a taker tonight.

Cupcake greets me at the door, like always, shaking her chubby booty as she goes. Only she has a big pink silk bow tied to her collar, and when I untie it, a tiny key slips into my hand.

I look around the dark living room but don't see Callen anywhere.

He must be home because there's a fire burning in the fireplace and candles lit on the mantle. Then I notice the giant white box tied with the same pink ribbon that Cupcake wore sitting on the coffee table in the center of the room.

What the hell?

"Callen—" I call out and walk over to the box.

It's huge.

If I sat this sucker on the floor, it would come up to my knees.

I look around again . . . "Callen—"

Still nothing.

I mean . . . it can't hurt to just untie the ribbon, right?

Of course, the lid accidentally comes off when I untie the bow, so I may just have to look inside. And since it's already open, I pull out piece after piece of pink tissue paper with small black kittens covering it until I find a smaller box under it all.

Box after box, like little Russian nesting dolls, and each one is bursting with more black cat tissue paper.

I laugh as the tower of tissue paper grows to the point that Cupcake is hidden, snoring underneath it somewhere, and I finally get to what I'm assuming is the very last box—a small antique jewelry box with a lock.

Wait . . . my key.

I pull out the key that had been attached to Cupcake and slowly turn it in the lock, then crack the box open and feel my heart squeezing in my chest.

"Callen . . ."

It's an old-fashioned gold locket, and when I open it, a miniature copy of our first ultrasound is taped in place with our initials engraved on the back.

"Do you like it, kitten?" this man I love desperately asks as he walks up behind me and wraps his arms around my chest.

"I love it," I tell him as I hand it to him and lift my hair. "Would you put it on me?"

He fixes the clasp, then fixes my hair, and I turn to face him, then burst into tears.

Because now, in his hand is a beautiful diamond ring.

"You didn't think it was going to just be that locket, did you?" He smiles and wipes the tears from my eyes. "Don't cry, Caitie. I love you. I want to spend my life loving you. I want to vow it to you in front of our friends and family. I want you and our baby to know you will always have me in this life and whatever comes next. Marry me, Caitlin."

I can barely push the words past my lips, the tears are coming so hard, but somehow, I manage. "Yes, Callen . . . Yes, I'll marry you."

If ten-year-old Caitlin could possibly be told this is how her life would turn out, she'd never believe it. Or maybe she would. I guess there's a reason I never gave up on this man.

our orgasms later, and I'm barely lucid, lying on the bed, my diamond ring reflecting the candlelight flickering from around our bedroom. This man thought of everything. He lies behind me, supporting my back as I tangle my legs with his, trying but failing to get comfortable. "Maddox wants to be my best man."

"Oh yeah? Maddox knew?" I ask with a lazy, scratchy voice.

May have screamed a little too loud.

Callen waits a beat as his hand stops the lazy long strokes up and down my arm. "Yeah. I needed his help finding out when your dad was going to be home."

I whip my head around so fast, I actually see stars. "What are you talking about? Why did you need to know that?"

I haven't spoken to my father since the day of the accident when I left his house.

He needs to apologize, but he never will because that means admitting he's wrong. And when it comes to his business, he'll never admit that.

Even when he did reach out, the messages he left were defending himself, not apologizing for hurting me.

"I wanted to ask him for his permission to marry you," he tells me as if that was the right thing to do.

"And. Did. He. Give. It?" I bite out, pissed and hurt. Pissed that my father would talk to Callen but not to me. And equally hurt for the same reason.

"His blessing, yes. I basically ended up telling him I didn't need his permission. I was marrying you with or without that, but giving his blessing could possibly be the first step in bridging the gap between you both." He tucks my head under his and tries to relax me into submission.

News flash.

It doesn't work.

"And what else happened?" I ask, needing to know everything.

"Well, let's see. Your mom gave Lucky shit. Your Uncle Cade offered me a shot. I wrapped my hands around your Uncle Becket's throat, and I got your mom and dad's blessings."

His hand restarts its journey as I lie here, dumbfounded.

"Are we just going to act like you didn't strangle my uncle?" I question.

"Yeah, babe. We're going to skip over that to the part where I think you should talk to your dad."

I want to sit up quickly and glare at him, but the giant fucking beach ball of a belly I'm rocking these days kinda prohibits that. "Are you insane?"

I know talking to him won't get me anywhere.

I've grown up in this world.

Until now, Callen has been on the periphery.

"And why would I do that?" I argue, unable to help myself.

"Because he's your dad, and you love him, and life is too fucking short not to, Caitie."

I lay my head back down on his arm and ignore the pain in my lower back and the way the light flashes behind my eyes from the sudden movement. I also choose to ignore the fact that Callen is right.

Damn him.

$\mathcal{I}$ wake up to a text and send my mom a picture of my ring.

MOM

You should have seen your boyfriend last night. He was incredible.

CAITLIN

My fiancé.

I correct her with a smile on my face.

CAITLIN

I heard he may have gotten a little pissed at Becket.

MOM

He wasn't the first, and he won't be the last.

CAITLIN

Ha. Ha. True.

MOM

So are we planning a wedding?

CAITLIN

For now, I'm just focused on the baby. Maybe we can plan something after.

MOM

You're going to elope, aren't you?

I don't bother to bullshit her. She'd see right through it.

CAITLIN

I don't know. Maybe.

MOM

Oh, my darling girl. You'll never know how much alike we actually are. I love you and am so proud of you.

CAITLIN

I love you too, Mom.

Can someone please explain pink camo to me?
Are we worried about blending in with flamingos?

—*Caitlin's Secret Thoughts*

"**I**'m allowed off the couch, Callen," I whine to my worrywart baby-daddy.

Yeah. That nickname is sticking. It's more fun than fiancé.

"It's a headache."

He comes back in with a bottle of water and two Tylenol. "Just humor me and take it easy, please. You're thirty-six weeks pregnant, Caitlin. Your head has been bothering you for two days."

"It went away and came back. It's not like it was two days straight, and it's not like I don't usually feel like shit in the middle of April in Kroydon Hills. The cherry trees are blooming everywhere. My allergies are always insane this time of year." I do take the Tylenol though. I'm swollen, fat, uncomfortable, and now I can add congestion and a serious headache to my list of complaints.

Callen grabs my favorite chunky, cable-knit red throw off

the back of the couch and tucks it in around me. "Please just humor me, Caitie, and lie down." He waits until I do it, then squats down in front of me and hands me the remote. "Take a nap or binge some Netflix."

Cupcake lifts her head up from behind my legs, and Callen immediately scratches behind her ears before she lays back down. I'm pretty sure she's got him trained—not the other way around.

"Just take it easy, baby. You're growing a human in there. It's okay to take a day off work. Everly told me she's been trying to get you to take time off, but you refused."

"Of course I refused. What am I going to do? Sit around here and watch cooking shows all day?" When he opens his mouth to comment, I cock my eyebrow, daring him to be stupid enough to do it. "Besides, I love what I do."

The doorbell rings, and Callen runs his fingers through my hair and kisses my temple.

Maybe taking it easy won't be that bad if I get to do it all day with him.

I hear muffled voices as I close my eyes.

"Caitlin . . ."

You've got to be kidding me.

Today? When I feel like shit. Today is when he shows up at my house?

I open my eyes to find my dad standing next to Callen, who doesn't look happy. "Up to you, baby. If you don't feel up to it—"

"I'm fine." I glare at my dad. "He can stay."

He's here. I might as well hear him out.

Lord knows, I've been waiting for him to show up for months.

Callen nods, then looks between us. "I'm going to give you guys some space. I'll be down the hall if you need anything. Just holler."

"Thanks," I whisper and will my body to comply as I roll to a sitting position.

I miss having a waist.

"Hi, Daddy." Cupcake doesn't move from the couch, and I'd laugh if I had the energy. My protective little bulldog. "Sit down. It hurts to bend my neck back far enough to look at you."

"You feeling okay, Caitie? Mom said you had your checkup this week and everything was looking great."

He takes a seat across from me, and I all but growl.

That little traitor has been feeding him information.

"Don't be mad. Of course she was going to tell me what was happening. You're my daughter, and that's my granddaughter. I love you. Did you think I wouldn't want to know?" My father has a level of cocky confidence that comes with the position he holds. You don't get the kind of power he has without earning that confidence the hard way, and right now, I find it frustrating.

"Why couldn't you have asked me yourself?" I refuse to cry. Not in front of him. Not about this. "If you wanted to know so badly, why didn't you ask me?"

I rub my forehead, wishing away this headache.

It doesn't work.

Damn it.

"I'm sorry. Did you call me back and I missed it, principessa?"

"Did you apologize and I missed it, Daddy?"

He didn't raise me to take any shit. From anyone.

"I don't apologize when I wasn't wrong. And I wasn't wrong. I did what I had to do to protect you," he argues calmly.

"Protect me from what?" I glare as the throb in my head intensifies.

"Caitlin, when have I ever shared my business with you? I

don't discuss it with your mother, and she's my equal, not my child. I've spent your life keeping you out of my business. Keeping you safe. That's not going to change now. It's not going to ever change. I don't know why you'd think it would."

"Are you really going to stand there and not even tell me if the threat is gone?" I yell, so unbelievably frustrated.

"Threats against you and my family will never be gone, principessa. They will always be there. There will always be something. But you are safe, and that needs to be enough, for now."

I feel my blood pulsing in my ears as I dig deep and try to control my anger. "You don't get to make decisions about my life without talking to me about them. Especially when you can't even tell me why. Callen is the best thing that's ever happened to me, and you tried to ruin it."

"I tried to save you," he argues back. "I'll do whatever it takes to keep you safe, Caitlin. I'm your father. It's my job and my right."

"Stop trying to save me. Stop interfering. Just be my father," I yell and grab my head as my vision gets blurry, and the room spins. "Daddy. Get Callen."

Shit.

Callen runs in a minute later and gathers my face in his hands. "What's wrong, baby?"

"Something isn't right," I cry, and he picks me up. "What are you doing?"

"Getting you in the car. I'll call Kenzie and see if we're going to her or the hospital. You don't complain, Cait, and you're scaring me."

Yeah . . . I'm scaring me too.

Callen

I stand in the hospital room, my back against the wall, out of the way, while they hook up monitors to Caitlin after Kenzie has checked her over.

"I don't understand, Kenz," I whisper as Cait asks the nurse something about the monitor. "She was fine at your office."

Kenzie slips on her professional face, and I want to scream at her. "Preeclampsia is like that, Callen. She could have a textbook pregnancy, which Caitlin had, and it can still happen. We're giving her a shot of corticosteroids today to help the baby's lungs develop and will try to hold off delivery as long as possible."

I fist my hair and stare at my entire world in one bed.

This isn't fucking happening.

"How long do we need to hold out?"

"Ideally, I'd like to give the steroids at least seven days. But that may not be possible. The good news is she's thirty-six weeks." Kenzie leans back against the wall next to me and presses her shoulder to mine. "Even though it may not technically be full-term, I deliver babies every day at thirty-six weeks who are completely healthy with beautifully developed lungs. I know I'm not going to be able to calm your racing nerves, but I swear to you, we're doing everything we can to get Caitlin and your daughter through her delivery as safely as possible."

"I need them to be okay, Kenz. Promise me they'll be okay," I plead.

And I know her answer before she ever says it.

She can't make that promise—because there's no way for her to guarantee it.

"Hey, man," I look up in the dark room and find Maddox leaning against the wall. "Sorry. I didn't want to wake you, but Mom said I needed to bring you something to eat."

I look at the bag in his hand and shake my head. "I'm good, man. Thanks."

"Callen, brother. You haven't left her side in two days. You've made sure she eats and drinks and sleeps. Who's doing that for you?"

I sit up in the pleather chair that doubles as a bed and face him. "I'm good. Both our moms have been here around the clock. Both dads too."

Sam hasn't seen her.

He hasn't wanted to upset Cait.

I'm pretty sure he feels responsible for this, even though it's no one's fault.

I don't bother telling Maddox I wish they'd all back off. Cait's scared and uncomfortable and hates having people fussing over her.

"Yeah. They're here. But you're surviving on coffee and sheer willpower." He lifts the bag again. "It's Nonna's chicken parm. She knows it's your favorite. Fucking eat it, so I can tell her I did my good deed," he whisper-yells at me, and I shake my head.

"You, I'm not scared of, asshole. But Nonna . . . I think Nonna may have buried a body or two," I tease, but I might actually be right. Either way, I take the bag and inhale the heavenly scent. "Will you thank her for me?"

"Yeah, man. I gotcha. How's she doing?" Caitlin doesn't want siblings and friends in here, and I agreed. She's supposed to be taking it as easy as possible. Our shit show families won't help with that.

"She's so fucking brave, Madman. I swear if she can will our baby girl into a healthy existence, she's going to do it. I'm in awe of her strength."

Maddox's chest vibrates with a silent laugh. "Maybe one day it will be normal to hear you talk about Caitie like that, but right now, it still freaks me out a bit."

"Better get over that shit quick. Soon, you're going to be Uncle Maddox. That's going to trip you out worse," I warn him.

"Man . . . You're gonna have a kid, and she's going to be my niece. Fuck . . ."

"Yeah . . . She's going to have us both wrapped around her little finger too. You know that, right?" I smile, so ready to meet my daughter.

"Yeah. Just like her mother always did," Maddox agrees, and I smile as I look at a sleeping Caitlin.

"Yeah. Just like that."

Until I deliver this baby, I have two brains to work with, Callen. You have one. Don't argue with me.

Not sure that's how this works, kitten.

The fact you're dumb enough to argue with me is proof enough.

—Argument between Caitlin and Callen.

"Callen—" Caitlin reaches out for me as they lay her on her left side, and a nurse rushes out of the room. "I'm scared."

I clasp her hand in mine and press my forehead to hers. "Don't be scared, Caitie. I'm right here. I'm not going anywhere. Try to relax, sweetheart. Your blood pressure is really high. That's all."

"It's more, Callen. I feel funny." Cait's voice shakes and breaks my fucking heart before she presses on her stomach and winces. "It hurts. This isn't right. Something is wrong."

"What the hell is going on?" I yell as the nurse changes one of the drips in her IV.

Kenzie walks in with her tablet in her hands, and the nurse who ran out moments ago is by her side, filling her in on what's going on, while Caitlin cries and squeezes my hand.

"Kenzie. What the hell is happening? This just started. She was joking around one minute, then crying the next," I yell at her, desperate for an answer.

Kenzie must see something she doesn't like because her face changes before she says something to the nurse, and the nurse rushes out of the room.

"Okay, guys. It looks like it's time to meet your baby girl." Kenzie, my friend, is gone, and our doctor is out in full force. The change is instant, and I'd be impressed if I wasn't scared for my fucking life.

"What?" Caitlin cries. "It's too early. You said you were shooting for seven days with the steroids. We've only had five. We need to give her two more days."

I lean over and kiss Cait's head. "It's going to be fine, Caitie. She's impatient like you," I try to comfort her but stare in horror as the color drains from her face. "Kenz—"

Kenzie hits a button on the wall and ignores me as everything happens all at once and somehow in slow-motion.

"Somebody get him out of here," she yells, but I refuse to let go of Caitlin's hand.

"No way. I'm staying," I argue with a nurse half my size before Kenzie gives me one look, and my heart sinks. "Kenz . . ." my voice breaks.

"You can't be in here, Callen. Go. Let me do my job." She turns away, dismissing me, and an orderly forces me out.

Someone yells, "I need a crash C-section!" before I'm escorted out into the hall, and the door is shut behind me.

We're not even in an operating room.

Families are milling about the corridor as I lean against the wall and slide down to the floor, staring in horror at everyone going on about their day while my whole world spirals in the room behind me.

What the hell just happened, and how did it go so wrong so fast?

"Callen?" Amelia asks as she walks my way with a tray of coffees in her hands. "What's happening?"

More yelling comes from the room behind us. Amelia looks at my face and drops the tray of coffee to the floor. The liquid splashes at her feet and mine, but I don't stand, afraid my legs might give out beneath me.

Seconds later, I have no choice but to get up as we're escorted through the corridor to the private waiting room our parents have turned into their space over the last few days. Sam stands when we walk in, but I can't focus on him or Amelia.

"Somebody better tell me what's happening," I argue with the orderly, as angry as I am petrified.

"I don't have any information for you yet, Mr. Sinclair. Someone will be in soon to update you. Please wait here." He turns and walks away, like that's supposed to make it okay.

Like there's anything that can make this okay.

"What happened?" Amelia asks as she steps into Sam's arms, shaking.

"She was fine an hour ago. Her blood pressure was high when she woke up this morning, but not that much higher than yesterday. She was arguing with me about eating. She wasn't hungry, and I wanted her to try to eat." I scrub a hand down my face, trying to remember what went wrong. How she went from smiling, because she loves arguing with me, to scared and crying. "Then her blood pressure spiked, and the machine started beeping. Cait said her head hurt, and a nurse rushed in to check on her. One minute, she was okay, and the next, she was in pain, and they were laying her on her side and rushing to get the doctor." I can't get the scared look on her beautiful face out of my mind. The way she said my name . . . "It all happened at once."

I can't lose them.

Neither of them.

Amelia takes my hand in hers and squeezes. "Our girl is a fighter. She's going to be fine."

"Girls," I correct her. "Our girls. My whole world is in that room."

"Mr. Sinclair . . ." An older woman in pale pink scrubs walks into the room, and my heart sinks. She's not smiling.

"That's me." I rush toward her. "What's happening? Is Caitlin okay? The baby? What the hell is going on in there?"

"Caitlin developed what's called HELLP syndrome. Her organs are failing. Dr. Hayes is performing an emergency C-section. It's the only treatment. Unfortunately, with HELLP, there are other complications as well. Your wife's platelets are low, which unfortunately can complicate surgery because her blood will not clot properly."

I don't correct her. I don't say she's not my wife. Not yet. She should be. She already is in every way that matters to me. And she's scared, and I'm not in there holding her hand. Keeping her safe.

I've never felt so fucking helpless in my life.

"So what do you do for that? Do you need blood? I can give blood," I tell her, and Amelia takes my hand in hers. "We can get the family here. We can all give blood."

"Caitlin is O negative. So am I. I can donate," she tells the nurse while Sam stands behind her, silent.

"Thank you. We never turn away donors and can get that set up for you. I'll be back as soon as we have more information."

"Wait—" I stop her. "Is she going to be okay? Caitlin? The baby? They're going to be okay, right? They have to be okay."

"We're doing everything we can, Mr. Sinclair."

And as she walks away, I feel my world fall out from beneath my feet.

That wasn't an answer.

I can count on one hand the number of times I've felt true fear in my life, but I've never felt fear like this before.

Within twenty minutes, half of both our families are crammed into the waiting room while we wait for Amelia's sister-in-law and Kenzie's partner at the practice, Dr. Wren Davenport, to get us more information.

My parents and siblings are all around me, trying to give support.

To give strength.

Everyone wants to be here for Caitlin.

But I don't want them here. We wanted it to be us. Her and me and our baby.

We didn't want a crowd. Not for this. And now I'm part of that crowd instead of being with her.

I'm supposed to be back there, not in this fucking room while she's fighting by herself.

I need to be with her.

With my daughter.

A different nurse, a slightly older one in darker pink scrubs, enters the room, and my heart stops beating as she looks hesitantly around at the massive amount of people filling the room. "I'm looking for Caitlin Beneventi's family . . ." she calls out, and Sam, Amelia, and I all stand.

I don't care that they're her parents.

That's my family.

I move in front of them. "That's me. That's my family. What the hell is happening?"

"Dr. Hayes will be out as soon as she can to fill you in on

everything. But I can take you back now to meet your daughter."

Someone could have hit me with a ten-ton anvil, and it would have hurt less.

I sway on my feet and feel the vomit crawl up my throat.

"What about Caitlin?" The room stands still. "Where's Caitlin?" My voice shakes as it booms in the otherwise quiet room, but I can't stop it. "I need to see her," I plead.

"She's still in with Dr. Hayes. I can't take you in there. But I can introduce you to your daughter."

"No—" I answer immediately. "We're supposed to meet her together."

The tears gather in my eyes.

Any man who says they don't cry has never been faced with the possibility of losing the love of their life. They've never been unable to save them, forced to stand by, useless.

My mom puts her hand on my back. "Sweetheart, Caitlin doesn't want you to leave Anastasia alone. Go. Stay with your daughter until you can introduce her to her mother. You'll be the first person they come to, no matter where you are."

My heart sinks. "Is she okay? My daughter . . . Are her lungs okay?"

The nurse nods. "Her APGAR scores were strong, and she came into the world screaming." She looks around the room behind me and smiles. "Your little girl wanted everyone in the room to know she'd arrived."

It might be funny on a different day, but right now, I just want both my girls in my arms. I'll laugh when Caitlin is with us.

I'm guided through the swinging doors, and my knees nearly give out when the nurse walks me down the hall, past the room Cait and I were in not thirty minutes ago.

Bloody rags are discarded on the floor, and Caitlin's bed is gone.

"Where is she?" I ask, more fucking scared than I've ever been in my life.

"Caitlin was taken to the operating room." She opens the door of a private room and steps aside for me to enter. A different nurse stands next to a tiny clear plastic bed on wheels, and a sob claws its way from deep in my chest at the first sight of my daughter and the reality that her mother isn't here with me for this moment.

This isn't how any of this was supposed to happen.

The nurse picks up my tiny baby girl, and it's like a sucker punch to the gut.

Her mother is supposed to be holding her.

Anastasia is wrapped like a baby burrito in a tiny white hospital blanket and a stretchy pink hat and matching big bow.

"Would you like to sit first?" she asks, and I nod, words failing me as I get lost looking at our beautiful baby girl.

I sit without answering and wait for her to place Anastasia in my arms.

Love and fear thickening each breath I take.

She's perfect and beautiful and looks so much like her mother, it hurts.

Tiny red lips purse, and I swear Caitie has given me that look before.

"Hi, baby girl," I whisper right before she opens her big blue eyes. "We've been waiting to meet you."

Caitlin

*E*verything hurts when I crack my eyes and open my mouth to call out for Callen.

But as my eyes adjust, I find him right here, next to me.

He's sitting in a chair, as close to me and the bed as he can be, and he's holding *her*.

Oh my God. She's here, and it all comes rushing back to me.

"Is she okay?" I cry as he turns to show me Anastasia's sleeping face.

"She's perfect, baby. You did so good." His voice is hoarse, and stress covers every beautiful line of his face as he gently grazes his lips over mine, then kisses away the hot tears I hadn't even realized were falling. "Kenzie said she's perfect. Her lungs are perfect. Her sugar is good, coloring is good. All the things they warned us could be wrong are fine. You did that, baby. You kept her safe. You protected her and got her here."

He kisses me again with tears in his own eyes. "You scared the shit out of me, Caitlin. You can't do that again, baby."

"I'll try," I whisper.

"You're gonna feel pretty crappy for another day or so. Kenzie said you've got to stay on a magnesium drip for at least twenty-four hours, but your blood pressure has already started coming down, beautiful."

"I want to hold her, Callen," I demand through my tears, even though my arms and legs feel heavy, like they're encased in cement.

"You lost a lot of blood, Caitie." He slowly stands. "How about I sit next to you and get her situated on your chest? You feel up to that?"

"Give me my baby, Callen," I cry, and he does exactly as he said and gets situated next to me. His big body moves so very carefully, when in reality, him just being here next to me gives me strength. Then so gently—*and if I wasn't already madly in love with him, I would be now*—Callen lays Anastasia against my chest and wraps an arm around me. Holding us both close.

"Hi, sweet girl," I say softly to our baby, so completely in love, it washes away all the fear and pain. "We're so excited to meet you. Mommy and Daddy love you so much already." I tug off her little beanie and smile at the crazy puff of black hair shooting in every direction, then notice the pink polka-dot blanket she's wrapped in. "You remembered?"

"The second they gave her to me in the itchy hospital blanket, I grabbed the one you packed and asked the nurses to teach me the baby-burrito trick. I knew you wanted her to be in the soft blanket you picked out for her."

I close my eyes for a second, trying to gain at least an ounce of composure.

"You scared me, Caitie," he admits with his head resting next to mine. "So damn bad."

"I'm sorry," I whisper and open my eyes to watch our daughter sleep, falling more in love by the second. With her and with him. "I scared me too, Callen."

"Never leave me, Caitlin. I don't think I'd know how to live without you," he admits quietly.

"I promise."

You can't get lost in the rain when you are the fucking storm.
Remember that when you're scared.

—Caitlin's Secret Thoughts

I told Callen I didn't want to see anyone, and for hours, I didn't.

For hours, it was just the three of us.

My new, perfect family.

Safe and sound and whole.

Every time someone came in to check on me—which was a lot—we were tucked into this bed. I think the staff gave up on telling him Callen shouldn't be there because he never moved. And I think Kenzie secretly loved it. Even if she lectured him at one point.

We spent hours with Callen's arms wrapped around Anastasia and me as she nursed on and off all afternoon between sleeping. The morning might have been hell, but the afternoon was heaven. It was everything I needed. It gave me perspective.

So when my mom and dad knocked on the door in the early evening, I let them in.

Callen didn't move.

He didn't even offer to move.

He made sure I was comfortable and safe and pressed a kiss to my head.

"My baby had a baby," Mom whispers as Dad stands silently behind her, but I don't miss the way he wipes at his eyes as Mom reaches out for Anastasia. "Can I hold her?"

"Sure," I smile, and the baby's eyes pop open as she's taken from my chest. She cries until Mom shushes her gently, swaying. "Oh, Caitlin. She's beautiful."

Dad tugs the blanket away from her face and swallows down his emotions. "She looks just like you, principessa."

But he can't look at me.

He looks at Anastasia, my mother—hell, he even looks at Callen—but he can't look at me.

"Daddy . . . None of this was your fault. You know that, right? Our argument didn't cause any of this," I try to tell him, but I can tell he doesn't believe me by the firm shake of his head. "Even the all-powerful Sam Beneventi couldn't cause this, Dad. I promise."

"Caitlin . . . I'm sorry. I wasted so much time." His eyes stay glued to my daughter, but his words hang heavy in the air. Dad doesn't apologize.

"I think I'm sorry too," I admit, and Callen tightens his hold on me. "I'm sorry you thought I was in danger and that you handled it the only way you thought you could to keep me safe. I won't act like it didn't hurt. That decision had such repercussions, and I still wish you would have talked to me instead of handling me like a child. But I think I understand it differently now. I've known my daughter for only a few hours, and I can't imagine there isn't anything in this world I wouldn't do to keep her safe. Even if it means doing something I know she'll hate me for."

Dad's agony-filled eyes finally focus on me.

"You don't know what pure love is until you have a child. You think you do when you meet the right person, but the way that love changes the first second you see your baby's eyes . . . It's the purest love and purest fear you'll ever feel. You're going to walk around for the rest of your life with a piece of your heart beating outside of your own body. I love you, Caitlin, and I am truly sorry I hurt you. I wish I could say I won't do it again, but to keep you safe, I'd do anything. Sacrifice anything," he admits more softly than I've ever heard him speak.

"Can you at least promise me you'll talk to me if it happens again? I won't ask you to share the workings of your business, Dad, but this is my family, and you've got to let Callen and me make the decisions about our lives."

Callen stays silent next to me, but his support is there in every squeeze of his arm around me.

"I can try, principessa."

"Sit down, Sam, and hold your granddaughter." Mom moves in front of him, and Dad sits and holds out his arms, and my heart is so full. This is how it's supposed to be. How it was always supposed to be. "Support her head."

His smile is ridiculous as he takes her from my mother. "I know how to hold a baby, Snow." He looks down at Anastasia and melts. The big, bad Mafia boss absolutely melts. "Hello, principessa. Welcome to the family." He runs the tip of his pinky down her nose. "That was quite the entrance you made today. You're certainly your mother's daughter."

Callen kisses my temple. "She certainly is."

One day, you're cool as shit.
The next, you're sitting in the back of an oversized SUV,
holding on to an infant car seat, yelling at your baby
daddy that he's driving too fast.
Not sure when 25 miles per hour became too fast, but
today, it is.

—*Caitlin's Secret Thoughts*

e park in the driveway, and Callen turns around to face the back seat, frazzled, like he's just driven the scariest racetrack anyone has ever ridden on. "Is she okay?"

God, we're pathetic.

I look at our baby girl sucking happily on her little turquoise binky that's half the size of her face. "Yeah. She's asleep."

He unbuckles her car seat and lifts it from its base. "Ready to be home, kitten?"

Emotions clog my throat like they won't stop doing lately. Stupid hormones.

Home . . . I'm *home*.

All the fighting.

All the uncertainty.

All the fighting and all the making up with all the people, and I'm actually home.

I run my fingers along Callen's face. "You are my home, Callen. So yeah. I'm ready."

The front door opens, and Maddox and Bellamy step outside. "Wait. We need a picture. Hold still and smile."

Apparently, everyone has keys to our home.

Luckily for us, it's just these two, and honestly, it's nice to have them here as we get settled. My fridge has been stocked with enough food to feed Callen and me for a week. Anastasia's room has been filled with diapers and wipes and diaper cream. Her clothes have been washed, and basically, anything I could have possibly done between now and her actual due date to prep us has been done for me. I could cry, I'm so grateful.

Not that that's saying much, considering everything has made me cry for weeks.

Bellamy sits down on the couch next to me as Callen and Maddox move into the kitchen to warm up some food. "How are you feeling?"

"Okay. Still sore from the C-section, but everything else feels fine. Everything except my boobs. Sweet Jesus, they hurt. It must be time for her to eat."

Bellamy eyes me curiously. "How fucking big are they? My God . . ." She pokes the side of one, and I wince and smack her hand.

"Ouch," I bitch.

"Dude, B," Maddox groans as he walks back into the room with an eggplant parm sandwich on a plate and a Diet Coke in his hand. He puts them both on the table in front of me, and I could weep with joy. "I can totally get behind you and a little girl-on-girl action, Bellamy. But it can't be with my sister."

"Dream on, Madman. You're not getting behind any of my action." She looks down at my sandwich and licks her lips. "But I'm gonna get behind one of those sandwiches. You need anything while I'm up, Cait?"

"No thanks." I grab the muslin blanket next to me and throw it carefully over Anastasia before pulling down my nursing tank and bringing her to the boob Bellamy poked. She roots around for a minute, and I hiss as she attaches, then relax as the tiny little mouth sucks.

When I look up, Maddox looks horrified.

"Oh stop." I laugh at him. "You can't see anything."

"Sorry. Just getting used to *mom* you. It's going to take a minute." He looks away, like I'm flashing him, when in reality, he can't see anything but a pale tan and white blanket. "It looks good on you, Caitlin."

"The blanket?" I ask and sink deeper into the couch.

"Happiness." My big brother leans forward and steals the small bag of chips that were sitting next to my sandwich. "This is who you're supposed to be. You did good, kid."

"Is that your way of saying you were wrong?" I tease and adjust Anastasia the tiniest bit so she slows down.

Maddox looks away again, like he can see through the blanket.

He can't.

Men are babies.

"I was wrong. I didn't see it. I got too lost in what I knew to pay attention to what you and Callen needed, and it was obviously each other."

He might have taken a little longer to come around, but now that he's here, I'm grateful to have Maddox on our side. It was always going to be Callen and me.

It had been obvious to me since I was a little girl.

One who finally got everything she ever wanted.

I roll over at two a.m., when my aching boobs tell me I either need to nurse or pump, but Anastasia isn't in the bassinet next to our bed, and Callen isn't in the room. *Huh . . .*

Getting out of bed isn't the easiest thing yet, a nasty c-section will do that to you, but I get it done, then go on the hunt for my loves. It's a quick hunt. The door is open to the nursery, and Callen is sitting in the pink velvet chair with his feet propped up on the ottoman and his eyes closed while Anastasia sleeps on his bare chest in nothing but her tiny diaper. My breath gets caught in my chest as I stare at the perfection of this moment.

One I wasn't sure I'd ever get.

"Like what you see, kitten?" he asks without opening his eyes.

"I love it, Sinclair," I say softly as I move in front of him. "Love you."

"I love you too, Caitie. So fucking much."

"I know," I tell him, suddenly unwilling to wait for the rest of our lives. "Marry me, Callen."

"Did you hit your head, kitten? I already proposed, and you said yes. Check out your finger. The ring is pretty nice." His smile is gorgeous. It's everything.

"I mean now. This weekend. I don't want to wait. I want to be your wife. I want to be a Sinclair like the two of you. I want the world to know I'm yours."

He cracks his eye open, and I get goosebumps.

"You want to marry me, huh?"

"Don't be an ass, Callen," I tease because this is us. This is the best of us. The quiet moments. The teasing. The pushing and pulling. The fire. It's all the reasons I love him and so much more.

"Pretty sure if you asked your mom to handle it, she'd have everything set up for you by the end of the week."

"You know marrying me is marrying my family, right?" I warn him, knowing he'll never walk away from us.

"Mine isn't much better, kitten. I'm not going anywhere. Never again . . ."

"Promise?" I ask because I'll never get tired of his next words.

"I promise, Caitie."

**Every eye in the room was on her,
but she fell in love with the only man who made her feel
seen.**

—Callen's Secret Thoughts

"You nervous, son?" Dad asks as he fixes my tie.

"Not even a little bit," I answer honestly. "Just ready to call her my wife."

"Don't ever forget this feeling, Callen. When you're tired and stressed and you and Caitlin have been fighting for days, remember how you feel right now. Remember how she makes you feel after you've had your ass handed to you on the field, or when the weight of the world is weighing you down. You think life has been hard this year, but there will be some really great years, and there will be years that make this one look like a cakewalk. If you always put each other first, you'll get through all those years together. It's when you stop doing that, that things go off the rails."

"Thanks, Dad." I hug him, so fucking thankful he's here for this.

Here for it all.

Not many people get the kind of dad I've had.

The kind of man I was given to look up to.

And with that thought, my brothers walk into the room, carrying the bottle of Maccallan I'm told is for the traditional pre-wedding drink in our family.

This group of men who've always been there for me.

My family.

"One more wedding in this house," Cooper smiles, probably remembering when he married Carys here, where Caitlin and I will be saying our vows in less than an hour. Less people this time, but that's what Caitlin wanted. No fuss. No muss. Just us, our closest family, and my brother Declan marrying us, like he's done for a few of the people who will be here today.

Guess it's kind of a good-luck tradition.

Not that it matters. We make our own luck. And when I look at Caitlin, walking down the makeshift aisle in our backyard an hour later in a soft white gown billowing around the beautiful body that gave us our daughter, I know I'm the luckiest man in the world.

This woman is mine.

She never actually gave up on me, even if I was scared she had.

Deep down, Caitlin loved us enough to give us this chance. Our second chance. And I'll never stop making sure she knows how loved she is.

Her father stops in front of me and kisses her cheek before he gives me her hand. "You don't need my permission, Callen. But you've got my blessing, and you've got my respect. You've earned them, and I don't give either easily. Be good to each other."

He shakes my other hand, then moves to sit next to Amelia, who has a sleeping Anastasia on her shoulder.

Caitlin and I turn to face each other, and her stunning smile splits her face. "You look beautiful, kitten."

She leans up on her toes and brushes her lips over mine, and Declan clears his throat. "You're supposed to say the vows first, Caitlin," he teases.

But she doesn't care.

Caitlin has never cared about what she was supposed to do.

"Then say the vows, Declan," she tells him with her eyes locked on mine.

"Do you, Caitlin Beneventi, promise to love, honor, and cherish Callen, even during football season?"

She flutters her long lashes, excitement rolling off her in waves. "I promise."

"Callen, do you promise to love, honor, and cherish Caitlin, even when she makes you go on a cookie run in the middle of the night?"

I silently laugh at that last part I have no doubt Cait snuck in at the last possible minute. "I promise."

Declan starts to give his proclamation of the marriage, but my girl doesn't wait for it. She steps into me, and I gather her face in my hands as our mouths meet. In the back of my head, I hear Declan say, "husband and wife," but it doesn't matter. No piece of paper changes that this woman is mine.

And moments later, when Amelia hands me Anastasia, and I hold my girls in my arms as the photographer poses us in front of the lake, I smile, without a doubt in my mind that I'm the luckiest man who ever lived.

Caitlin tips her chin up to me and kisses my jaw, then Anastasia's head. "I love you, Callen."

"I will always choose you, Caitlin. In every life. In every way. I will choose you to love. I promise."

The End

Want more Caitlin & Callen?
Download their extended epilogue!

The Philly Press

NOT READY TO SAY GOODBYE YET?

Are you ready to see which of Kroydon Hills men falls next?

There's plenty of secrets they've been keeping from you and you're not going to believe what they are.

Make sure to preorder *Enticing,* book 2 in *Red Lips & White Lies,* to see what secrets Leo's been keeping…

Preorder Enticing Now

#KroydonKronicles #Enticing

Are you curious about the other characters mentioned in Redeeming? Cooper and Carys and Sam and Amelia have their own stories you can read today.

Read Cooper and Carys's duet starting with Worth The Risk free on on KindleUnlimited.

Read Sam and Amelia's story, Rise of the King free on KindleUnlimited.

If you haven't read the first book in the Kings Of Kroydon Hills series, you can start with *All In* today!

Read All In for FREE on KU

ACKNOWLEDGMENTS

Thank you so much to my family for all of your support. My husband and children are my world and my time with them often gets sacrificed for my time with these characters.

Thank you to my amazing team. I cannot imagine doing this without each and every one of you. Dena, Callie, Jen, Tammy, Emma, Kelly, Vicki, Morgan, Valentine, Val, Julie and Shannon - I have no words big enough to show my appreciation. And to my Happy Hunting girlies, thanks for cheering me on. Callen & Caitlin are better because of you.

And to my incredible momager, Bri. One more down and an infinite number of books still to go. Thank you for managing my business and my life.

As always, my biggest thanks goes to you, the reader, for taking a chance on Callen & Caitlin, and this fictional town I love so much. I hope you enjoyed reading Redeeming as much as I've enjoyed writing it.

ABOUT THE AUTHOR

Bella Matthews is a USA Today & Amazon Top 5 Bestselling author. She is married to her very own Alpha Male and raising three little ones. You can typically find her running from one sporting event to another. When she is home, she is usually hiding in her home office with the only other female in her house, her rescue dog Tinker Bell by her side. She likes to write swoon-worthy heroes and sassy, smart heroines. Sarcasm is her love language and big family dynamics are her favorite thing to add to each story.

Stay Connected

Amazon Author Page: https://amzn.to/2UWU7Xs
Facebook Page: https://www.facebook.com/Bella.
Matthews.Author
Reader Group: https://www.facebook.com/groups/
bellamatthewsgamechangers
Instagram: https://www.instagram.com/bellamatthews.
author/
Bookbub: https://bit.ly/BMBookbub
Goodreads: https://bit.ly/BMGoodreads
TikTok: http://tiktok.com/@bellamatthewsauthor
Newsletter: https://bit.ly/BMNLsingups
Patreon: https://www.patreon.com/BellaMatthews

ALSO BY BELLA MATTHEWS

Kings of Kroydon Hills

All In

More Than A Game

Always Earned, Never Given

Under Pressure

Restless Kings

Rise of the King

Broken King

Fallen King

The Risks We Take Duet

Worth The Risk

Worth The Fight

Defiant Kings

Caged

Shaken

Iced

Overruled

Haven

Playing To Win

The Keeper

The Wildcat

The Knockout

The Sweet Spot

<u>**Red Lips & White Lies**</u>

Tempting

Redeeming

Enticing

Captivating

Teasing

Breathtaking

CHECK OUT BELLA'S WEBSITE

Scan the QR code or go to http://authorbellamatthews.com
to stay up to date with all things Bella Matthews

www.ingramcontent.com/pod-product-compliance
Lightning Source LLC
Chambersburg PA
CBHW052155160726
47990CB00015B/1793